I read *The Muir House* in one day, alternating between wanting to put down the book and not learn the secrets of Willa's life and reading each page as fast as possible so I could get to the next. Mary DeMuth is a rare writer whose vulnerability can only come from laying her head on the breast of Jesus and tapping out his heartbeat onto the page.

Tracey Bateman, author of *Thirsty* and *Tandem*

You know the minute you open a DeMuth book that you are in the hands of a superior storyteller. Rich, masterful, poignant, and spellbinding, *The Muir House* is DeMuth's best yet.

Tosca Lee, author of *Havah: The Story of Eve*

A captivating read filled with mystery and drama, *The Muir House* has you cheering for Willa as she searches her past in order to come to terms with her future. Mary DeMuth's well-crafted story makes readers ponder what home really means — for her characters and for each of us.

Alice J. Wisler, author of *Rain Song*,
How Sweet It Is, and *Hatteras Girl*

Willa Muir is one of the strongest twenty-something characters in modern fiction. Her quest to reconnect with her past before embracing the future will resonate with anyone who has ever left loose ends untied. *The Muir House* is a fascinating coming-of-age tale with twists and turns that constantly leave the reader wanting more. It is Mary DeMuth's finest work yet and it shouldn't be missed. Whether young, or young at heart, you will find yourself enraptured by Willa's determination to finally find home. In fact, this book just might lead you home too.

Shannon Primicerio, author of *The Divine Dance*,
God Called a Girl, and the TrueLife Bible Study series

The Muir House is no light read, no thin, cotton blanket, but a rich tapestry of words and story, an artistic expression of dark threads that reflect Light.

Mary DeMuth uses these pages as a canvas upon which she paints her most powerful story. *The Muir House* grips you in an elegant tale that is part mystery, part love story, and wholly human in its portrayal of our deep need for belonging and a place to call home.

Perhaps nothing is more powerful than the secrets we keep — and the ones that keep us. Can the truth really set us free? Mary DeMuth confronts that question in unexpected ways through a soul-stirring, page-turning story about home and what our hearts need to know most.

As the director of Proverbs 31 Ministries' fiction division, She Reads, I select and promote the best inspirational fiction out there. I wait for new novels by Mary DeMuth because I know I can recommend them wholeheartedly. *The Muir House* does not disappoint.

Mary DeMuth is an expert at delving into the human heart and revealing profound beauty in the complex lives of even the most troubled characters. A gripping tale, *The Muir House* is an illuminating narrative about the true meaning of family and faith. This well-crafted story left me with a singing heart.

"There was a time when a man wanted to marry you." Have you ever played fickle with another person's soul, pulled him along, then lost him forever? Mary DeMuth weaves a remarkable story of hesitation, rejection, love, and stability melted at last into a circle of lasting relationships. Naked fingers are out of place in her world where gold endures and rings bind the hearts of best friends forever.

Austin W. Boyd, author of *Nobody's Child*, The Pandora Files series, and acclaimed Christy nominee *The Proof*

Mary DeMuth writes with extraordinary beauty, grace, and originality. *The Muir House* is a powerful and mesmerizing work that takes you on a journey to discover the secrets of your heart.

Tom Davis, author of *Red Letters: Living a Faith that Bleeds* and *Scared: A Novel on the Edge of the World*

With the skill of an artist, Mary DeMuth perfectly captures the desire within us all to know and be known, to love and be loved, and to understand the meaning of home. *The Muir House* is a captivating read to the very last page. I loved it.

Emily Freeman, author of *Grace for the Good Girl* and *Chatting at the Sky* blog

What a challenge family relationships can be, often rife with conflict and rich with love. With a deft pen and thoughtful insights, Mary DeMuth has given us a story of just such conflict and love guaranteed to touch the heart.

Gayle Roper, author of *A Rose Revealed* and *Shadows on the Sand*

Mary DeMuth has once again captured my soul with a story that resonated long after I closed the back cover. DeMuth is a master at immersing readers in another world—one of hopes and fears and triumphs. She's done it again with *The Muir House*. Her finest novel yet.

James L. Rubart, bestselling author of
Rooms and *Book of Days*

Mary DeMuth uses vivid language to unpack the mysteries haunting Willa Muir, the heir to both a past and a house she'd much rather forget than embrace. The metaphors are rich, the story unique. Just when you think you've figured out the ending, DeMuth's *The Muir House* takes yet another dark turn in this story of redemption and yearning.

Patricia Hickman, bestselling author of
The Pirate Queen and *Painted Dresses*

Mary DeMuth is a master at telling relevant stories that explore the wrenching need we all have to find love and affirmation outside of ourselves. Her characters in *The Muir House* are as real as the sun on your face, the rain on your sleeve, and the breath in your lungs.

Susan Meissner, author of *The Shape of Mercy*

THE
MUIR
house

Also by Mary DeMuth

MARY DeMUTH

THE MUIR *house*

A NOVEL

ZONDERVAN®

ZONDERVAN.com/
AUTHORTRACKER
follow your favorite authors

ZONDERVAN

The Muir House
Copyright © 2011 by Mary E. DeMuth

This title is also available as a Zondervan ebook.
Visit www.zondervan.com/ebooks.

This title is also available in a Zondervan audio edition.
Visit www.zondervan.fm.

Requests for information should be addressed to:
Zondervan, *Grand Rapids, Michigan* 49530

Library of Congress Cataloging-in-Publication Data

DeMuth, Mary E., 1967 –
     The Muir house / Mary E. DeMuth.
          p.   cm.
     ISBN 978-0-310-33033-2 (softcover)
     1. Self-realization in women — Fiction. I. Title.
PS3604.E48M85 — 2011
813'.6 — dc22   2010052105

Published in association with the literary agency of Fedd & Company, Inc., Post Office Box 341973, Austin, TX 78734.

Cover design: Michelle Lenger
Cover photography: Dan Davis Photography
Interior design: Michelle Espinoza

Printed in the United States of America

11 12 13 14 15 /DCI/ 23 22 21 20 19 18 17 16 15 14 13 12 11 10 9 8 7 6 5 4 3 2 1

To Rockwall, a stable home, a great place to raise kids,
a special city in my heart

It takes wisdom to build a house,
    and understanding to set it on a firm foundation;
It takes knowledge to furnish its rooms
    with fine furniture and beautiful draperies.

Proverbs 24:3 – 4, *The Message*

one

Seattle, March 2009

In that hesitation between sleep and waking, that delicious longing for dawn to overwhelm darkness, Willa Muir twisted herself into the sheets, half aware of their binding, while the unknown man's face said those words again.

You'll find home one day.

She opened her eyelids, forced wakefulness, maligning sleep's lure. Her two legs thrust themselves over the side of the storm-tossed bed. Toes touched hardwoods, chilling her alert, finally. She pulled the journal to herself in the dusky gray of the room, opened its worn pages, then touched pen to paper. She copied the words as she heard them. The same sentences she'd written year after year in hopes of deciphering its message, understanding it fully. But they boasted the same syntax, the same prophecy, the same shaded sentences spoken by a dream man with a broken, warbled voice. A faceless man of the South, words erupting like sparklers from the black hole of Willa's memory.

Why couldn't she remember the man? Understand his cryptic message?

Something stirred then. A flash of recognition. Willa closed the journal, placed her pen diagonally on top, then curled herself into a sleep ball, covers over her head like a percale cocoon. She forced her eyes shut, willing her mind to remember the glinting.

There! Like an Instamatic from her childhood, the flash-bulb illuminated a gold ring. The man didn't cherish it on his finger. He held it like a monocle, as if he could see through it clear to eternity. Through that ring, a circular snapshot of the man clarified. Though the rest of his face faded into blue mist, his eye, wrinkle-creased and wise, focused like an eye doctor's chart under the perfect lens. A crocodile-green iris circled a large black pupil, its whites streaked pink with lacy vessels. It winked at Willa, or maybe it merely blinked. Hard to decipher, looking at one eye. The eye held sadness and grace, laughter and grief—and an otherworldly hint of promise. Willa memorized that eye behind the gold ring.

But like every other snatch of Willa's memory from that vacant memory of a four-year-old, the eye vaporized.

So familiar.

Yet so unfamiliar.

Nearly the green of Blake's eyes so long ago, those bewitching, enticing eyes she'd made herself turn away from, breaking her heart. Shattering his.

She returned to her journal, sketching the ring, the hazy face. The muddy-green eye she highlighted with an olive pencil. Light played at the window shade. She tugged it down so it would fling ceilingward, which it did in flapping obedience. She opened the sash, ushering in Seattle's evergreen perfume. The crisp air stung her Southern arms with goose bumps as she inhaled its scent. Fifty-five degrees in the morning felt like ice to Willa, even now. But facts were facts: You just couldn't compare the air's pristine cleanness to the South's sometimes thicker-than-mud humidity. And if she could help it, she'd never breathe Texas again.

Mother made it quite clear. Not even Southern hospitality could woo Willa back, not with Mother's hateful words swirling through the heat.

Willa fingered Mrs. Skye's letter atop her pile of books. "Come home," the caretaker wrote, in plainer-than-plain English — dark blue letters on crisp white stationery. "I need your help remodeling the Muir House. Need your expertise. Besides, your mother needs you. She's fading as fast as the house's paint peels. It's time."

Willa shook her head in response. "No," she said to her room, her heart, her will. "I can't. Won't."

But something deep inside told her it was time to find home.

Willa folded Mrs. Skye's letter in half. Instead of quartering it and returning it to its envelope, she tore it into confetti. When she left the room, the confetti stuck to her bare feet.

two

"If you ask me," Hale said, "it's a sign." He took a drink of sludge, what the Oasis Café called Vitality, and smiled. Green bits clung to his perfectly white teeth.

"Rinse," Willa said.

"Green teeth again?"

She nodded.

He emptied the small water glass, a throwback from fifties diner ware, swirled a bit, then swallowed the whole mess. He smiled. "Satisfied?"

"Quite." She picked at her smoked salmon frittata. "I saw an eyeball, Hale. Nothing more."

"You said it was green, right?"

She nodded.

"So it wasn't mine, then." He held a hint of sadness in his blue eyes, the color of Seattle sky after the fog lifted.

Willa kept her gaze there, willing herself to forget Blake's envy-green. She held Hale's carefree blue to her heart.

Hale made a circle with his index finger. "Au contraire. You saw a ring. A golden ring. The Egyptians—"

"Quit it with the Egyptians. For you, everything goes back to the Egyptians."

Hale shook his head. He pulled her hand to his, held it perfectly. Not too tight to make her palms sweat, not too loose to make her wonder. "The Nile River," he said as if he hadn't heard her scolding, "provided the first rings, woven from the sedges and rushes nestled next to papyrus plants." With his other hand, he circled her naked wedding finger. "The symbol of eternity."

"Quit getting creepy and stalkerish on me."

"I'm not Blake."

"I know."

"Then don't pull the stalker card."

He withdrew his hand, then winked one dusk-blue eye. "A ring has no beginning or end. Like life, it circles around itself, returning from where it came." He shaped his free hand like a spyglass, looked out the café's window onto the sidewalk. Then he spied it on her. "It's a symbol of the sun and moon, this shape. And the inside isn't dead air, it's a portal to the unknown."

"I have no portal."

"Everyone does."

"Nope, you're the one who told me I had a wall. Perhaps I am a wall."

Hale sighed. "I didn't say you were a wall. Just that you're so afraid of love that you've built fortresses around yourself. Like your mother. Like the Egyptians. But I—"

"Focus," she said. She squeezed his hand, then withdrew. "This isn't about my mother—who, by the way, hollered at me, told me to leave once and for all. It's not about ancient Egypt or you storming my walls. It's about my life." She sipped her green tea pomegranate infusion, then nibbled on dry flax toast.

"I'm well aware of your life. Of your obs—"

"I swear if you say obsession one more time, I'll break up with you."

He laughed, and when he did, his brown curls bounced in the effort. Hale's goatee, longer than a real goat's, swayed in the mayhem. She did love this man, loved him right on down

to his Salvation Army shoes. He drank more sludge, not bothering to rinse. "I'm in your life for the long haul, Wills," he
said. "Besides, who else would accompany you on your valiant
quest?"

He did have a point. All those years piecing together her
past in yellow notebooks, journals, and scraps of paper. All
those newspaper clippings. Most men — most people — would
think her, well, obsessed. But since when did seeking the truth
equal obsession? "You know where you came from," she said.

"Raised by wolves." He howled.

She shook her head. The Oasis Café's patrons didn't even
look their way, didn't seem to care that her boyfriend fancied
himself a werewolf. Stranger folk than he frequented this off-
beat place. "Maybe I was too," she said to the coffee-drenched
air between them.

"You weren't. You had a mom and a dad."

"Had is the appropriate word. I'm a twenty-six-year-old
orphan," she said.

"She's still alive, Wills."

"She said, 'You are worthless and ugly and stupid and not
my child!'"

"Why do you keep revisiting her words?"

"You're the one who brought it up. And having to talk
about it again breaks my heart. She's a closed subject, you
understand?"

Hale nodded. "But your parents loved you, right? Before
she sent you away, your mother took care of you."

"Rote, Hale. Something she had to do because Daddy made
her. Sometimes she tried to fulfill requirements of mother-
hood, a miser with affection, but most of the time she scowled.
Daddy? He loved extravagantly." She felt her voice quaver. Daddy's eyes sparkled like Hale's, the purest azure, which made her

longing for Hale make sense, in a pathetic sort of way. Like her counselor used to say, always looking for a father.

She looked out the window, noting one cumulus cloud shaped like an anchor, only to dissipate.

Hale spooned multigrain hot cereal into his mouth. "Gruel," he winced. "I hate the cholesterol specter."

She shook her head, weary of his health kick.

"Sorry. I'm becoming a me-monster again. Listen." He twirled his spoon in a flourish. "Wills, I know we don't know the inciting incident – that empty place in your memory. But we do know the rising action, the climax."

She looked at her lap, brushed a crumb away. "Neither of us knows the ending."

"But perhaps together, we will." He reached again for her hand. She let him take it. "Maybe we'll be the denouement."

"I have too much baggage." She speared a wedge of grapefruit.

"How colloquial."

"I think the word you're looking for is cliché."

"Touché!"

"Come on, Hale. This is real." Another grapefruit piece. She wished she'd doused it with evil processed sugar.

"Maybe it's not."

"Maybe you're annoying," she said.

"Maybe. But you like me, remember?" He smiled.

She returned the favor.

He took another bite of gruel, then swallowed. "You're why the *vena amoris* is so important to me." He wiped his hands on a patchwork napkin, pulling her left hand across the table. He pointed to her ring finger.

"You've completely lost me."

"Exactly. But I hope to gain you."

She raised her eyes to his, and she understood. His face, unlike the man in the dream, snapped into perfect focus. Those eyes, that face, that man, his heart — wanted to marry her — empty memories notwithstanding.

His left hand held hers, but with his right, he fumbled through his thrift-store khakis. He pulled out a simple gold ring. "One ring to rule them all," he said.

Willa's heart hiccupped. She wanted to pull her hand away, wanted to run out of the Oasis Café screaming, but fear magnetized her to the metal chair. "I'm not easily ruled," she choked out. Panic fluttered inside. Memories of yelling, shrieking, hating swirled in the cavity of her heart. Daddy. Mother. Willa. The big white house. A broken heart.

He glided the ring onto her finger. "The *vena amoris* is the vein of love. Originating here." He touched the simple gold ring on her finger, "And venturing to the heart." He pointed to his own, thankfully.

"You know I don't do marriage." As the words passed her tongue, her teeth, her lips, she saw his wince as if she'd slapped him.

"You love me." Hale's hand still rested on his heart.

She nodded. That truth, she knew. Willa felt the ring ruling her finger, threatening to travel the *vena amoris* to her heart. "I need to go." She gathered her purse, her hand, that ring, and stood.

Hale didn't stand. Didn't chase after her. He sat there, wet-eyed and slapped, his face like a scolded boy's, not a man's.

She wrestled with the ring, expecting it to glide off as easily as it slid on, but it wouldn't. "I can't get it off."

"Keep it. Let it remind you." Hale said these words to the patchwork napkin, not to her.

"I need to go home," she said.

He lifted his eyes to hers now. Cleared his throat as if he wanted to unclog his voice of emotion. "What if home is a person, Wills? What if *I* am your home?"

She tore away from his eyes while his words chased her all the way home.

three

They say a woman's wealth, her true identity, rests in the richness of relationships, but "they" have it all wrong. What a woman really needs, what truly defines her, is four solid walls. A house with good bones, a yard sprinklered in the summertime, a creaking porch swing, overflowing window boxes. Castled there, she safeguards her secrets, particularly if those mysteries lie concealed in cardboard boxes in the attic.

Willa sanded the importance of both — hearth and secrets — into her marrow, nailed them like Luther's treatises to her heart while she walked seven blocks toward home, still trying to pry Hale's ring from her finger, his hopeful words from her heart.

Hale was beautiful. In every way. She knew this. Others confirmed it. He worked on behalf of Seattle's working poor, helping secure affordable housing. Homes for those without houses. And he loved her. Why he did, she couldn't quite make her heart understand.

With every logical step toward home, while Green Lake glistened under the morning sun, she scolded herself in cadence.

He loves me.

I should marry him.

He should marry me.

We should marry each other.

Should, should, should.

Such a mathematical equation. Hale plus Willa equaled

marriage, the ring being the plus sign making it all balance. She would have the security a fatherless girl wanted. He would have someone needy to rescue and coddle. A perfect match.

Willa pulled the locket from behind her tank top. A heart dangled as faithfully as it had years and years before. She opened it. Blue-eyed Daddy on one side, five-year-old Willa with crooked teeth on the other. She wanted to ask Daddy what to do, how to react to Hale, what to say, but his smiling picture said no words. And his death confirmed that he'd never speak life over her again. In that recollection, grief moistened her eyelids. How long would she miss that man? Forever? With every milestone, the pain augmented like a terrible exclamation point to his absence.

She squinted back the tears in the sunlight, pulled in the halcyon air, and smelled fire. Odd that someone would stoke fire from kindling this time of year. The chill of spring left weeks ago, replaced by Northwest heat – a balmy seventy-two degrees at high noon. Still, some folks relished cozy liked they chugged their coffee fix – often.

Willa looked at the ring, how it captured the sun. Hale said its innards were a gateway to the unknown, yet now her finger filled that void. He must've thought she was his unknown. But was he hers? Could a person become a home?

She wanted to holler a yes, jump on Hale's back under the watchful eye of Gas Works Park, and let him run her down the grass incline toward Lake Union while she screamed and laughed and hung crazy to his shoulders. She could picture such a thing. Could feel her hair windwrapping her face, could smell the faint hint of Hale's evergreen cologne. But she couldn't make the daydream a reality. Which is why she had to go home now, to sift once again through the large box of clippings in her attic, to carefully weave the broken story of her past so she could finally make sense of today's reticence.

A fire truck screamed by her, glassy red. She smelled its exhaust, tasted it on her tongue. It turned right.

Onto her street.

Something inside, a primal horror, made her run flat out.

She turned the corner. Four houses down on the right, it squealed next to others of its kind, catty-corner this way and that. Hoses hooked up to the block's fire hydrant spewed water onto her fuchsia house.

She rushed to the sidewalk facing her porch, a cry leaving her mouth. But in the cacophony of fire, no one heard the scream. Willa's skin absorbed the heat of her bungalow's flames licking, tasting, biting, consuming her home, its secrets, while firefighters sprayed pathetic sprinklers onto the rafters that buckled beneath the attack of flames. Still, she rushed at it. If she ran fast enough, she could rescue her journal, the drawing of the man's green eye.

But arms caught her. "Stand back, miss," a fireman said.

"But that's my house. My—"

"I'm sorry." He said it like he might've meant it, but she knew he couldn't possibly. Had he not interrupted her, "my everything" would've been recorded by the day, showing all of Seattle that her research was her everything. Even more than Hale and his ring. More than white window boxes or a rickety porch swing or fuchsia siding.

She'd been so close. And now every shred of evidence belched flames and smoke. She struggled against the fireman's embrace, smelling soot. He held her back, saying I'm sorry over and over again. She looked up to see the roof implode on itself, sparks twirling to the sky like unwanted confetti after a parade.

Home lost its fight. The fire won—everything.

Willa sat on the sidewalk below the cobble-stoned retaining wall while firefighters clodded heavy boots on her once-pristine patch of clovered lawn. They shouted indecipherable words above her in a strange whirlwind. She told herself now would be an appropriate time to cry, but no tears obeyed, her eyes as dry as the lathe and plaster of her once-preening home. This was the way of it, right? Throw your life into one single pursuit, only to see fate roar away everything in one nasty spark. She could almost feel the wall around her heart erect itself as it had in the aftermath of Blake's suffocation.

She opened her phone, then closed it. The small act burned isolation into her. Once again she'd given her entire life to one person – a man. She had several girlfriends she could call, but none she felt comfortable sharing the fire. Hale was it. Before that Blake. And always Daddy. Willa tasted the fire on her tongue, and felt its hiss inside.

She didn't even own the home kindling before her – a rental leased to her by a distant friend of a friend's grand-mother, the rent ridiculously affordable as reimbursement for her decorator skills.

Splintering caught her attention again, the crackle of flames overwhelming her home dreams. *The truth will set you free,* she heard on the singeing wind. Call her sentimentally religious, but she believed those things. Believed if she knew the truth of the past, she'd be free in the great big Now.

A fireman lifted her to her feet, his grip stronger than her resolve to resist. Now that every shred of evidence wafted northward on an erratic breeze, she would never know the hole, never unravel the mystery of the months she lost, never understand the fickleness of her parents' marriage – or figure out why she couldn't say yes to Hale, or why she ran from Blake.

Should she call the man she ran from? She touched her phone, let her finger rest on Hale's number, and settled on snapping it shut. Again.

Not Hale. Not now. Not with the ring burning a circle

around her finger like a heated expectation she could never fulfill.

Where would she go?

No, not there.

Mother would holler those words again. Words that burned more than the crumpling house before her.

four

Willa picked a piece of fire-defiant grass pushing through the crack in the landlady's sidewalk, then ripped it into tiny pieces, littering the pavement while ashes stirred by a breeze dandruffed her hair. She plucked a dandelion. The insurance adjuster didn't notice this act, too occupied as she flustered around Willa's collapsed rental home. At the place she'd severed the poor dandelion, white milk circled the stalk. She pressed the juice to her tongue, grimacing as she did. Its milk was not sweet. Anything but.

Last night as she reclined in the middle of a king-sized bed at a nameless hotel, Hale texted her ad nauseam. He'd apparently driven by to check up on her and spied the charcoal house. "I'm freaked," he texted. "You okay?" said another one. "Where are you? I called all the hospitals and you're not there, so you're either with Jesus or staying somewhere." "Please tell me you're okay." "Text me back!" Must've been forty or so of them, all unanswered. She felt cruelty in the act of ignoring, but she couldn't bring herself to let Hale into her pain. This she would go through alone.

She signed papers, nodded toward the empathetic-faced woman, trying to assure all would be well. Willa hated the sympathy of people who didn't know her, so she deflected. "Thanks for your time," Willa said. "I'm sure you have other disasters to attend to."

The woman nodded, shook her hand. "I'm so sorry. You're far too young to have such a thing happen. Everything you owned inside."

Tell me about it, she almost said, but kept her words behind clenched teeth. Instead, Willa turned away, waving as she did, indicating the conversation was over.

She waited for the adjuster to pull away from the sidewalk before she sat on her scorched lawn. The smell of firewood mixed with burning plastic seeped into her. There was truly nothing left, and with the wiring gone bad in the attic first, God had assured her he'd burned every shred of evidence. Every one of her boxes.

There'd been a time, not many years ago when Willa lived for her carefully constructed reputation, that she'd rather die than talk to God in broad daylight, where passersby on their way to Green Lake could watch the crazy girl rail at the heavens. She'd rather have ankle tattoos laced over bone than be heard like that. But that was before Hale authenticated her, as he put it. Taught her the value of sharing secrets, being real. He prayed out loud during all sorts of occasions—lamenting Seahawks games, hiking Tiger Mountain, delivering bad news to a client. He didn't mind voicing his concerns where folks could hear them. And that carefree, uncomplicated relationship with Jesus rubbed off on her. Tainted her in a good way. Thanks to Hale, Willa threw underfoot some of that irrepressible need to be liked. Since God saw fit to point his electric finger on her roof and burn every bit of her investigation to cremation, she figured what could it hurt?

She didn't kneel.

Didn't stand either.

Just sat on what was left of the green patch and crossed her legs. Her temper too. As her ancestors put it, she hollered. "God, I get it, okay? Get. It. You've been messing with me to stop the detective work from afar and just get on with it. Well, congrats, Almighty. You've done it now. Every single piece, every opened path, now closed for eternity."

A couple walking a golden lab strolled by. The man raised an eyebrow, then saluted her. She saluted back. "Carry on," he said.

"Thank you," she said. So she carried on.

"And how am I supposed to head back to her lair? Mother's not exactly wanting me back, regardless of her state. Not to mention other folks back there who want nothing more than for me to disappear. You hear that? You want me to disappear too? Are you ticked off that I wasn't in my house so I could incinerate right then and there, collapsed under all my boxes? I would've made interesting compost." At this, she severed clover, head by head, only three-leaf ones, though. "Ah, come on. Say it, God. You wished I'd been in there. Then you wouldn't have to trouble your sovereign self with my nagging."

A Boeing jet spewed its carbon tailprint in a long white streak across the periwinkle sky, creating a skyway from the Olympic Peninsula toward the summit of Mount Rainier. Since its trajectory headed southeast, the precise direction she needed to go, Willa took the exhaust as another breadcrumb in God's Hansel and Gretel ways. He'd been coaxing her with pieces of the trail all along her sojourn in Seattle, but she hadn't budged. With the nightmares, how could she? And with Blake back there, why would she? Why would God tell her to go back to the place where the darkness began? Wasn't he the Father of Lights? And wasn't that precisely why she did her research from a safe haven? Besides, she couldn't bear the smell of that house again.

But Mrs. Skye's email seemed hopeful — a strange thing for a woman often reserved. When Willa wrote she'd be willing to fly back and do the design job for her old home, now converted into a bed and breakfast, the caretaker welcomed her. Told her to come, that she'd have a room for her. Her old room.

No doubt with strings attached to visiting Mother. But where else would she go?

Ashes dotted her skin, brought her back to Seattle, a day post-fire. She brushed away the memories in like manner — the embalming room with black and white checkered floor. The voices around the corner she couldn't make out. The curtain closing on the memory. She shushed her mind, told it not to stray. Even then, she couldn't resist the pull from her pocket. She took out the slim picture holder and removed the Polaroid. There she stood, a pale yellow dress above her knees, mismatched socks, black shoes, pigtails. A man's hand rested on her head as if he would prevent her growth. He stood in shadows beneath a giant tree, his shaded face blending into gray.

Sometimes when Willa strained, she swore she heard the faceless man sing, but when he did, he opened up a gash in her soul — the gaping wound that started her cutting all those years ago. All that cutting for nothing.

five

Two weeks later, Willa fingered a *House Beautiful* under trembling hands as airplanes muscled overhead. Thomas Wolfe was right. You couldn't really go home again. Even as the fluorescent lights of the kitschy Seattle gift shop hummed, she tried to convince herself of the author's fallibility. After all, a 767 parked in the North Satellite of SeaTac Airport denied the fact — she was headed home. In twenty minutes she would shuffle her feet down a too-narrow aisle, cram her body between two strangers, and wait for the plane's nose to aim Texasward. A few confined, hungry hours and it would spit her out on Southern soil. She'd be home.

And Hale would be safely tucked into his life in Seattle. He could pursue a better girl — the kind of Larabar-nibbling knockout he deserved.

"I'm not letting you go." His words wafted skyward on misty breath. He stood anchored to the drop-off deck while cabs whirred by and she told herself not to cry. Through the miracle of drugstore Vaseline, she managed to dislodge her engaged finger and re-gift the ring to him. Yet he held it out to her, those not-letting-go words still playing in the cold air between them. He placed its circle in her left palm, then closed her fingers in his. "You keep it."

"Hale —"

"Please don't say anything else. Let's just keep it at me not letting you go because that's the truth. And truth is something you value, right?"

She nodded, hoping the motion wouldn't dislodge her tears.

He pulled her to himself, wrapping strong arms around thin, weary shoulders. "I'll be in touch," he said. He kissed the top of her head as if he were her brother sending her off on a trip to Europe, not her brokenhearted ex-fiancé. He stood back, held her upper arms, and dazzled her with his clear eyes. "I mean it."

House Beautiful didn't keep good company on the plane, so she recycled it in the seatback pocket. Too many austere, architecturally dry homes with pristine furniture suited for museums, not living. She preferred eclectic – a holy mishmash of tokens from life, scoured finds from garage sales married to midcentury modern furniture. The contrast, the hominess, the collaboration of styles would culminate in her own home, someday.

She thanked God for an interior design job with portability, particularly with Mrs. Skye's job offer in front of her. And although the renter's insurance money had yet to kick in, she thanked herself for the wisdom of backing up all her design files on an exterior server. From a now-depleting bank account, she bought a new Mac, some clothes and toiletries, and several pairs of Toms shoes, one pair of which graced her feet today. She checked her phone for messages, half hoping she'd see a clever text from Hale. Nothing. Didn't he say he'd contact her?

She rented a Prius, in honor of Seattle, and started the monotonous drive around 635, a looped freeway that circled Dallas. No mountains shouted hello. No Indian-named towns announced themselves on highway signs. No Puget Sound let the sun dance on its choppy waters. Just a sea of large vehicles heading on a cement serpentine to Lord knew where while the blue sky loomed terribly large, unbroken by topography, while strip malls cloned themselves every four miles. How many Mattress Giants did a city need?

"So this is home," she said to the Prius. With its computer-game-like console, she half expected it to answer her back.

When she took the Interstate 30 overpass, she announced to her fellow Texans, "Take in the vista, folks. This is as high as you'll get." For a second, maybe two, she drove above the world, just concrete below, while Wal-Marts and subdivisions spread before her street after street. Though a forty-degree spring chill had cut through her that Seattle morning, a balmy seventy degrees hugged her the second she exited the airplane through the non-air-conditioned tunnel. Now she let in the Texas air. Her hair tickled her face, no doubt stringifying itself. With one hand, she pulled it back, her eyes on the gray horizon, straining to see the water.

When the sun caught Lake Ray Hubbard, she felt her chest concave. The size of Lake Washington, it sparkled under the day, reminding her. Fishing for catfish, bass. Swimming behind their too-small boat, the elation of water skiing the first time in the boat's minimal wake. Memories with Daddy attacked her, shotgun-like. So much all at once. It'd been one thing to play CSI with her past on papers organized into files, tucked into now-torched boxes. It was quite another thing to smell the humid air, watch the lake's waters dance. And as the air flew through her window, she wondered why it didn't smell like the Puget Sound.

It wouldn't be long before she'd face Mother, untangle her memories. Then everything would be okay. She had to believe that. She drove toward a Rockwall she didn't remember. A new lakefront development rose like a gem to the right of the I–30 bridge. Her town had grown as she had—in just a few short years. It practically preened new.

She exited, all the while telling her stomach to stop flipping, turning, churning. She'd emailed Mrs. Skye, the caretaker, days before, telling of her intentions to stay in the family home. She'd received a tepid reply, but expected that. Would the woman crack this time? Enough to shed some light? Or would she remain the caretaker of darkness? In a handful of minutes, Willa would know.

She turned left on Goliad, the quasi-highway, broken up with lights and mom-and-pop stores. To her left, she spied Joe Willy's Restaurant, a haven of many fun and food memories. On her right, she spotted the veterinarian—where Sanka, her ancient cat, had let out her last breath. Willa could still picture Sanka's eyes, how they pled not to send her to the back of the office. Willa's heart broke with every meow.

Just beyond that, she spied the florist, where Blake sent her on a romantic scavenger hunt. When she'd found the florist and walked inside, the clerk handed her one dozen pink buds. She blushed rose-red precisely the minute he jumped up from behind the counter, scaring her half to death. She threw the roses when she jumped, twelve pink long-stems flying hither and yon. The florist laughed, gathered them again, and re-presented them. And when Blake kidnapped her away from her car, he bent near and kissed her, long and slow. Delicious, really. Her first kiss.

Willa shrugged away the memories, or tried to. Somewhere along this stretch of road rose a convalescent center, where Mother inflicted nurses with her charm, the site of Willa's heartbreak. Three years it had been, before the Alzheimer's took vicious root, according to Mrs. Skye. For the past three years Willa had read the caretaker's guilt-laden letters, blasting Willa's ingratitude, her neglect, her stupidity. Three years of letters she seldom answered. She viewed them then as evidence, every page detailing her mother's decline in painstaking detail. Though Mrs. Skye's letters were ash now, the words still screamed at Willa.

She no longer walks.

She yells obscenities now.

She doesn't know me.

She never asks about you.

She wets herself.

She is alone in the world, and you have abandoned her.

Her mother, so alive, so angry, so full of words, now reduced to bed-living, crying at old shows, locked away in her mind. Would Mother remember the words she spoke over her? Would she recognize her face when she dared to visit? Would apologies leave her mouth? Willa shook her head, hoping to shake the guilt. What kind of daughter, an only daughter at that, let her mother rot away in a convalescent center?

A diversion rose bright and bold in the same place it'd been: Sonic. She turned right into its lot, angled her car into a slot and ordered cranberry limeade from the dismembered voice. Maybe a drink would soothe her conscience, would erase the jumpiness in her stomach. She looked at the bright menu, telling herself to relax. In Seattle, she'd missed the mini ice cubes of Sonic fame. Never had it been replicated. Not a slushy. Not crushed ice. Something in the blessed in between. The roller-skating waitress handed her the drink. Willa placed her delicacy in the cup holder, backed out of the angled spot, then continued toward old Rockwall, minutes away from the house of mysteries.

She dodged construction through the town square, then

picked up speed. Old timber-framed homes lined the widen-ing street, some proud, some crooked from disrepair. The sun hovered in the left hand pocket of sky, warming the side of her face. At least she'd have the sun, its warmth, its happy hello nearly every morning. For all it lacked in mountains, Texas did have its sun.

Willa slowed when she saw the house towering on the right side of the road. She told herself to breathe, told herself to suck in sunshine air, but her lungs held her breath. The Muir House Bed and Breakfast, the sign said. Established 1895. She parked out front, marveling at the transformation — from funeral home to bed and breakfast in a few short years. Didn't folks have memories? Of touching Grandpa Clark's icy hand right there in the front room? Of mourning Elda Perkins who made the best pies in Rockwall? Of forming lines of cars and driving over yonder to the cemetery? Could a place morph from embalming to entertaining?

But then she remembered the place wouldn't serve as a respite for fellow Rockwallites; it would welcome visitors from out of town who didn't know the home's death roots.

But she knew. All too well. The utility shelter — her haven — on the house's right side knew.

Living above a funeral home had its macabre moments. The family quarters were spacious for just the three of them: Mother, Daddy, her; and the back carriage home housed Mrs. Skye, always watching. But the bustling below her footsteps, inter-rupted by long bouts of quiet, weighed on Willa once she was old enough to understand death. For a time, she wondered why people wailed and wept when they first saw the plastic people, eyes closed, dressed in their Sunday best. Why the tears for a mannequin? Somewhere around five years old, death dawned on her, and the great hereafter made its presence known.

Willa shook her head of the memory, willed it to die, but it stayed perched in the back of her consciousness as it always had been, teasing her. She opened the car door, then looked long at the old house, her heart catapulting inside. The left front door opened. Willa shoved down her fear. Told herself to be brave.

six

Mrs. Skye walked like a matriarch onto the wide, white porch, her arms crossed over a sagging chest like they were intended to rest there – always. Her smile pressed thin. She made no gesture to wave at Willa. She planted herself, a fixture on the swept-bare porch, nothing more.

In that empty place between them stood tense static. Instinctively, Willa offered her hand to Hale, the one she knew would hold her through this, but he was gone.

Instead she hefted a suitcase – Hale's actually – and picked her way over cobbled steps. She strained up the crooked wooden stairway, noticing the peeling paint beneath her feet.

"Here you are on your quest for answers," Mrs. Skye said.

Willa shook her head. Tears ran unheeded down her cheeks. Seeing the house again, encountering a hard-to-read Mrs. Skye, mixed together to form a pit of dread. "Nice to see you," she choked out.

Mrs. Skye opened one of two tandem doors on the porch, the left one, to be exact. It creaked on old hinges. "Go ahead. Come in out of the cold."

"The cold?" Willa laughed while she lugged her things inside.

"Don't be a Northerner, now. It may be March, but it's still winter a few more days, so it's cold. And this house is hard to keep warm." She shut the door behind Willa. "Now let me get a look at you."

Willa dropped the suitcase. The smell hit her first. Mrs. Skye might've painted and spruced up the place, but she couldn't deaden the smell of musty death. "Here I am," Willa said. The words held more longing than declaration, she knew. Her voice echoed off the twin parlors.

"You're too thin." Mrs. Skye's eyes narrowed a bit. Her red-flecked gray hair didn't dare grow long, preferring to be cropped close to her white scalp. Age spots dappled her face as she stood between the left parlor and the hallway behind.

"You look great," Willa said.

Mrs. Skye looked beyond Willa toward the kitchen. "I have work to do," she said.

"The bed and breakfast, right?"

"Eventually. It's in process. You'll be staying in your old bedroom. You're as good a first guest as any, I suppose. Right next to the embalming room."

"You named it that?"

"Of course not, but that's how you know the room, right?" Willa nodded.

"Now, don't let the closet door fool you; it's a small bathroom now. You should be quite contained."

Willa kept her mind on embalming. She knew Rockwall to be a conservative, grit-of-earth place, not exactly a destination where folks wanted to stay in embalming rooms, conjuring up ghosts. "Have you come up with a theme for the rooms? I remember you struggled with that."

Mrs. Skye nodded. "Of course. We're going to capitalize on Rockwall's famous rock wall. Your room will be the Rockwall Room. The others will follow in the wall theme. The Great Wall of China, Wall Street, the Berlin Wall, and Hadrian's Wall. But as you know, they're just decorated any old way. Let's hope you can pull everything together."

"At least you didn't choose Jericho." Willa tried to frame her interior design mind around the woman's theme, but had a hard time thinking of bedding for the Berlin Wall room.

"Funny. Now, I expect you to be efficient. I want to open the bed and breakfast July Fourth. That gives you four good months to complete the rooms. Then you can get back to your life in Seattle. I imagine you have clients waiting."

Four months? Could she last that long under Mrs. Skye's strange distance? "Yes," she said. "I can have it ready by then, Mrs. Skye."

"Save the formality. Call me Genie."

"But I've never called you that."

"Get used to change." She paced through the front room to the kitchen.

Willa followed. New cabinetry, sleek and dark, hollered at her — ripped right out of this year's Ikea kitchen catalog. In this ancient house, white bead board cabinets made more sense. European cabinets seemed as incongruous as a great-grandmother wearing a string bikini. Why did she say yes to this job? How could she bring everything together to make the décor cohesive? How did Hadrian's ancient wall meld with sleek cabinets?

Genie pulled a large pitcher of tea from the stainless steel fridge, poured herself a glass. She drank it long, her red lipstick kissing the rim. "My first name's actually Eugenia. Even after all these years, I bet you didn't know that."

With Willa's boxes of investigation, she did know. But as Eugenia left Mrs. Skye's lips, all Willa could think of was the word *eugenics*, the idea of making a better human race through selective breeding and elimination. She hated that her warped mind doubted Eugenia'd make the cut. But she held her mind, then tongue, in check. "All right, then. Genie it is." Saying the new name gave Willa an odd sense of hope. Perhaps the old girl would share every secret now, and Willa could start living. The sun angled through the side window, practically inviting a look outside. Willa leaned toward its beckon, then spied the carriage house out back, the same white peeling paint as the larger house. "You still living back there?"

Genie took another drink. "It's my home. You read the will. You should know."

"I just thought —"

"Thought I'd tire of the old place and rent a condo? If I were you, I'd stop pretending to know the mind of someone else. Leave that to the prophets. Or your mother."

Hearing the word *mother* in the echo of the house panicked her. She stood in the home where nearly all her grief birthed. The words. The fights. The deception. And now, as she occupied this space, in the town that housed Mother, the obligation to visit loomed greater than Genie's snark.

Genie pulled out a smooth sliding drawer. "This came for you today, FedEx. I'm guessing it's for that job you have." She handed Willa a sleek white envelope.

Willa didn't look at it. She tucked it under her arm. "I best get settled."

Genie bit a fingernail between white incisors, ripped it horizontally, then spat it on the shiny tiled floor. It stayed there, as dead as many of the funeral home's former visitors. "In terms of food, you're welcome to fix anything you want. But I expect payment." She pointed to a file folder on the counter. "Here's an inventory of what I have, including prices. Just check off what you eat, then include payment by the end of each month."

"I wasn't expecting to freeload."

"Your correspondence seemed to indicate you wanted free room and board." She gave Willa a hard look, keeping her eyes on Willa's. "If you don't mind me asking," she measured. "Will you be staying beyond your four-month job?"

Willa made herself smile. "Well, that depends on how long it takes me to unearth the truth. You could tell me now, and I'll book my return flight on Independence Day. Out of your hair in no time flat."

Genie shook her ancient head. "I'm a caretaker of more than this house."

seven

Willa let Genie's words meander through her mind as she mounted the side steps, one of two stairways in the house. In daily life, Mother forbade her to take the fancy stairs, which opened wide to the funeral home on the first floor. The side stairs cricked under her feet, a protest they'd made since she was five.

A sign hung above each room in the U-shaped hallway. She didn't bother reading them because something else struck her. All the bedroom doors were closed, she noticed. Except one. The embalming room. Her hands chilled. She snuck past it toward her room, reading the title above: The Rockwall Room. She jiggled the glass handle until it shimmied open. At least Genie had the sense to keep the hardware.

Willa told her heart to stop racing while she unpacked her scarce belongings. She'd been prone to panic, and had learned to talk herself down, thanks to her kindly counselor. She sat on the bed. The room didn't smell the same, thanks to a scented plug-in on the north wall, permeating the ancient room with an artificial apple orchard — as if Rockwall had orchards. In truth, Rockwall developed on the backs of men and women who picked cotton from the black, clay earth. The old wardrobe was all that remained of her things, but it had been painted black, then distressed, which distressed Willa greatly. Curly grain maple, knotless as could be, now hid beneath Walmart paint. The travesty.

She wondered if Genie perked her ears, if she'd measure

Willa's steps from below. Willa slipped off her shoes and pulled on a pair of fuzzy footies. No sense in rousing the woman's curiosity. She practically tiptoed back to the embalming room, now donned "The Berlin Wall Room" by a hand-painted sign, white letters on black. She turned to comment on the irony, half expecting Hale to materialize behind her, but emptiness shouted back.

She paused before she stepped through the double French doors, backed by gaudy burgundy taffeta. She stood on the threshold of memories. Only these were the ones she already remembered in painful clarity.

When Genie was Mrs. Skye, she'd told Willa she decorated the rooms to her fancy without theme. Though the room now preened Southern charm with a dark canopy bed, forest green curtains, and a double wedding ring quilt slung over a quilt stand, she saw it through little girl eyes. In a flash, the bed melted into the floor, the curtains rolled in on themselves like the Wicked Witch of the East's shoes under Dorothy's house. The walls, once tan, now pickled green. The steel gurney rose. Black and white tiles checkered themselves over the distressed wood floor. The embalming room.

She remembered standing here before the funeral home's last funeral — Daddy's — after he battled his heart, then his mind, and lost. Daddy held his own for a time, as if he were trying to live long enough to tell Willa her stormy story. But the attack sapped his strength and the stroke killed his words. And Mother never left the two of them alone to write it down. As if to add a dagger of an exclamation point on Willa's grief, Mother's mind slipped here and there, her façade of civility giving up its fight in lieu of frank honesty, though never enough to give Willa the information she needed. Before she threw Willa from her life, she must've created some sort of internal pact with herself, that she'd never spill the beans, the secrets, the mystery. And her mind obeyed, even as it slipped from sanity, hijacking her secrets in a final act of defiance. Mother's memories left quickly, like an August thunderstorm.

It all happened right here, she thought. The final goodbye to Daddy, and though she didn't know it at the time, the end of the already-tumultuous relationship with her mother. Genie must've known, must've remembered the awful goodbyes, which was why she flung open the doors, no doubt. As caretaker of the Muir estate, she'd been entrusted to manage the home and its secrets. Perhaps this was her way of declaring battle, of showing her strong intention of winning the silence.

Willa ran out, her heart racing. She returned to the Rockwall Room, then sat on the four-poster queen-sized bed. The room's decor, stolen from Pottery Barn (page 23 of the winter catalog, to be exact), didn't shake hands with its bones. Floor-to-ceiling drafty windows, a wide-planked fir floor with divots to spare, and a bead board ceiling surrounded the showplace but didn't touch it, as if it were afraid to be tainted by modernity. Pottery Barn and the Muir Funeral Home just didn't see wall to furniture.

Willa remembered the envelope. She retrieved it, then shook her head. Not a client. Not a job.

Hale.

She pulled the paper rip-strip, revealing an envelope inside. It was one of Hale's inside-out envelopes. So intent on saving the environment, and quite married to thrift, he thought each envelope arriving in the mail a divine gift. He'd unglue its seams, then turn it inside out, re-pasting it with glue he made from organic flour. "Oh Hale," she said to her old room. The ache inside threatened to burst like Mount St. Helens, spewing her heart in one billion ashen particles. She should've said yes. Should've jumped into his arms at the Oasis Café. Should've let go of her past when her house incinerated.

She opened the envelope, then smelled it. Evergreen Mist. Oh, how he knew her. They'd found the scent in a tiny home store tucked into the recesses of Pike Place Market, amid the room atomizers of patchouli and musk. It smelled just like a Christmas tree, and although Willa warned him that a home scent was not meant to be cologne, he braved her worries and wore it anyway. And now he tortured her with it.

For a wicked second, she willed Evergreen Mist to battle Fake Apple Orchard in a duel to the death, to rid her room of artificial fruit in lieu of pure blissful Douglas fir. But the mixture of the two smells edged her toward a headache, making her miss Hale even more.

She unfolded the letter.

Dear Wills,

You know I'm not one for quick delivery and all, but I couldn't stand the thought of you arriving without a letter from me. So I threw my carbon footprint convictions out the tailpipe and had the quick-mail powers-that-be scurry this to you ASAP.

I won't say much, just remind you that I'm your home. I've known it since we first met. You remember that night, don't you? That streetlamp? The rain? My umbrella? You were feisty and strong, not wanting shelter, but so chilled you accepted the gift of my protection. I hope you'll do the same again someday.

I'm not going to be emailing or even texting you — that feels too impersonal. I'd rather you see my heart through my handwriting, through taking the time to spill words with ink and good recycled paper. Besides, it's hard for me to send jaunty little notes here and there through cyberspace. And I can't bear to hear your voice. So, we'll do this the 1970s way.

Hale

She held the letter to herself. Life availed itself to far too many goodbyes. Daddy who cherished. Mother who despised, then banished. Hale who blessed. And the house that held shreds of secrets, now burned clear to heaven. Hale fancied himself a poet of sorts, and Willa agreed. Words didn't flow from her the same way his leaked out. But she felt a primordial urge right then in the corner of the house while the sun set itself for the night—an uncanny need to write. So she picked up her laptop, roared it to life, then found the Muir House wi-fi connection.

She created a private blog in a flurry, choosing the plainest skin she could. The words she typed would be between her and Hale only. No need for the world outside to know her heart. Though he said he wasn't texting or emailing her, she figured he hadn't totally unplugged, so she sent him the exclusive invite. She flustered over what she'd say to him, but decided on *This is the best way I know to communicate with you. It's just between us, okay? Willa.*

The empty post box beckoned her fingers to write. So she did.

Title: So *now* I'm home.

Hale,

 You'll be happy to know I received your letter as soon as I arrived. Thank you. I can't pour everything out right now, though I feel I could, finally, so I'll stick to something we both admire: architecture.

 You would like Rockwall, I think. At least you'd like the old part. The new part looks like every other American suburb. Big box stores. Chain restaurants. A movie theatre multiplex and the like. But if you take Goliad north, you eventually end up in the town square, with the requisite courthouse in its center. (Aside: Can a square have a center?

I suppose so. I've never been one for geometry.) You'd like the 1930s – era art deco courthouse, though I've seen pictures of the old sandstone one, and I know you'd like its elegance even more. But the mortar between the stone disintegrated, making the ancient courthouse unsafe, so the WPA built this "new" one.

Little shops flank the square, mostly in ancient brick with wide front windows beckoning you in. A cake shop. A trendy secondhand clothing store. A trattoria. A coffee shop. On my trip through town, I read they hold a Saturday farmer's market there. I'll have to check that out. But be assured, I'll miss you as I do. I know how much you like Swiss chard and fresh oregano and those brown, free-range eggs gifted from happy chickens.

I'm not sure what else to write right now. So I'll stop.

Wills

Oh, and don't pester me about Mother. I haven't seen her yet. I'm still deciding.

She didn't write the word *love* before her name. Truth was, she didn't much love herself right now as she lived with the sticky regret that comes from saying no to Mr. Right. Why couldn't she just be like every other marriage-hungry girl out there, leap to her feet, nurse tears in her eyes, and holler a blessed, "Yes, I'll marry you!" But she had this terrible premonition that if she'd done that, within a month of the wedding she'd become one of those runaway brides, splintering Hale's heart.

No, it was better this way, she told herself. The right thing to do. Better for Hale. Better for her. If their love was meant to be, to borrow a cliché, it would survive this forced exile. She turned off her computer, tried to sleep, hoping dreams would outweigh the nightmares of being home.

eight

In the light of the next day, she knew one thing. The bedroom would never look right, would never be home. That Thomas Wolfe: Willa was beginning to think him genius. She heard bustling downstairs — the front door opening, the hollow sound of voices. She looked outside, expecting to see a serpentine of cars pouring into the expansive parking lot, but only one lonesome Nissan accompanied her rental. This was no longer the Muir Funeral Home.

She scanned the room, then spotted magazines fanned out on the apothecary nightstand, enticing Willa, seducing her. Her hands itched; her breath cut itself short. Maybe she was home, after all. *This Old House, Better Homes and Gardens*, and *Country Living* hollered at her.

Willa started cutting at age eight, not the cutting you hear about where rich, sad girls draw blades across pink skin. Cutting houses. She'd been clipping houses for twenty years now. She did it to know *why*. Or *what*. Or *who*. She already knew when.

Her first scissors didn't fit right. Her staunchly right-handed Mother, determined Willa'd not be cursed with left-handed crazy handwriting, forced her fingers into right-handed contraptions — straitjackets for fumbling fingers. Willa risked tortured knuckles so she could snip homes from magazines.

Mother hoarded a glossy stack next to the toilet, nearly as high as the toilet paper dispenser. Willa dared move the magazines once. Only once. Mother grabbed her head, cold hands pressing the sides of her skull inward toward her nose. "You mustn't move them," she hissed. "Mustn't!"

It was night, always night, when Willa slithered along the hard floor, snaking toward the bathroom. Mother took several blue pills every night, so Willa knew she wouldn't wake up. She snuck to the stack of magazines, slipping one from the bottom of the pile, barely breathing.

She weaseled the magazine to this room, shut the door, and started cutting. Nothing but houses. Tiny clip art homes. Mansions. Cartoon houses. Blueprints of cottages intended for the sea. And if by accident she'd rip one, she mended it with tape, glue, whatever she could find. If a part was missing, Willa glued it to her house notebook anyway and drew the rest. She couldn't bear a house half built.

She still couldn't.

That's why she had to know. Despite what Mrs. Skye wrote once, that the truth wasn't good in the telling. It might've been crazy, her pursuit, might even get herself in a heap of trouble. But she didn't care. She was dead already, numb to the bottom of too-long feet — a restless wrestler who desperately needed to know. A hole bored into her heart shaped like dormers and pier and beam — lathe and plaster too. No matter what Willa did, who she dated, where she lived, she couldn't fill it. Couldn't find it.

In Blake's eyes, she felt an odd sense of fitting, of being right. Of being loved, wanted, obsessed over — though the suffocation got to her. But before that, she found safety in the utility shelter.

She'd scouted home in the little shelter that hugged the house's south side, bunkering herself away from all the pain of her microcosmic world. Inside those walls, sitting next to the electric meter, she watched the dials move slowly in circles, proof that her home boasted life. A little window the electric man used to read the meter became her view to the world out-side. Inside, though, she felt havened. At least for a time. But even there, she couldn't prevent the pain from entering – in the form of another person. Proof positive that you couldn't protect a life with walls and a window, but you could rampart a heart, with enough determination.

For one blessed hiccup of time she felt a breeze of content-ment in the four walls of her Green Lake bungalow with its porch swing and perennial garden. *I am home,* she believed. Only to have a spark from antiquated wiring ignite the hole in her heart and roar despair inside. Only she could never hold the despair, grab at it like something tangible; it ran clear through. Her heart a sieve, containing nothing. Not even grief. Not until she found out where she came from. Who she was. Why her mother hated her.

She hugged *This Old House* to herself, then opened it, smelling the gloss inside. And like a crack addict, her hands grabbed for her orange-handled scissors.

nine

Willa had practically redecorated the entire wall-themed bed and breakfast in her mind when her cell jangled. She startled at the noise, but then relished it. Hale must've quit his technology-is-evil nonsense. But when she looked at the number, she didn't recognize it. Something local, though.

She debated whether to answer it, then finally decided to against her own advice.

"Hello?"

"It's true!" the voice squealed. "You're here. I can't believe it."

"Rebbie?" Could it really be Rebbie Porter? She hadn't heard from her in years, not since high school. How did she get her number?

"One and the same."

"But how did you know?"

"Oh come on, Willa Zilla. This is Rockwall. Everyone knows everything."

"But—"

"No buts about it. We're doing dinner, all right? I'll pick you up."

"I'd rather—"

"I'm actually on my way. See you in five!"

Willa stared at the phone as if it'd been hijacked by deliriously happy aliens. Rebbie would be here in five minutes. At first the thought horrified her. They hadn't exactly parted with happy words. But, then again, if memory served her right, Rebbie knew everything about everyone. She'd discovered Willa's plans, apparently. Maybe she knew her secret too.

Before Willa could pull on her shoes, she heard a car drive up—not just any car, but a boxy behemoth gas guzzler, painted sunshine yellow. Hale joked you could house a large extended family in one of those—along with their neighbors, and several pets, maybe even a walk-in closet.

Willa pulled Hale's letter to her nose, whiffed in his scent, and missed him all over again. She'd have held his words to her face longer, but the doorbell tinked, and she knew Genie would chastise her poor friend if the noise continued. She hurried down the central staircase in a flurry and opened one of the front doors. Rebbie, the fabulous former brunette with ice blue eyes now stood before her, blonde as a Dallas Cowboys cheerleader.

"Girlfriend!" She nearly leapt into Willa's arms. Apparently, Rebbie held no grudges, or simply forgot their high school feud. "Let me look at you!" Rebbie pushed back, swaying her long blonde hair in the effort. "You look positively Seattle!"

"Is that good or bad?" Willa snagged a glance Genie's frowning way. "Oh, I'm sorry. Rebbie, do you know Mrs. Skye?"

Genie splayed her bony hands, as if to say *I give up.* "Of course, of course," she said. "We've met at the Chamber."

"Genie's the dearest woman." Rebbie smiled.

Genie shook her head no, but her eyes seemed to agree.

"Well," Rebbie said into the foyer between the two parlors, "we best be going. Great to see you again, Genie. You've really beautified this place. A real showstopper. And that kitchen!" Rebbie kissed the fingers of her right hand, then lifted them heavenward. "Pièce de résistance!"

"We'll have to have you cook for the Chamber again," Genie told Rebbie.

"You know I'd adore that." She ruffled around in a gold purse as large as her vehicle. "Where did it go? Hmmm. There it is. I wanted you to have my card." She handed it Genie's way. Willa caught a glimpse of it—a stylized apron with her name in funky print.

Genie placed it in her pocket.

Rebbie clapped her hands. "Willa? You ready?"

Willa nodded, then followed her blonde cooking friend to the beast.

Zanata's host seated them near a window, then poured two ice waters.

"Are you here to see your mom?" Rebbie looked around her, not into Willa's eyes, as if she knew this wouldn't be the easiest question to answer.

"Not exactly."

"Oh."

"Yeah. I should see her."

"I can go with you if you like," Rebbie said. "You might find this strange, but I like visiting those places."

"I'll let you know."

Bread arrived like a period at the end of the conversation. Willa tried to think of things to say, ways to steer the conversation away from Mother.

Thankfully, Rebbie leaned in and smiled. "I know Jason Castro," she whispered.

"And who is that?" Willa took a long drink, shell-shocked that such a trendy joint lived on Rockwall's square. She could smell sautéing garlic mingling with the aroma of the wood-burning pizza oven. She loved the thick-rimmed hand blown glasses, the pottery-unique plates, the menu rife with specials.

"What? How could you ask such a thing?"

"I could ask it because I have no idea what you're talking about."

Rebbie knocked on her own temple. "Hello! Don't you watch *American Idol*? Season seven? Number four?"

Her lips moved, but she spoke a language Willa didn't understand.

Rebbie shook her head, then sighed. "He's from Rockwall, and he's famous. A singer. And his dreadlocks! Girl, you need to wake up!"

"Apparently," Willa said.

Rebbie scanned the menu, then pointed to the left hand side. "I know this might sound weird, but the chicken pizza with grapes and that fancy Italian cheese is to die for. Want to split it?"

"Well—"

"And their salads are huge, so let's split the spinach pecan one. Deal?"

Hungry, Willa didn't have the will to push for her own choices. "Okay," she said.

Rebbie flagged down their waitress, who, by the look of things, was her new best friend. She ordered. "Okay, so all I know about Seattle is that movie *Sleepless in Seattle* where Meg Ryan is in that café with Billy Crystal and she fakes—"

"Wrong movie. That was *When Harry Met Sally*."

"Was it?"

"Yes. Trust me."

"I guess I'm all confuzzled."

"Listen, Rebbie." Willa leaned in. "I'm sorry about Blake, about what happened."

Rebbie batted the air between them. "It's so Egypt."

"What?" Hale's kitschy fascination with Egypt roared into her head, then her heart. Would she ever escape his influence, even though her phone and computer kept silent?

"Ancient history, Willa Zilla. Don't worry a thing about it. He liked you since before you wore your first training bra back in elementary school. He probably still does. Want to see him? I can arrange it. You'll find he looks different, and he's softened a bit. And he's single."

Too much information. No wonder Hale railed against meaningless pieces of data. Rebbie was a data entry specialist's worst nightmare. "Um. No. I'm actually here for a different reason." But her heart thrust itself against her will. She wanted to see Blake, wanted to feel his arms, those eyes, that desperation he possessed for just her. Why did he still have a hold on her? Even now?

"Forbidden love? It must be. It's written all over your face."

Willa took another drink. "Listen, don't take this the wrong way, okay? But you don't really know me anymore. I've been away since graduation, eight years now." And there's Hale. She toyed with letting Hale into the conversation.

"You forget you were here when your daddy was passing."

Daddy. Willa sighed. "Yes, that's right."

"How long since he died?"

"Fall of 2005. Four years ago."

"I'm sorry," Rebbie said.

"A lot has happened since then."

"Don't I know it." Her eyes winced a bit as she said it. "I'm sorry. I come across too strong, don't I?"

"A little. But it's okay. I'm just thankful you've forgiven me. And to be honest, I'm glad you kidnapped me tonight. It feels good to see a familiar face."

Rebbie twisted her bottle blonde hair through manicured fingers. "What about my hair? You don't think the color is too much?"

"No, it suits you."

"I hope so. I'm single, you know. I'm hoping this is the new me—the me who will attract a new *him*." She swallowed. "What about you? Is there a *him* in your life?"

"Hale," Willa heard herself say. But was it true? Was Hale hers? Was he a *him*?

"Great name."

"Great guy," Willa said. "But it's complicated. I'd rather not talk about it right now."

"Suit yourself. But when you want to, I'm all ears." Rebbie smiled.

They spent their meal catching up, mostly from Rebbie's side. Willa now knew who'd married whom, which people wrecked their lives, who'd already divorced, who moved away from Rockwall. Rebbie had her own catering business, mostly personal chef things for wealthy ladies. She spoke nothing about Willa's family.

The waitress brought the check. Rebbie, slick-as-a-salesman, whisked the check toward her. "I'll take this."

"No, I can help. Let me help."

"Don't be ridiculous. I invited you, remember?" She handed a card and the check to the waitress. Willa and Rebbie spoke about the restaurant, how great the food was, how interesting the clientele. Rebbie signed the receipt with a flourish and stood. "Let's go. I want to show you my dream."

The night held a crisp edge to it. Instead of turning left toward the courthouse, Rebbie pointed right. "There it is," she said.

"What?" Willa noticed the old, empty church. "You want to start a church?"

Rebbie grabbed her hand and led her toward the old Methodist church on the corner of Fannin and Rusk.

"You can let go," Willa said.

"Oh, I'm so sorry! I get so excited, is all!" She jogged across the intersection.

They stood before the old brick church with two squared towers, arched transom windows holding stained glass, and large white doors facing each street. "The Methodists built this in 1913. Isn't it beautiful?"

Willa agreed.

"When we were babies, the congregation moved to that new building toward the freeway. This building's been waiting for me, I just know it. Wouldn't it make the most beautiful café and coffee house?"

"It would."

"I don't have the money collected yet, but someday I will. Someday I'll cater from this place and provide Rockwall with a unique gathering hub. With great food, of course."

As they walked back to Rebbie's car, Willa felt a tinge of envy. A dream. Other than redecorating other people's homes, what was her dream? Once she knew the truth about her past, then what? And how did God figure in now that Hale wasn't there to be all Jesusy for her?

Safe inside the steel walls of the large car, Willa cleared her throat. Had her whole life been a giant throat clearing exercise, just waiting to say something, then choosing not to? Remembering Genie's reticence to share, she hoped to lean back on an old friendship, gather data there. "I need to ask you something important," Willa said. "About my family."

The animated face chewing bright blue gum contorted, ever so slightly. For a good long minute, Rebbie said nothing.

"When I was four — "

"That was a long time ago."

"Do you know anything about my life that year?"

Rebbie clicked left fingernails on the steering wheel. "I'm sorry. I'm one of those people who can't remember a thing, particularly anything before the age of seven, and even then, it's blurry. Wish I could help."

"That's okay."

Rebbie took a deep breath, then let out a soliloquy of words, more gossip than Willa'd heard in years, all strung together in rapid fire. As Rockwall whirred by from the vista of the high-riding vehicle, Willa counted houses — her way of grounding herself to the strange old-yet-new surroundings.

"Is that your car? It's cute." Rebbie shoved her truckish vehicle into park.

"For now," Willa said. "I'm renting."

"So you're not here long, then?" Willa heard a strange catch in Rebbie's effervescence.

"While I redecorate the upstairs rooms, I hope to find what I'm looking for so I can get back to my life." Such a simple statement, really. But was it an impossible venture? Can anyone really get back to that which was utterly lost? Her home? Her inability to commit? Willa jumped from the vehicle, landing on a dormant mound of fire ants. Thankfully it didn't teem to life.

Rebbie didn't get out. She automated Willa's window after she'd shut the door. "I had a good time tonight. Let's do this again."

"I'd like that," Willa said. She hoped she meant it.

ten

She used to believe the old house was haunted. Not by ghosts of corpses lying cold in its rooms, but by voices of her parents. As if the home had walls crafted of sponges, absorbing every argument, then releasing them back into Willa's room at night. While the stars winked outside under a warm Texas evening, she tried to shush the words, but failed.

They flurried around her now, but none stayed coherent long enough for her to record their fury. Last night, she'd been the epitome of concise words, recounting the timeline she put together all those years. Though her box had burned to the Seattle ground, her memory released the ghosts last night. She looked over her handwritten notes, thinking of Hale, his architect handwriting. Hers was loopy, unorganized, slanted left and right—the ultimate insult to her mother's right-handed tutelage. But what she scratched out last night still didn't hint at the mystery.

She remembered several three-year-old memories, now chronicled afresh. She recalled some five-year-old adventures, punishments, and kindergarten capers. The timeline she sketched out, best as she could muster, still gaped empty somewhere between four and five. She'd re-doodled the man with the ring, his eye. She scribbled rudimentary sketches of other dreams that came to her, some nonsensical like a carnival ride on steroids, others clear and obvious. She remembered her mother's looks, her father's eyebrows raised. Her questions to them both about the empty months of her memory once she grew old enough to realize its absence. Always the same answer, told in different ways. "Chances are," Daddy said to her one summer break during college, "you don't remember because nothing remarkable happened. It was just a few months, anyhow. I can't even remember when I was ten years old, Willa Bean."

But she remembered. Practically everything. Even little details like the feel of a rocking chair's arm, or the flight pattern of a butterfly the summer of her seventh year, how it looped above, landing on a bird's nest, how it pointed both wings like prayer to the sunshine. Willa saw her mother's face, knew the flecks of hazel in her eyes, the feel of her clothes against Willa's skin when she tried to sit next to her but received rebuff. She knew the way Daddy smelled after shaving. When she was six, she remembered walking to school, encountering a disheveled man, probably homeless. Willa walked past him, crunching a can beneath her feet. It hadn't been hers, but it impeded her path so she stepped on it. The man said, "Would you kindly pick that up and dispose of it for me?"

She retrieved it, remembering the grit, the sticky ooze coming from the can's mouth. She wanted to ask the man why, but he answered before she could.

"This world is my home. I'd like to keep it clean."

She could feel the grass under her feet when she was nine years old, running a race with Rebbie at her heels, through Harry Myers Park. They'd raced to the gazebo near the small fishing lake. The warm wind brushed her face. Willa felt her legs strengthen, elongate, as if she were growing in the running. In a hiccup of time, her big toe met a rock anchored to the grass and she toppled, crying. Rebbie hadn't bothered to pick her up. Instead she ran straight to the gazebo, gasping for air while Willa writhed. She could still taste the grit from the fall, still recall the flap of skin hemorrhaging from a smashed toenail.

Her drawing-studio professor at Seattle Pacific University praised her for the realism she portrayed in her pieces. "You have an uncanny ability for small details," she said. True. Except for those empty months. Except for just those.

Willa sat poised on the hospital-cornered bed, fingers above her keyboard with a cursor winking on a fresh document, her new Day One of investigation on the field, in the place of her memory loss.

For a brief time, she thought she'd blog her thoughts to Hale, but her mind wouldn't release words for him just now — only questions.

What did she feel?

Who was she?

What kind of girl blurted a fleeing no to Hale?

And how could she respond to him when she didn't have any idea why she denied him?

Of course it all had to do with untangling the past, but why? And for what purpose? What if the past was meant to be iron-locked shut, and her tampering with the combination would send her entire world into a pain-filled trajectory? What if knowing the truth imprisoned her?

Willa shook her head. She fingered the locket still encircling her neck. Daddy kept his smile from a faded photograph, seemingly trying to say something. But words never came. She heard the hum of traffic commuting, but her own walls hollered hostility. Her mother's artificially high voice. Her father's calm demeanor, his soothing voice tinged with bitter words. Both combining into a stew of wrath.

Another voice broke through, taking all the space in Willa's mind.

You'll find home one day.

She sat on the bed, within the four walls of this home, but

those words didn't confirm anything. Here, home? Not really. So where would she find it? And who was the man who uttered such assurance?

A knock startled her. The door opened with a screeching creak.

Genie stood in its jamb, looking less formidable beneath the transom window. She held a mug. Steam circled from the cup's belly like incense. "I made some hot chocolate."

She said it like an obligation. "Thanks," Willa said.

Genie brought the cup to her, steps steady on the groaning wood floor, and placed it on the nightstand. "Enjoy your evening," she scripted.

"I intend to." Willa smelled tinny roses, the cologne Genie'd always worn. She tried to look Genie in the eyes, but the woman wouldn't allow such intrusion. So Willa tried another tack. "Do you hear voices in the house at night?"

Genie recoiled, almost as if Willa had gathered her fist and struck. "Are you crazy, girl?"

"Perfectly normal. But sometimes if I listen hard, I can hear my parents arguing. Can you?"

Genie backed away until a padded chair caught her knees. She sat. "Your parents were good to me," she whispered.

"Do you remember their voices?" Willa took a sip of hot chocolate. Definitely not the powdered kind with lumps littering the bottom. Pure homemade — milk swirled with melted chocolate. How could a woman prone to prickles make something so hospitable?

"Of course I remember their voices."

"So being here all the time doesn't make you hear them in your head?"

Genie stood. "Ghosts don't exist, nor do their voices. And they certainly don't haunt a home."

"*My* home." Willa measured those two words like a stingy woman measuring sugar. The word *home* echoed in the room, or at least that's how Willa felt. *You'll find home one day.*

Genie crossed arms over herself. She smiled, then looked Willa firmly in the eyes. "Yes, *your* home. I know my place—a place your mother was kind enough to offer me. I am a caretaker. Nothing more."

Willa stood. "But you said you were a caretaker of secrets too. I heard you."

"True."

"Why is the truth so hard to tell? And why would that change everything? What are you so afraid of?"

"I am not afraid," Genie measured. She paced away, leaving the door ajar. The scent of her cheap perfume lingered like a slap's sting.

eleven

The ring held her finger, which confused her since she remembered taking it off and placing it inside a matchbox from the Oasis Café. She knew it rested next to the bed, yet its circumference pressed in on her left ring finger as if it were mad at her. She looked down, and sure enough, there it circled, taunting her. She tried to pull it off in the semi-dawn darkness of the room while early birds chirped good morning. No budging. Hale's voice lilted in, at first sounding like doves calling, mourning. But as she squinted the night's sleep away, his voice became distinct, as clear as one wine glass celebrating another in toast.

"You know I love you, Wills," he said.

"Where are you?"

"Right here." She felt him near, felt his breath, his heart, his presence.

Willa shuddered at the delicacy that was Hale, his voice with a tinge of gravel, poetic words new on his tongue as if he composed them right then. "Hale," she said, as she reached for him.

Air, stale and half-humid, grasped her. But he didn't. He faded.

"I can't," she said. She couldn't finish her sentence, not out loud. Though she thought several completions. Can't think. Can't unravel the mysteries. Can't say yes to Hale. Can't stand this house under Genio's fist. Can't abide by a town held in secrets. Can't visit Mother.

So many can'ts. Never enough cans.

Hale's voice hummed a tune, indistinct. It thrummed through her, and for a snatch of time, she felt peace. But his hum abruptly ceased, replaced by *her* voice. Mother's.

"I can't stand looking at her," Mother said. In a flash, Willa was six again, peeking around a door two rooms away. Mother's voice careened into itself, a soprano shrieking words Willa couldn't stand to hear. She held her ears, but Mother's pointed words, the ones she wanted Willa to taste, swallow, and digest, stood out from her murmuring.

"Lousy."

"Inconvenient."

"A waste."

"Useless."

"Ridiculous."

"In the way."

Willa's groggy mind begged Hale back, but his silence made sense. She'd pushed him away; surely he'd not return, no matter how kindhearted his intentions. The words continued, higher each time. She pressed both index fingers into the soft flap of skin covering her ear canal, pushing until her skull ached and she heard the blessed whoosh of her heart pumping blood through her brain. Whoosh. Whoosh. Whoosh.

Mother's sentences diminished, her accentuated words now silenced. The gold ring shrank from her finger. Willa flung open her eyes to the sun's awakening, breathing hard, her heart thrumming her ribcage. A dream. A nightmare. All pushed together into one.

The dream gave her focus. After showering, she'd start the morning by blogging to Hale, then head to the library to dig up the mystery of Mother. Though she'd had little luck on the Internet from afar, surely she could find information about one of Rockwall's most beloved citizens between a binding. Maybe

Hale was right about the impersonal nature of a computer and the inability of a cursor to convey information of the heart. Perhaps paper and ink held the solution to everything.

Blog title: You smell great.

Dear Hale,

I loved the way your letter smelled, reminding me of you. I wish I could say that a few nights in Texas have solved all my issues, but they've only reopened wounds. I hope to God you'll still want me after my heart breaks in every possible way.

I know you're not one for investigation, but you're smarter than the average bear, so any insight you might have would be helpful. Why do families hide their secrets? And if one wanted to uncover them, how can she do that? So far the direct approach has added up to a big fat zero.

I met an old friend for dinner. Don't worry, it's a she, not a he. Rebbie, from high school. I asked her about my missing memory, but she didn't know. At least I have to take her word for it. But it makes me wonder. Could it be that the entirety of Rockwall proper knows my secret but won't tell? Will the city implode on itself if I find the truth? If you hear about an atypical earthquake east of Dallas in the next few weeks, you'll know what happened.

If you don't mind, would you please pray God would send a truth ambassador to me, someone who will shoot straight, caring more about disclosure than secrecy? It's a big prayer, one I pray in the in-between times. I half believe God will answer, half believe he's happy with me investigating the rest of my life. And, no, Mother doesn't hold the key. Remember, she told me to scat. Told me to —

The doorbell chimed. Then chimed again. A third, fourth,

fifth time. When the sixth chime echoed upstairs, Willa hit *publish*, then pulled a sweater around herself and hurried downstairs. She opened the door to an older man, clad in a scratchy looking overcoat, old khakis, and dreadfully worn shoes. He wore a plaid Sherlock Holmes hat. He held something in his hand.

"Sorry, ma'am. Would Genie be around?"

"I'm not sure where she is."

"You work here?" His voice sounded like Hale's might in old age, a hint of laughter, a scratchy undertone.

"No, sir. I'm ... " What would she say? And why would she tell a stranger that she was the true heir of this home?

"No matter." He looked uncomfortable there on the porch, not cold or put out, just that he didn't belong. So Willa beckoned him in. He put down the tissue-wrapped object, then took off his hat, planting himself on the red velvet couch near the fireplace. "Rheus," he said. "My name's Rheus."

"Nice to meet you, Mr. Rheus."

He laughed. "No, that'd be my first name. Last name's Aldus. Rheus Aldus. Yeah, my mama liked the poetry of it, I suppose. Not sure why."

"Well, it's nice to meet you, Mr. Aldus."

"Likewise. But just call me Rheus, please."

"Can I get you something to drink?" Willa wasn't sure what to do other than this. Should she try to find Genie? Ask the man to wait?

"No, it's fine. Just give this to Genie, will you?" He unwrapped a rectangle of metal, then held it up — a light switch plate. "She's been looking to convert all the plates here to originals. Had herself a good hollering when she found a few plastic plates scattered here and there in the house. Knew the Muirs probably meant to replace them with originals, but Mr. Muir died before such frivolous things could be done, I suppose."

She took the plate from him, then sat across in an old Morris reclining chair. She looked behind her, strained her ears to hear noise. "Did you know the Muir family?"

"Only through Genie's stories. I've only been in town just a few years, not long after Mr. Muir passed."

Willa sat back, felt the smooth wood of the chair's arms beneath her hands. At least Genie got this part of the furniture right. "I'd love to hear those stories," Willa said.

"I'm afraid a tale's not good in the telling once it's reached me. I get things mixed up awful."

"That's okay. I'd love to hear anything."

"You a reporter or something?"

Willa smiled. "In a way."

"Well, let me see. I met Genie soon after she started converting the house from hosting dead folks to live ones. Right about two years ago now. It's been a long process, apparently. Said she was caretaker of the place since the daughter abandoned her to go chase dreams up north in Yankee territory."

Willa laughed, then cleared her throat to cover her slip. The Northwest? Yankees?

Rheus sat back on the couch, his gray eyes distant. His face was a roadmap of sorts, wrinkles crossing over like country roads going here and there. Yellowing teeth smiled back at her. Gray hair lay flat over his head where the hat had been, but curled outward around his ears where it hadn't. He cleared his throat while a look of confusion crowded his face. "Where was I?"

"The daughter left."

He winked at Willa, as if he knew. "Genie started redecorating the home." Willa found herself straining forward, her neck and shoulders taut, waiting for a shred of truth.

"Yes, her way of honoring the Muirs, she said. Reclaiming the old house to beauty, I think is how she put it."

"Does she ever talk of the Muirs?" Willa heard a faint rustling. Her pulse quickened. Just a few more words, Rheus, she wanted to say.

"Of course. They're her favorite subject, particularly Mrs. Muir, though now she takes time to visit her over yonder." He pointed toward town.

Willa's guilt settled once again in her stomach.

"They're like sisters, the way she tells it."

Clicking heels. A sharp intake of breath.

"Mr. Aldus, how nice to see you." Genie's voice didn't convey the niceties of her words. Slightly edged.

Willa stood and turned. Genie, perfectly preserved, wore a pale pink sweater and what older women call slacks — gray to be exact. But her eyes seemed black. Willa filled the silence. "I was just talking to —"

"I'm sure you were." Genie stepped between the Morris chair and velvet couch. "Mr. Aldus is kind enough to find treasures for the house."

Rheus barked out a laugh. "Yes, I'm good for that, right? But I thought you said we were friends, that you liked our conversations."

Willa smiled at Genie's awkward expression, though she felt the weight of Hale's disappointment as she did. Hale always seemed to love folks who acted unlovable, who spouted unkind words. He had an uncanny ability to see the good in folks when they acted their worst. Another reason Willa didn't deserve him.

"Of course," Genie smoothed. "That too. And he's the best Scrabble partner." She patted Rheus' shoulder in a matronly way as he stood, a sort of patronizing *there-there.* "Now you know I need to work, right?"

He nodded, a fiery look in his eyes. Willa couldn't discern if it was anger or sadness or both.

"I brought you another light switch plate." He pointed to Willa. "I gave it to your guest."

"Guest?" she said, narrowing eyes Willa's way.

"I best be scooting," he said. "Wouldn't want to interfere with your work." Rheus didn't rush his way out. He folded the tissue paper that once held the plate, placed it in his rag-tag pocket, put on his plaid hat, nodded, then padded to the door in those world-worn shoes.

Genie followed as if she were pushing him out the door with her will. In a way, that was probably how it happened. She nudged him forward through the left-hand door. He tripped over the threshold, then splayed in a ruckus on the porch. For a second he didn't move.

Willa rushed to his side.

Genie half bent down.

He stirred, rolled over to lie on his back. His eyes flickered open, revealing not cloud gray as Willa originally thought, but Texas sky blue.

"Are you okay, Rheus?"

"It's Mr. Aldus," Genie said.

"Your eyes," Rheus said to Willa. "They're just like –"

"Now don't try to talk, Mr. Aldus. You need your strength. Let's get you standing." Genie pulled him to his feet, dusted him off, then shook her head. "Be careful on these stairs. Thanks for the light switch plate."

"Rheus," Willa said. "You were saying something about my eyes?"

He shook his head under the bead board porch. A cardinal flew through the eaves between the three of them, circling to alight on a barren tree. Rheus followed the bird, watching, keeping his eyes on the creature. No one spoke or moved. The bird fluffed its red feathers, then flew away toward town. "He always tells me where to go next," Rheus said to the sky. "That dang bird'll be the death of me."

Willa almost said, "Or Genie will," but she kept her words inside.

"Well, I'm sorry you had a spill," Genie said. "Will you be okay to walk?"

Rheus tipped his hat. "Lord willing, I'm always okay to walk wherever he leads me."

Willa touched his arm, looked into his eyes. "I enjoyed our talk," she said. "I hope you'll come back again."

"With an invitation like that, I surely will."

The stairs creaked as he labored down them into the brown yard. He didn't look back, didn't say goodbye. He put one foot in front of the other in a determined trajectory toward town. Genie huffed inside, but Willa watched Rheus walk, marveling at his slow but determined pace. He held a piece of the puzzle. She saw it in his eyes. An oddly answered prayer.

twelve

The library loomed now. When Willa frequented it as a girl, the library had been crammed into a former post office, sandwiched between two one-way streets, barely enough space to park. But now thanks to the Friends of the Library the new building shot heavenward, a monolith to Rockwall's love of books and reading and knowledge—least that was how Genie put it in her infrequent letters. Willa entered the foyer, then the lobby. On a wall to the right, something glinted—a tree with golden leaves, clinging to vertical rocks, each with a name. She paused before it, scanned the names. So many people she didn't know. So many folks she left behind. The name *Muir* caught her eye. On the upper right hand branch of the tree, the Muir House had donated generously to the library. Had it been Mother's doing? Or was the donation something Genie had given later, in memory of Daddy? Or simply a way to advertise the upcoming bed and breakfast? Most likely the latter.

She turned left toward the checkout counter, heading toward a younger girl with a friendly face. "I'm wondering if you can help me."

"What do you need?" The girl with cropped black hair and a nose ring looked up, then tucked a short pencil behind her ear.

"Research. I'm writing a paper on the history of the Muir House."

"Second floor," the girl said "Top of the stairs and to your right. The reference librarian should be able to help you."

Willa said a quick thanks then took the stairs. She didn't want to admit the longing, the hope, the inclination that Blake would be that librarian. His dream, he'd told her. And when Rebbie said he was in town, she couldn't think of a better place to find him. She rebuked herself for playing such games, for letting her heart beat toward Blake again, but the force of her desire compelled her upstairs, hoping.

A guy sat in the chair behind the reference desk, head down, blond highlighted hair covering his face. Not Blake — who'd been an avowed brunette. Still, the form seemed familiar. "Excuse me," she said.

He looked up. "Willa?"

She met those eyes. Blake's. Something inside her fluttered. That familiar pang of desperate love winded her. The obsessive need flooded back into her all at once.

A blond-flecked Blake laughed back.

"Blake?" Though his eyes remained muddy green, his appearance was entirely altered. Different hair, filled out, taller.

"It's okay. Don't feel bad or anything. I've been working out." He stood, then moved around the desk. He lifted her into an embrace, squeezing tight, stealing her breath.

"What a surprise," she said. Upon closer examination, Blake did have the same smirk, the same sassy eyes, but his face looked fuller, his stature considerably less thin. Though Rebbie had pined for all things Blake Alderman back in high school, Willa claimed him for herself through junior and senior year, calling themselves fellow outcasts. In this embrace, she missed him all over again, though she remembered the reasons they broke up all too well. That smothering of young love. Remember that, she told herself. Remember his ways.

He pulled away, held her eyes captive.

"What in the world brings you back here?"

She heard the pain in his voice, regretted it, wanted to

remedy it, kiss the pain away. "I'm back for a short period of time – redecorating the Muir House and doing research for a book I'm writing." The last part slipped so easily from her tongue she wondered if she'd become pathological.

"Can't you get everything online now?"

"Aren't those heretical words for a librarian to utter?"

"I was being facetious."

"Twelve gold stars," Willa said.

"You're still giving out stars, then?"

"Only to you." They'd survived Rockwall High School by giving each other stars when they endured another day, slipped away from a painful conversation, made a smart aleck look bad. Not exactly full of virtue, those stars. But they were fun to give, even if they were imaginary. Partners in petty crime. And in obsessive love.

Blake looked entirely different in his tight black t-shirt and oh-too-cool jeans, both wrists circled in some sort of hieroglyphic tattoo. She reminded herself of the matchbox next to her bed, of Hale's intentions, of her wayward heart. She'd typically been great at initiating a flirtation, at conjuring her way into the graces of good-looking men, but she seldom sustained the flurry-of-the-first-kiss revelry. Except for Hale from his steady persistence and Blake who bewitched her, kept her next to his beating heart. Could he hear it now? But beyond those two, no relationship flourished beyond the first tentative kiss.

"So you're researching." Blake's words brought her back to books, research, her quest.

"My family, actually. A memoir."

"You? Your family? I thought you left here to put your family behind you. At least that's what you told me." His voice hitched, just a hint. She looked at his lips, then dared another look into his green eyes, remembering how she'd steal glances in high school, how he'd return the favor when she least expected it. They'd stared plenty. And he kept good tabs on her. Sometimes way too good.

"Everyone leaves home sometime."

"Sometimes," he said, "you find everything you need in one place. I left for college like you did, but Rockwall called me back. And now I'm doing what I love."

"Point taken. I'm sorry."

"No need. Here's the funny thing. You're here, and you need me. So I'd say this is a divine way of things working out." He winked.

Willa felt the wink in her gut. She wondered what divine being he spoke of, but left the topic unanswered — something Hale taught her. He'd shown her, through myriad examples, to restrain herself from blurting out every thought. "The world doesn't need your running commentary," Hale once scolded. And he'd been right.

Willa placed her hands on Blake's desk. "Yes, I need your help. Do you have any yearbooks? Women's league cookbooks? Church directories? Anything that might help me research the Muir family?"

Blake didn't answer. Instead he clicked his way through databases, fingers flying over keys. She took the time to gaze out the large rectangular windows overlooking an empty field, Interstate 30 just beyond. Cars whirred past on an exceedingly wide freeway, going here, there. Always a destination. Always hurrying. Always motoring on a defined trajectory. Willa'd known hers, mapped it out in faraway research, yet now she stood — stopped in one place, on the verge of arriving. It niggled her insides, tremored her thoughts. Would knowing the truth really set her free to love? To move forward?

"Here we go," Blake said. "We have five volumes — all checked out. I'm sorry."

"Checked out? When?"

"Yesterday morning, apparently. I can contact the patron, if you'd like. Oh wait! No need."

"Why?"

"You're staying at home, right?"

"Um, yeah."

"Mrs. Skye has them. She probably checked them out as a courtesy to you."

"No doubt." This time she did roll her eyes.

"Sarcasm?" Blake smiled, showing perfect white teeth. She remembered him with crooked ones years ago. Loved the taste of his mouth, as he did hers. She shook her head, trying to dispel the memory. Concentrate, she told herself. "I doubt I'll ever see those books if she has them."

"She'll have to return them in three weeks."

"Mrs. Skye does as she pleases."

"She may, but she doesn't know the Stealthy Librarian!" His voice raised above the silence of the room. A man to Willa's left turned and stared, as if he were the librarian whispering hush.

"Oops," Blake whispered. "Anyway, there is a thing called microfiche, dear. And we have a lot of archives, particularly about Rockwall history. You're welcome to peruse that. I can help you find Muir references."

"I'd love that. I'm particularly looking at anything unusual that happened in 1987."

"Why that year?"

"It's, um, pivotal to the memoir. Kind of the linchpin."

"We were both four years old then," Blake said.

She remembered his devotion in high school, how he talked about love and "us" and how marriage would be perfect when they made a go at it. As Willa smelled his cologne, she reminded herself of his increasing need to be near her, how he followed her, checked up on her, got terribly jealous if she spoke to another guy.

In Blake's clutches, she hadn't yet connected the dots of her empty memory then, hadn't been bothered by the hole. College ripped open the wound, so Blake wouldn't have known the extent of her curiosity. And he wouldn't know about the significance of her losing her memory at four. "Yes," she finally said. "Four." She couldn't say more, didn't want to. Keeping Blake in the dark would propel him to dig without unneeded curiosity, perhaps.

Only Hale knew the scope of her desperation. She couldn't put into words exactly what she searched for, and standing here in the middle of Rockwall proper, helped by someone who'd stalked her past, paralyzed her tongue. What could she say? There was a man, an eye, a picture, an inkling? She sighed. "Did you say something?"

"No biggie. Let's see what we can find."

They spent the morning side by side at the microfiche machine, perusing but finding very little to fill the empty memory. Every once in a while, Blake sat so close, she could feel his arm against hers. The longing, locked behind walls, broke into her. While she uncovered her family's past, she willed herself to forget about Blake, his warm breath, their shared lives, their plans. How he needed her like air back then. How he happily breathed for her, gave her the attention she craved like iced drinks in summertime. Her obsession to a point. His to the nth degree.

She puzzled over Blake many years, wondering why she'd allowed herself to be nearly owned by him. How all that happened. And she wondered why in the world she'd felt entirely alive, as if every cell in her body electrified in his presence back then. She'd played every sort of feminine game to lure him near, finally hooking him. And once hooked, she tried to accustom herself to the strange feeling that perhaps it was all a great reversal, that the hooking had been a part of his plan all along. He said their love was of the ancient sort, wiser than seventeen years. Deeper too. And she believed his words. For a long, long time.

Now she fidgeted with her naked finger, telling herself to remember Hale's blue eyes when she caught glimpses of Blake's unworldly green. Blake wanted to own you, she told herself. While Hale graced her with freedom.

Still, she found herself holding his eyes, cradling them to herself like dark chocolate. And Blake returned the favor.

"I've missed you," he whispered.

She tried to focus on the research, the screens in front of her. She felt his breath on her ear. "I know," she said.

"You know?"

She shook her head, scolded herself for letting his eyes captivate her again. "We weren't good for each other."

"Speak for yourself." He put his hand on her upper arm, turned her toward him. "My life's been incomplete without you, Willa. You have to know that. I can see it in your eyes. The longing's there."

She remembered his forward ways, even back in high school when his geek-persona didn't seem to affect his honesty. Willa kept his eyes, feeling hers tear up. What in the world was she doing? She looked away. "I can't."

He reached for her hand. Held it. She pulled away. Though part of her longed for the familiarity of a man who knew her before Daddy's death, understood her story not from the recounting but in the living it.

Silence stole between them. The microfiche machine smelled hot.

"You can't," he finally said. He kept her gaze.

"I'm confused," she said. At least her words were honest.

"I'm not." He backed away a bit, chair rolling across carpet. "I know you, Willa. You know that. I actually knew you were back in town. Just like I knew you'd find me. So I waited. I didn't chase after you."

"And I came," she hushed.

"Yes." He turned their chairs to face each other, let their knees touch. "You might remember me as awkward. I'm not that man anymore. I've made up for that lack. And I know you still want me."

She pushed away. Such brash audacity. Yet his eyes burned into hers. A confidence that he would hold her again. She battled his grip, fighting for words. But none came in the silence of the library.

"Excuse me," a voice interrupted.

Blake stood quickly, nearly overturning his chair.

An older librarian shook her head. "I believe you have some database work to do."

"I'm finishing up here," he told her, all the while stealing glances Willa's way. "Just a few more clicks."

The librarian clucked, then said, "Soon."

He sat next to Willa again, this time the epitome of professionalism, as if he'd never boldly staked his claim in whispers, glances, and grasps just heartbeats before. He breezed through a few more screens, revealing the extent of the Muir family's influence, how Willa's mother and father intertwined with town politics, helped create citywide endowments, and scholarship funds for smart but poor kids. Legendary didn't begin to describe them, though the *Rockwall County Herald* used that word effusively.

"You come from good stock," Blake said.

Great, she thought, *I'm uncovering dirt on Mr. and Mrs. Mother Teresa of Rockwall. I'll be a real hero!* But all she could say was, "Apparently," while the librarian stood nearby.

"Let me keep digging." Blake's voice stayed librarian soft now. He stood. "Anything you can give me to go on?"

She stood now, gathered her purse, nodded for him to follow her away from the librarian's smirk. He did, to a study room. She kept the door open. Willed herself to talk business and not dignify his forwardness with her own tumbled feelings.

"Look into Mrs. Skye. Her name's Eugenia Anne Skye, and she's somewhat of a mystery." She wanted to let out her whole sordid tale, to have someone other than Hale shoulder this burden of a blocked memory. But she kept her mouth shut, the only sensible thing she chose that day. She'd loved Blake once, and she knew he loved her. He told her as much under a firework-ignited sky before their senior year, before his obsessiveness took over. They sat above the shores of Lake Ray Hubbard, red blanket beneath them. Chandler's Landing, a local country club, opened its iron gates long enough to let its Rockwall citizens dot the hillside with chairs, blankets, and toddling kids.

While the rockets' red glare burst through the air, she shared everything she could about her parents' explosive marriage. Every burst of gunpowder punctuated her anguish. "I don't want to be them," she said.

"Don't you think it depends on the people, Willa?" He slipped his arm around her shoulder.

"I've heard the stories," she said. "When they first met, they were like us. In love. Infatuated. Smitten. All those words the romance writers use. But something happened."

"Well, nothing's going to happen with us because we love each other."

It was the first time he gave her that word, *love*. He seemed shocked to have said it. But then he bent near, brushed his lips to her, and whispered, "I'll never stop loving you."

Willa dismissed the memory. Told herself to be sensible. Scolded herself to remember Hale, not a high school romance, that did end, by the way.

Opening up her heart and sharing this piece of her memory might usher in something she didn't want right now — Blake's love. And yet, schizophrenia reigned, if she were honest. She told herself to be strong, to resist, to redirect. Her quest to find truth didn't involve Blake. Couldn't involve him. But his intrusion flustered her heart, reminding her of the kind of love that felt like fireworks on a sultry summer night. That kind of hometown, knowing love. Slightly forbidden, wholly embraced. No, she told herself. No. The less Blake entangled himself with her, the more apt she'd be to uncover information. Best to keep her heart hushed. Best to keep to the quest. Best to remember what it felt like to be smothered.

He took her hand again, this time looking around. "What else can I do?"

She pulled away. But the memory of the look he gave her stayed with her. That look of longing, of neediness. The way Rheus looked at her came back to her. "There's a man I met named Rheus Aldus. He may play into the Muir memoir somehow. Can you look into him?"

Blake smiled his crooked smile, but with perfectly straight teeth. "He's a character. Sort of a fixture here at the library. I'll see what I find, but he's not one for silence. Take him to Route 66 and order their two-egg breakfast with bacon, eggs over easy, and biscuits. But be sure to ask for country gravy alongside. He'll spill anything for biscuits and gravy."

"Sounds like you know this from experience." Willa stepped out of the study room. She'd taken enough of Blake's time. And he'd taken enough of her.

"He's a friend—an interesting friend."

"As you've been to me today. Thanks, Blake."

He stood, moved toward her. They both noticed the librarian then. He extended his hand, not offering a hug. "My pleasure. Come back soon."

She scribbled her cell number on a slip of paper next to the microfiche and handed it to him. "Call me if you find anything."

"I'll call you even if I don't."

thirteen

When she was nearly four years old, Daddy held Willa while she cried from a cement-scraped knee. He kneeled there, in front of the big, white house, his eyes squinting. She smelled soap while whiskers scraped her cheek. She'd been riding her red and orange bike without the aid of training wheels. Daddy let go, told her to ride, but she panicked, letting go of the handlebars, then toppling over, her knee crashing onto the parking spaces in front of her home. He shushed her. Petted her head. Helped her stand. Told her they'd get a bandage eventually. Put her back on the bike, promising not to let go this time. But he did, and she flew, this time down the pavement, not into it. She felt the rush of air past her face, the thrill of riding against the wind. She felt every part of her come alive, a four-year-old doing the impossible.

Daddy cheered her home, gave her a walloping high five. He laughed alongside her. "I knew you could do it," he said.

Mother appeared on the porch. Willa hadn't seen her exit, but she saw the dark expression on her face. "Get. In. Here," she said. Three somber words that ushered in the missing months from her memory.

Then black. Not one detail. Or thought. Or inkling. Her counselor blamed it on trauma, that kids lock away a painful memory in order to survive. But Willa thought perhaps she could outwit her memory through investigation, through fact-finding. If she wanted it bad enough, she'd uncover it. But she hadn't. And although Hale tried to understand the queries, she knew he grew tired of it all.

Her first recollection after the black hole surfaced in another one of Daddy's embraces. She was five, alert, alive, and seemed to be happy to be so. Her hair pigtailed, she remembered the way the sun angled through the giant pecan tree out back. She'd been playing house in the utility shed again, the window now adorned with curtains she fashioned from old cloth napkins, a string, and some tacks. She heard hammering in the basement of the carriage house, a sure sign that Daddy would be working with his hands, nails spitting out of his mouth like porcupine quills. She thrilled at the thought.

So she left the little shelter, preferring to find Daddy. She spied him standing in front of the carriage house.

"Come here," he said.

Pecans rolled around under bare feet that ran toward him with abandon. She tripped over a root concealed by the nuts, hurtling headlong.

Daddy ran to her, picked her up, righted her to the earth. "Willa Bean," Daddy said, "don't worry about spills. And no matter what happens, you know I love you, right?"

She nodded.

He wiped her tears clean on the sleeve of his shirt.

She wore a bracelet, beads made of wooden letters, spelling out Willa. Daddy knelt before her, pushing the bracelet around and around her slim wrist. "Willa." He said her name like it was Yahweh's — hushed, reverent, as if the trees listened, ready to scold him for letting it out so casually.

"Why'd you name me Willa?"

Daddy directed her to the swing beneath the pecan tree. He patted the seat. She noticed everything in vibrant color, as if God turned on the rainbow lights in an instant beneath the shade of the pecan. Yellow dust rose after Daddy's hand patted the seat. A butterfly, blue and magenta, flurried between them, fluttering the still, humid air. She put out her finger as an invitation, and the butterfly responded for a hiccup of a second, then ventured toward the house.

"Willa, Willa," Daddy said. He scratched his head, his fingers tanned by the summer sun. "Well, if you want the boring version, I could tell you that Willa means helmet."

"Like the Rockwall Yellowjackets wear when they play football?"

"In a way. But more like helmets used for protection during war."

"War?" Willa looked up at Daddy. His head seemed haloed by the sun, his smile, though crooked, gleamed dentist white beneath the tree.

"That's a subject for another time. Let me tell you the real reason, sweetheart. Will means choice, like I choose to smile today. Does that make sense?"

It didn't really. She thought Daddy took to smiles naturally. But she nodded anyway.

"And I've made the best choice in my life to love my beautiful Willa. Every day I love you. Every day I smile because you're in my life. You're my sweet little girl who decorates my life." He squeezed her shoulders, held her next to him. "And nothing that ever happens in this world can change such a thing as my love for you."

"I love you too, Daddy." Her words seemed to delight the wind because it picked up, rustling the leafy expanse above. A few pecans lost their struggle to hang on to branches. Daddy's hands protected her head like a helmet, letting a few plunk him on his head, instead.

fourteen

The tree canopied itself over the house like it cherished its job to protect the roof from a Texas hailstorm. When Willa spied it as she turned into the Muir House, she rehashed the Daddy memory again, except that now the pecan's swing marred the remembrance. She opened, then slammed the car door, hoping to shut out her weakness for Blake's blatant overture.

She marched to the swing, hung askew by one end. For all the spiffing up Genie'd prided herself in, the swing screamed of her strange neglect — an odd thing since it hung directly between the carriage house's front window and the back door of the house. Genie would walk a path directly into the swing if she took a straight route.

Willa pushed the swing slightly, allowing the one remaining chain to creak against a high branch. She lifted the other chain, now a rusted snake at her feet. If only she had a ladder, she could right the wrong. Life should be so simple. Seeing it broken there, the tree a steady, willing anchor, she wondered again if such a thing as a neat, understood life was ever possible. Or if finding the memory would be the anchor, only to have half of her fall to the ground to rust in the grass. She dropped the chain. Where it had pressed warm into her hand was a mark, a rusted chain tattoo that reminded her again of decay.

The carriage house's door opened to the day, Genie's form inside its frame. "I've been meaning to fix that," she said.

"I can," Willa said. "If you can get me a ladder tall enough."

"I suppose you'll charge me for that too." She motioned for Willa to follow her into her home.

Willa hesitated. In all the years Genie haunted the carriage house, she'd not invited Willa upstairs, which now struck her as strange. Funny how things that seemed perfectly pedestrian in childhood blared odd in the light of adulthood. Why hadn't Genie, a fixture in the Muir family, welcomed Willa in her home? In her mind, the place became like a forbidden chocolate factory—a scary but enticing place.

Willa stood next to the broken swing, feeling broken. Her hand itched to hold Hale's, to forsake Blake's flirtations in lieu of something healthy, more reliable. She remembered how right Hale's hand felt in hers, like God had knit them both together as a matching pair of mittens. But Hale didn't stand beside her now. Didn't climb a ladder to fix a swing, though he'd done his best to mend her heart. She stood here alone, bereft of hope, mired in a mystery that threatened to never unravel. Perhaps the dead did spirit away their secrets to the grave.

"Don't just stand there. Come on up. I have something for you."

Willa told her feet to walk, convinced herself that maybe her fact-finding mission would consummate in the confines of the carriage house. But the fluttering in her chest heightened her nervousness.

Genie left the front door open, not standing beneath it to usher her in, so Willa walked on through, then shut the door. She mounted the steps that flanked the garage until she stood in front of another entrance, this door shut. A strange welcome. She knocked.

"Come in."

Willa shut the door behind her.

"Good. You're learning." Genie stirred something on a stove in the one room studio.

"Learning?"

"To shut doors, keep the cold out."

This place smelled like a memory, one she couldn't connect to. She nearly touched the past in a flashback, but like the man telling her she'd find home, it recoiled in an instant. While Genie busied herself in the small kitchen, Willa took in the room, fighting to remember. But the fleeting memory slipped away.

The great room, decorated entirely in Shabby Chic, belied the Ikea kitchen cabinets in the house. An arrangement of fake gardenias sat on a distressed dining room table, mismatched chairs sidled up. Gauzy curtains made from what appeared to be very old calico dressed the wide windows like an afterthought. An old braided rug in tones of rust and blue circled under an inviting, well-worn couch. On nearly every flat surface, vases in every style boasted more fake flowers. Just exactly what was Genie's style? She could always fall back on the word *eclectic*, which could mean anything, and would be too close to her own style for comfort.

"You can sit yourself down there." Genie pointed to an overfluffed white chair, which, upon closer examination, had faded cabbage roses in pink and the palest green embossed on the slipcover.

So Willa sat. Sank would be a better word. She felt the goose down immediately and secretly vowed again that if she ever owned her own home, she'd buy feather-stuffed couches. Definitely from Restoration Hardware.

Genie brought two mugs of something steamy to the sitting area. She placed one mug next to Willa on an old trunk, being careful to place a coaster beneath. Then she sat opposite her in a many-times-painted rocking chair. "So," Genie said. Steam rose toward the woman's face.

"So. You said you have something for me?"

"These." She pointed to a stack of books.

Willa hadn't noticed them next to the fluffy chair. The library books! Really? And here she thought Genie had spirited them away. "I went to the library to find those," she said.

"I figured as much."

Willa took a drink of that heavenly hot chocolate. "This is amazing. How do you make it?"

"It's a family secret," Genie said. Then she laughed. Not a friendly laugh, but not an unfriendly one either.

Willa fidgeted. "Well, it's spectacular."

"I know."

"So, thanks for the books."

"You won't find what you're looking for."

Willa felt the air move out of her. Of course. Censorship. She should've known Genie hadn't originally intended to lend her the books. She had to inspect them first. Willa shook her head. "I really don't understand."

Genie settled back into the rocker. It creaked slowly as if it were too old to rock anymore but had been forced. Beneath the rocker, Willa noticed how the painted wood floor (oh the travesty!) showed its brown roots. Genie must've worn that rocker out. Lord knew how many times the woman rocked it until the paint surrendered its color. "Contrary to what you might be thinking, I'm not a stubborn woman," Genie said. The words halted this time, not as confident as her earlier snappiness.

"You have a compelling way of convincing me otherwise."

"You and your high-minded words. For heaven's sake," Genie said. "Just speak English."

"I am." Inside, she laughed. It was Hale who crafted words.

Perhaps some of his wordsmithing had rubbed off on her. Willa lifted one of the books, leafed through it. Old faded pictures stared back at her of faces and places she didn't recognize.

"Those are your history, your kin."

"I suppose so." She said the words disconnected-like. Home and family felt like an appendage to her now with Daddy gone. How, exactly, would these nameless faces connect her to the reality of family?

The *scritch scritch* of Genie's rocker ceased, leaving the room empty of noise except for the ticking of a distant clock. She leaned forward.

Willa noticed the way her chin reclined on her hands. She took note of Genie's well-manicured fingernails, not a flashy heat of red, but a simple French treatment of pink and white.

"I'm going to tell you something," Genie said. "And when I'm done, my inkling is that you'll finish the job I've hired you to do, then pack your bag, jump into that silly rental car, and skedaddle back to Seattle where you belong."

"So you're going to tell me the truth." Willa settled back, letting the feathers cocoon her. At last the truth. She steadied herself, or tried to. She was surprised at how fluttery she felt, how nervous. Did she really want the truth now? Could she receive it? Hold it? Truly embrace it?

"I'm going to tell you a story. And as you know, every story has truth in it."

"That's vague."

"By intention." Genie stood. She clicked over to the broad, wide windows that looked right into Willa's bedroom window on the second floor—at least when the pecan tree hadn't leafed out. It made her shudder to think of Genie spying on her that way. She made a note to keep the plantation shutters shut on that side of the room.

Genie didn't face her; she looked beyond the windows,

her voice small. "I used to think as you did. That learning the truth would set me free. Would save me. Would tie up what went loose."

Willa let the clock tick her response.

Genie paced, but said nothing for fifty-seven tocks. She seemed to be debating within herself, several times her mouth opening, with nothing coming out. Then she'd take a breath and clamp her mouth shut.

The clock ticked more, only this time Willa didn't count with its rhythm. She watched the branches of the tree between the windows and the funeral home, realizing finally that the picture she held was taken beneath it. She'd known it all along, but somehow didn't connect the image with the actual tree until right now, from this strange vantage point. The dirt clinging to her shoes had been the same dirt of the empty memory. Surely Genie knew the man.

"A long time ago." Genie broke the silence with a sentence fragment, filtering through the room's quiet. She didn't complete the thought. Genie held her elbows, pulling them tighter to her chest.

Willa wanted to say, "in a galaxy far, far away," but kept her mouth shut.

"I had a memory," Genie said. "An incomplete one. Like you. So I put on my investigator hat and went hell-bent on discovering what it was that bothered me. I spent years of my life digging, only to find the truth."

"So you know how I feel, then? How I need to know."

She turned and faced Willa, the sun behind her shadowing her face. "I was impatient and wrong. I should've let the buried things stay underground."

"Interesting words for a woman who works in a converted funeral home." Willa knew her sentence slapped, but she didn't care.

"Yes, interesting. But I think there's much to be said about the ritual of death, about folks finishing their lives and being done with things once and for all. If we dredge up their shenanigans, we're marring their memory, unsettling their death."

"Life's for the living," Willa said. She hoped the words to be true. And yet her heart felt six feet under.

"A touching cliché, that. But one we rarely live, wouldn't you say?"

Willa stood in a flash, upsetting the hot chocolate, which toppled onto the floor, splashing the rose-covered chair brown. "Oh, I'm sorry."

Genie said nothing. In a fluid motion, she crossed the room to the kitchen, grabbed several towels, and handed them to Willa. "Sop it up," she said.

Willa dirtied her knees while the towels absorbed the liquid. "These are slipcovered, right? You can wash them."

"Yes," was all Genie said as she loomed over Willa like Cinderella's stepmother.

Willa handed her the towels, then stood, eye-to-eye with Genie.

"You clean up well," Genie said.

Willa nodded.

"I'm only going to say this once." Genie held her gaze. "Turns out there was truth to my story, only it wasn't a good truth. All that malarkey about truth freeing folks. You know I'm a Christian woman, but I'm not sure Jesus had it right when he made truth equal freedom. I found out that—" She looked away, covered her mouth, stifling something—a cry? "My cousin Timmy had no good intentions. And finally remembering what he did destroyed my life, you hear? It did not set me free."

Willa stepped back until her calves touched the wet chair, but she didn't move away. Genie's words stunned her to the wood floor. Was Genie trying to tell her something? That the trauma she'd forgotten could be some sort of abuse? Is that why she couldn't say a hearty yes to Hale's proposal? Had she been violated as her counselor suspected, but she dismissed? She chastised herself for thinking only of herself and not considering Genie's pain, so obvious in front of her. Maybe Genie's rough edges had extremely good reasons.

Genie returned to the nearly floor-to-ceiling windows. Their ancient panes blurred the house, softening its angles. "If I were you, I'd let things lie."

At the word *lie*, Willa felt her soul recoil, if such a thing could be said about a soul. Would she ever know the truth? Of a girl with an empty memory who agonized over filling it back up? She said nothing. Instead, she returned the empty cup to the small kitchen, set it in the uncluttered sink, and left.

She didn't shut the door.

As Willa descended the stairs, she heard the rocker creak against the floor joists. Halfway to the house, she touched the pecan's trunk, wondering what secrets it could tell.

fifteen

They kept to themselves, Genie with her spilled secret and Willa with her determination to splay hers. Willa worked on her designs, starting with Hadrian's Wall, researching the ancient ruin, scouring the Internet for Scottish décor. How would she ever decide? And would she settle on plaid, crests, and pub paraphernalia?

She couldn't decide. And after several sketches that looked like tartan vomit, she read through a short volume of Rockwall history. The city received its name from an excavated ancient rock wall, which could just as easily have been a geological phenomenon. The excavators at the time believed it to be a marker of earlier ancient settlements. But others said the horizontal giant bricklike formation was more or less the handiwork of Mother Nature and her fault lines. Apparently those who excavated the wall had mouths as big as the wall was long, because the name stuck. Rock Wall. Rockwall.

She spent another evening with Rebbie, patronizing the new cineplex on Lake Ray Hubbard, thankful for a comedic break, but longing for Hale as the romance between the two perfect people with minimal personal problems heated up. Why couldn't she be a normal girl with normal issues, holding Hale's hand? And why did Blake's eyes invade in such strange moments?

Now, a week under her Rockwall citizen belt, she sat immobile on her bed, the shutters closed to her back, but the windows bare to the front of the house. She watched the cars speed by, wondering if Genie watched her through the blinds, if she had x-ray vision into Willa's broken heart. Genie who understood heartache mixed with a heavy dose of regret and bitterness — how could such a person be a vehicle of truth?

The mail truck pulled toward the Muir House, idling while the lady inside fished for something. Not hearing from Hale, not listening to his voice, not smelling his earthiness had driven Willa near crazy, but as she watched the lady shove an envelope into the mailbox, she knew. It would be the heart of Hale, sent just to her. Just in time, since she nearly did a search on Blake minutes before.

Like a high school girl lunging for a note from a crush, Willa skipped downstairs, opened the door, let it hinge into the sunshined day, and hurried to the mailbox. She pulled everything out, focusing only on one envelope. Yes. Hale. Written to her. She ran back into the house, placed the rest of the mail on a three-legged table, and trotted up the stairs. After shutting the door, she curled on the bed again, then slowly opened the recycled envelope. As she opened each flap, the envelope's former usage materialized — an insurance company offering multiple-coverage discounts.

Inside she found an origami note, pressed into a six inch butterfly. So Hale-ish. She unfolded the letter, wondering if he had the ability to unfold her heart.

> *Dear Wills,*
>
> *I'm feeling like a moth larva today, wanting so desperately to break free from my prison, but I can't. I'm too weak. With you in Texas, I can't seem to fly. And yet I know that God's greatest gifts come through the discipline of patience. So I wait in this dark place, praying my emerging wings, which feel leaden, will know what to do once the light hits them.*

My one solace: This little cocoon will take its own flight next week to Southernville.

"You're coming here?" Willa said. Hearing her voice in the empty room made the heartache and longing more apparent, seemed to amplify it. Seemed to place her strange longings for Blake in proper, ridiculous perspective.

By the time you read this, I'll be in the Big Easy. You know how I've always longed to make a difference with my life, to truly impact a community? Well, God smiled on me and sent me a chance to work among the still-houseless in New Orleans, to get a whole new block of individuals out of FEMA trailers into their own stick-built homes.

New Orleans? A lifetime away. May as well have been New York, for that matter. Willa let out the breath she'd been keeping. How many hours of driving would that be? She kept reading.

I had a chance to stop through Dallas on my way, but I'm on a Willa fast right now—my way of letting my heart heal. If you've seen a plane traverse the sky southeasterly, chances are it was probably me, looking down on you. I guess I'll be flying after all.

I'll be up to my armpits in building houses and hope. Hopefully I'll have a spare minute or two to send you a proper letter. Don't mistake my wordlessness for careless-ness, though. I wouldn't have asked you to marry me unless I meant it. And I still do.

I hope you find what you're looking for. When I was seven, I lost a ring—one of those Happy Meal trinkets that decoded mysteries. It was made of metal! I prized it, cher-ished it, then lost it. Months later, I found it between my bed and the wall, tangled in flannel sheets. Its pristine silver had molded, and though I scrubbed it, after I placed it on my finger, it greened too. I ended up throwing it out. I hope what you find doesn't green you, Wills. I hope it shines pretty in the sun. Because I want to kiss you beneath that sun, want to hold you until the pain gushes out and you feel home. But that's a road I can't travel right now.

Don't write until you receive a letter from me. I'm unsure of my address until I land and survey the project. Perhaps a true fast from written words will do us both good, help us gain proper perspective.

Until then, I remain cocooned, praying that you'll make your way out at least, stretch your wings, and flutter on a spring breeze. I ache without you.

Hale.

So he hadn't been reading her blog. Strange, since she saw he accepted her invitation. He must've really meant a fast from her, a separation.

Something else picked at her after she finished the letter. Something different. She pulled out Hale's original letter. Yes, there it was, or better said, *wasn't*. A period. He'd ended his first letter with his name, then white space. But this letter he finished his name with a dot of completion. She'd normally not notice such a thing, but she knew Hale to be meticulous, knew him to be cautious about his punctuation. He lectured her once about her overuse of exclamation points, equating it with shouting. And how many times had he talked about the dot and the line?

"Our life is this dot, Wills." He'd pushed a fountain pen straight down onto a piece of recycled paper, then lifted it before the ink bled. She sat next to him at what you might call a dining table, though it really started and ended its life as a few fruit crates and a "discovered" piece of Formica countertop. She wanted to hold the hand that held the pen, but kept hers pocketed. She felt the heat of him next to her in the cold, barely warmed apartment. In the genesis of their relationship, Willa barely knew Hale thought of her in a romantic way, and with his explanations of the universe on an unsteady table, she resigned herself to friendship only.

He repositioned the pen, then flourished it clear across the paper, running the inked line beyond the paper's boundaries. "This," he said, "is a line."

"I see that." Willa tried not to laugh. "Thanks, Mr. Geometry."

Hale shook his head. "I'm trying to tell you something."

"I see that."

He smiled, then grabbed her hand. Thrill zinged through her, welcoming his touch. But he didn't hold it to himself, or even squeeze. He reformed her hand to point, then traced it across the line. His grip lingered a blessed millisecond after the motion, but then he let it go. She placed her hand on her lap.

"The line is forever. Eternity. The hereafter. Infinity." He grabbed the sides of his head in both hands, then pulled, Bozo-ing his curly hair. "It never ends. I don't want to live for the dot, Wills. Don't want to live a shortsighted life."

"What do you mean?" She shivered.

"You." He offered no more words. She wasn't sure exactly what he meant, but was so enraptured by everything that was Hale that she dared not voice a word. He'd shunned any romantic involvement, said it kept him from focusing. So when he paid particular attention to her, Willa secretly hoped she'd be the one to refocus him. And now they sat in silence, two unconnected dots.

"I'm sorry, Jesus," he said to the ceiling. "I don't know what to do. I have to be sure." He put his head in his hands, then looked at Willa. "Maybe you should go."

She nodded and left his third floor apartment, taking every step in grief. So this was it, wasn't it? Every step down, she felt her heart trip, then deaden. On the last step, she turned and looked up. Hale stood there, paper in hand, pointing to the dot, then the line. "I love you," he shouted for all Seattle to hear.

"Me? Or Jesus?" How could she be sure he wasn't praying out loud again?

He smiled. "It's you," he said.

Running the upstairs felt like flying. With his arms around her like that, she felt almost whole. She whispered her love in his ear. It carried to him in foggy mist, like the rainy cold mingled with her words and delivered the message softer. He didn't kiss her then; he didn't have to. The dot and the line said it all.

And now he ended his name with a dot. An inked finish. A completion. What did it mean? What could it mean? Was he done with her forever? Now that he pursued his dream on the tangible streets of post-Katrina New Orleans, would he stop dreaming about her? Would the joy of work replace Willa?

She told herself not to cry. She scolded herself, letting her head berate her, call her stupid for stringing him along, for refusing his hand, for walking away from the boyfriend who loved her. *It's all your fault, you stupid girl,* the voice said. And she listened to it, believed it, soaked in it. *Hale ended his letter with a period. All because of you.*

sixteen

Before she could soak herself in tears, the knock came. She heard Genie's determined steps across the downstair's hardwoods. If a footfall could sound impatient, Genie's embodied the word.

Voices chattered below, indistinct.

"Willa," she heard Genie call.

"Great," she muttered. Willa ran index fingers beneath both eyes, trying to mop up the mascara races. She pulled in a few regulating breaths, smoothed her clothes, then walked downstairs.

Rheus Aldus, disheveled still, stood there, his hands behind his back. "The red bird brought me here. I'd like to take a walk," he said. "Want to come?"

Genie wrung her hands, looked at her shoes. Clearly not wanting Willa to say yes.

"Of course, I'd love to."

He smiled, then turned to leave. "See you later, Genie Anne Skye. You'll love me yet."

Genie huffed, but Willa noticed a smile briefly flash across the woman's face.

Outside, the sun cut through the slight crisp in the March air. Willa inhaled spring that always came early in Texas. Magenta bundles on redbud trees looked near to bursting. She marveled that a simple change in scenery from bedroom to God's great outdoors nearly salved the memory of Hale's letter. She almost broke into prayer right there, a vestige of Hale's strange tutelage, but then thought the better of it. No use in scaring off Rheus.

Rheus turned toward town. "I want to show you my home," he said. "And treat you to the best burger in the world."

Willa quickened her pace to match Rheus' tempo. "I don't know about that," she said. "Seattle invented Red Robin. Their Banzai Burger is the best I've ever had."

"Too fancy. Too strange. Nope, I promise. This burger will change the landscape of your culinary world."

"You sound like a food critic."

Rheus' face took on an injured look, something Willa hadn't intended. "I may not look like I have things together," he said, "but I'm smart, Willa."

Willa reminded herself to be Hale-like, to treat those who looked different as equals, or better than equals. "I'm sorry. I didn't mean anything by that comment."

Rheus laughed. "I know. I'm just messing with you."

A car zoomed by dangerously close. Rheus pulled her toward him, away from harm. "I wish they'd use some of that transportation money to make more sidewalks," he said. "But I suppose folks don't walk much anymore. A tragedy, if you ask me."

She heard Hale in his voice, his desire to see communities with porches and sidewalks and open-air markets and conversation. Rockwall seemed to be moving that way with its revitalized downtown, old courthouse, and cute, trendy restaurants. Still, not a soul but the two of them walked. The sun smiled on them, though, and the scent of flowers hinted the air.

"This way," Rheus said, directing her down a side street. "I'm not sure how long you'll be here, so I wanted to make sure you experienced this before you leave us."

His *us* sounded interesting, like he had another half – or longed for one. Before she could answer him, she smelled burgers. He smiled. "Though perhaps you already know the secret."

"You mean that smell?"

"Boots Burgers," he said with a flourish. "The best-kept secret in Rockwall."

Immediately, she remembered the place, thought of the hushed way her high school friends revered the place. She'd been in her vegetarian stage then, and took to taunting and making fun of all those beefeaters. Thankfully, she did away with her disdain for eating animals, particularly preferring beef. The first time she had a burger in Seattle, at Hale's gentle prodding, she nearly cried with joy, though hours later her stomach made her pay for it.

Rheus pointed at a lean-to that sat next to a blue home in a residential area. Hand-painted signs invited them there, but not for long. "Boots Burgers," one said. "No eating on the premises."

"So it does exist," she said under her breath.

"Howdy, David," Rheus said to the man behind an awning. "Where's Russell?"

"Over yonder in the house." He pointed to the home flanking the lean-to. "Had to use the facilities. Don't worry, he washes his hands." He directed that comment Willa's way. "Who's this?"

"Oh, this is Willa Muir. She's my friend."

"Muir? As in the Muir House?"

"One 'n' the same." Willa nodded his way.

"Good family," David said. He flipped a burger, then placed a square of cheddar on top. "The usual?"

"Yeah, two Double Doubles." Rheus looked at Willa. "Boots has been here near forty years, and you've never been here?"

"No," she said. The place stood practically in her back yard. How could someone live in a place, really live, and not know everything about it? But her life had become that way, with mysteries tucked into the crevasses like Boots was hidden from foot and most car traffic.

"Well, get ready for the best thing your mouth ever tasted."

Russell returned, clapped Rheus on the back before turning to the grill behind the counter. A line formed behind them from nowhere and everywhere, cars dotting the side road. He plunked fresh buns on the grill, searing grill grease into them. "You want chips?" he said.

She noticed the chips flanking the cash register. She didn't notice any deep fryers, which meant no fries. But seeing how the hamburgers danced in grease, she said a polite no.

David wrapped the burgers, bagged them, tallied their order, and finished the transaction in a quick flurry. "Never frozen," he said.

"What?"

Rheus laughed. "You trying to impress the pretty lady?" He turned to Willa. "Everyone knows they only use fresh ground beef, and when it runs out, they close for the day." With that, he whisked the bag away so the next customer could shout an order.

"You mind if we eat these at my place? They're pretty sloppy."

"No problem," she said.

She enjoyed the warm almost-spring afternoon as her stomach growled for that blessed burger. She took note of every house along the way, of the clapboard homes so different from the outskirt residential neighborhoods, all clad in brick with soaring two-story entries. With clapboard, you had the potential of variety, what with paint colors and wood-wrapped trim. To her delight, every house boasted different colored paint.

"Here we are. It isn't much, but it's home," Rheus said.

He told the truth when he said it wasn't much — a tiny, leaning home grayed by the elements.

"I've been meaning to paint it," he said.

"I'd be happy to help you choose a color." She could imagine it a fern green with cocoa trim.

Rheus opened the door without unlocking it. "I trust my neighbors," he offered as an explanation.

Inside she let her eyes adjust. After facing the sun, it felt like orienting herself to a cave. The home smelled of must and old coffee. When she blinked the fourth time, she could make out the living room and a small dining room behind it with a table and three chairs, all different.

Rheus sat, then directed her to sit across from him.

She obeyed.

"I'll bless the food," he said. "Lord, God of mysteries and misplaced memories, come now. May these burgers make us wise and strong and happy. Amen."

"Amen," she said. She pulled away the wrapper, opened her mouth, and bit into heaven on earth. She felt her eyes rolling back in joy. Oh. Dear. Lord. She wanted to say every complimentary adjective that came to mind, but her mouth kept itself busy chewing, swallowing, then biting again. She downed the burger. Did it consume her? Or she, it?

Rheus laughed. "Warned you, didn't I?"

She wiped the corners of her mouth, no doubt decorated in mayo, pickle juice, and ketchup. "So good. Thanks. Even beats Chick-fil-A!"

"Those are fighting words around here," he said.

Right then, she came to herself, as if the beefy goodness had lulled her into an alternative universe. Now she felt alive, alert. Maybe this would be when she'd learn the truth. She lifted her eyes to the living room walls, lined by shelves on two walls. They were unstained one-by-sixes, lipped by a toe-kick molding, supported by those triangular metal shelf holders. On the makeshift shelves were pictures, tilted against the lip. Some yearbooks stacked flat from various schools. She stood, moved to get a closer look. Different looking people of several nationalities smiled from family portraits. She couldn't find one picture of Rheus.

"My unsolved mysteries," he said.

"What do you mean?" She picked up a smiling family. A father with a black beard to match his hair. A mom with mouse-brown hair parted on the side and straight. Two children—a boy probably ten, with a smirk and mussed up hair. A younger girl, maybe five, with blond pigtails. It was an Olan Mills moment. Or maybe the Wal-Mart portrait studio. Very posed. "Do you know them?"

"I feel like I do. They're the Andersons. Carla and Bob."

"Why do you have their picture?"

"I bought it."

Willa sat on the gray velvety couch that had seen better days, still holding the Andersons. "You bought a family picture?"

Rheus sat opposite her. "In a way, yes."

She readied herself to hear a sordid tale of Rheus' former life as a cat burglar, but he said nothing.

He simply smiled as if that were the only explanation she needed. He exhaled, then said, "God gave me a mission."

"Buying people's framed photographs?"

"No, restoring memories."

At these words, Willa's heart pounded harder in her chest. He spoke her language, a man who spent his life, apparently, on a God-ordained memory-giving spree. She almost brought up her own fragments, almost blurted them out into the quiet room, but something held her back.

"I make my living buying entire lots of abandoned storage units," he said.

"Oh."

"Disappointed?"

"No. It's just that restoring memories sounds different than buying junk from storage units."

Anger flashed across his face. Just as quickly, it vanished. Willa regretted her words, but wasn't sure why.

"Well, it's time I get you back to your place. I reckon you've got a lot of investigating to do. At least that's what Genie tells me." He opened the front door, but didn't step through. He invited her to walk home alone. What had she done?

"Thanks," she said. "The burger was the best I've ever had. Even better than Red Robin."

"I tell the truth." He shut the door before she could say anything more.

seventeen

Willa's memory often came in the dawn of sleep. Dusky, hazy black and white movies flittered through her head like a wayward butterfly. One remained, replayed. Willa held a plastic flower to her nose, whiffing nothing. The room spun. It had no shape. No color. Just stark walls, windows covered with heavy drapes, no pictures, no furniture but a few boxes. Oddly, it wasn't the funeral home, of that she was sure, but it held a familiarity.

"It's not real," a woman's voice said. It wasn't an angry voice. Just indifferent, as if the woman were a school bus driver or a grocery checker. Impersonal. Detached. But somehow known.

"I know," Willa muttered.

The woman's hand manhandled the flower. "That's mine. Nothing is yours, not right now. Nothing, you hear me?" This time she heard a slice of anger in the woman's words. Willa looked into the woman's face and saw uncanny eyes there, but couldn't place the image. Who was she?

She woke before the tiny *her* asked the familiar-but-not-familiar woman why the flower is hers and why nothing is Willa's. Every night before bed, particularly now at home, she prayed that her dreams would play on longer. Just a few seconds more. But this ripped-away dream didn't obey such petitions. God paused the memory, freezing little Willa in the spinning room, flowerless, standing across from a stern woman who seemed like family.

What did it mean? Willa's mind buzzed with the possibilities. It certainly was something new, something she hadn't remembered before. She picked up her notebook, placed next to her bed for such a time, and sketched what she remembered while the sun heated the left side of the room, turning the dark gray curtains nearly white with the shining.

After she finished the drawing, a knock pounded the door. Willa stood, looking down at herself. Pajama bottoms and a threadbare tank top, suitable attire. "Come in, Genie," she said.

But Blake stood there. She registered the shock on his face, her clothing choice (not to mention her fuzzy head from a night's worth of dreaming), and hollered. She slammed the door on him, and hurried to find something to wear. She heard an "I'm sorry," from behind the door.

"Just a minute," she said. She looked at the clock. 9:30. What person came to someone's room at 9:30 on a Saturday? Blake's "I'm sorry" echoed through her. She remembered his crazy intrusions, how he suffocated her, then apologized. She told herself to push back, to make him leave. Instead, Willa pulled on jeans, a tank, and a t-shirt, slipping into a pair of flip-flops. She ponytailed her hair, gargled briefly with mouthwash, then answered the door, all while her heart thrummed her chest. Why did she still want to be near him?

Blake smiled. "Just in the neighborhood." He ran a hand over his stubble — something he certainly didn't have in high school. And yet, he did have this gumption back then, the ability to find Willa at vulnerable times. Part of her sounded the alarm in her soul, told her to run far away from this man who knew how to capture her off kilter, but the delicious part inside that still longed for a dangerous man silenced it. What was it about bad boys and good girls? And with Hale, the best man on God's green earth, haunting her, why in the world would she risk everything? She couldn't answer that.

Instead, she opted for fake anger, wanting to smack him

for making his presence known so early. Didn't anyone sleep in anymore? But here he stood, looking a bit forlorn and needy — something she liked in a man, though Hale seemed to pawn off his needs on God and had sufficiency in himself.

"Wanna go have coffee?"

"Sure," she said. She grabbed her purse and a hoodie in case Texas decided to be cold, then followed him down the central staircase, lecturing herself as she did. Don't fall for him, she scolded. Don't you remember his intrusion? His obsessiveness? But the other part of her pushed her toward him, relishing his scent, noting the confidence in his gait.

Blake drove the perfect car, at least in her imaginary universe where folks lived in hamlets and country markets replaced Kroger. A Mini Cooper, bright red with black and white racing stripes. "I love your car!" she said. She ran her tongue over her teeth, hoping the sweaters weren't there, but they were knitting themselves.

Guilt, the same kind she pushed down about her mother and her visitless ways, hollered in her head. Hale, in the shelter of the Oasis Café, presented her with a ring and a promise, and here she was slipping into a cool car with her old love, the one who brashly re-declared his intentions. She should've run away. Instead, she sat in the idling car, waiting for it to take her away. She entertained the thought of Hale sheltering a girl in his old VW, rushing over to open her door, holding an umbrella over her head. It made her sick.

"You okay?" Blake backed the car out of the bed and breakfast's expansive driveway.

"Yes, just shocked to be awakened."

"Mrs. Skye said you'd love the company."

Willa laughed. "I bet she did."

"We're going to Texas Roast," he said, as if that would square everything right with the world. What in the world was

Texas Roast? She briefly remembered the cut of meat impossible to find in Seattle, but the one she pined for more than wild sockeye salmon: brisket. For all its fishy glory, the Northwest couldn't compete with a slow cooked brisket over smoky wood. Heaven. On. Earth.

They neared downtown, just a few blocks from the Muir House. He turned left, then parked behind an old brick building that used to be something else. She reached for the door, but he held up his hand. "Hold on a sec."

He ran to her side of the car, then opened it. He bowed. "After you, my lady."

Willa's stomach lurched. So oddly like Hale. Had Blake memorized Hale's mannerisms, mimicked him, and then decided to torture her with them? It seemed so.

He opened the door to the place, which immediately brought Seattle back into sharp focus. The wafting of roasting and brewing coffee, black gold in her mind, made her smile. In that blip between smelling joy and making her way to the counter, she suddenly felt caught between two homes. One in Latte-land with mountains and rivers aplenty — and Hale's love. One here, where the mysteries threatened to either confound, destroy, or restore her — mixed with Blake's flirtations. Where was home?

Blake ordered an Americano with room. She stuck to her old standby, a skinny tall hazelnut latte. Sitting in the warehouse-like dining area, with old brick walls that no doubt had stories to tell, Willa settled back. "So," she said.

"I've found something," Blake said. He pulled a piece of paper from his jacket and slid it across the café table to her.

"What?" She unfolded it. Read the words. Shook her head. "I don't understand."

"It looks like your mother filed for a legal separation. Check the year."

"1982. The year before I was born."

"I don't know if it means anything or not, but I do remember all our talks about their rough and tumble ways." He winked at her. "This seems to confirm it, at least. You don't have to think you're crazy anymore."

Willa laughed, then sipped her very hot drink. "I don't know if I'll ever get beyond that hurdle. With Genie in the house, lurking and saying all these nice things about Mother, you'd think they were as close to sainthood as could be."

"Some people need to believe their myths," he said.

"All of Rockwall seems to need that myth."

"There's more to this town than rumors and patriarchs never making a mistake. That's why I stayed. I wanted more for Rockwall, more life, more authenticity, more vitality." He gestured to the Texas Roast walls. "Like here. Look at how beautifully they've remade this place. It's new, but old."

Willa saw more Hale in Blake's face. What were the odds? He'd been married to his skateboard back in the day; now it seemed he'd be comfortable on a city board for rejuvenation. "You've changed," she said.

"You too." He looked away. "But you're still beautiful."

"I doubt that."

"Don't doubt what has always been true. Besides, the truth I knew happened. You came back here as I knew you would. Back to me." He held her eyes while steam from their coffees continued to rise as a barrier between them. "I don't know what your status is, Willa, but I tend to think in terms of sovereignty."

"As in kings?"

"As in God's sovereignty. He brought you back here, clearly. And he gave me skills you need. I don't know why you need to write this memoir, though I have my inclinations. But I can help you. Maybe restore — "

"Don't. Please don't say anything more."

He backed away, a smirk on his face. "Let me finish my sentence. You're still one to jump so fast to the next word before it's even spoken. I was going to say maybe I could help you restore the missing pieces."

"Oh," she whispered, feeling her face warm. "But in the library—"

"I shouldn't have presumed." He put his hands in the air. "Shouldn't have said those things. It's just when I saw you, all these memories attacked me. Made me want you again." He reached toward her, touched her shoulder, then withdrew. "Sorry."

She wanted to punch him for playing with her emotions, but she kept her left fist under the table. This was classic Blake. His words held a hint of patronizing, as if she needed rescuing and he would ride in on a white stallion, flagging his newfound information like Super Librarian. Still, she needed him. Why he seemed to need her felt elusive. She took another drink. "Don't apologize," she measured. "I'm still thinking about my parents' separation. It's something I hadn't discovered."

"So you've done research already?" He remained stoic. Kept his eyes and hands to himself, thankfully.

"If you only knew." Try a boxful or two, she almost said.

"Do you mind if I offer some advice?"

She weighed his words, wrapping both hands around her mug. "Why do I have the feeling you'll offer it, even if I don't grant permission?"

"Because you know me. Always one to speak my mind."

"True, true," she said.

He sipped, said *ahhhh*. "Truth is a finicky thing."

"That's your advice?"

He nodded.

"Well, I disagree," she said.

"How so?"

"Truth is truth is truth. It's not distorted when it gets burned away to its purest form. It just is. Simple as that."

"And you need to find it on Rockwall soil, is that it? Return to the scene of the crime?"

The word *crime* gave her pause. "Is there something you're not telling me?"

Blake laughed. "Heavens no. Just using a figure of speech. Why all the paranoia?"

She pulled in a breath, choosing not to stop the words about to flow. "Because, Blake, I need to know what happened in my life. I have this hole, you see. A deep, dark, blank that I can't remember." Oh God, why did she release this? To him? To Texas Roast? She half expected everyone to crane their necks her way, jotting notes about her words.

"This is the first I've ever heard about it." He looked at his fingernails, perfectly cut and clean.

"That's because I didn't know about it until college. The counselor said—"

"I don't trust counselors."

She wondered at that. This was the first fundamental difference between Blake and Hale. Where Hale welcomed any outside help when it came to issues of emotion and heart, Blake, apparently, shunned such a thing. "Why do you say that?"

"I have my reasons." He gathered his cup, then hers. He stood. "Let's go, all right?"

She nearly muttered, "Quick date," but kept quiet.

Outside under the unrelenting blue sky, she smelled Rockwall, a mixture of sweet spring blossoms emerging from trees, a hint of wetness from the dancing lake, and something she couldn't discern. Blake opened the door. "Sometimes you have to embrace the chaos," he said. "Sometimes things don't tie up neatly." With that, he shut the door. She felt its reverberations on her right shoulder.

He drove her home, or what was momentarily home. In that brief trip, she wondered why so many of her conversations ended in a huff. Of course with Genie, but also with Rheus. Now Blake. A darkness crept over her heart. She felt it. The deepest of worries that maybe everything was her fault. That maybe her parents argued solely because of her presence. That maybe she was crazy and everything had been blossoms and joy growing up, only she'd become forgetful. Or delusional. Maybe she camped on the whole awful story solely as an excuse to say no to Hale. Or anyone for that matter.

But when Blake pulled into the Muir House's parking lot, she reassured herself. This house held many secrets. Secrets that dared to be told, but never without penalty. She knew that now. If she were to uncover the truth, she'd lose any popularity contest with folks happy with the status quo where Mr. and Mrs. Muir reigned sovereignly, unblemished, untarnished, clean, right.

Blake breezed a "thank you" her way. He didn't open her door. She pushed against it, stood, bent down, and thanked him back — the proper Southern thing to do. As he pulled away, the memory came back to her. How that woman told her that nothing was hers. She felt the paper in her pocket, proof that the perfect marriage on the outside was not the case, at least for a time. That paper was hers. As was her fractured memory. No one could take those away.

She bent low, examining the emerging green grass, wondering at it. Texas and Seattle proved opposite in their grass cultivation. Seattle blanketed itself in kelly green grass most of the year, but not in summertime when its beauty faded to brown. Texas kept its brown in winter, erupting into glory for spring until late fall. She saw the tiny green sprigs emerging from the lawn flanking the house, and with it a tiny white flower — a mini daisy flanged in pink. She picked it. It was hers. Hers alone.

eighteen

A new week found her walking through every room upstairs, taking notes, letting her mind conjure up new décor. Though she knew Rockwall had few furniture stores, Dallas would provide when she had a chance to explore. Today? The beauty of a few catalogs Genie ordered enticed her. Itching fingers cut out pictures, placed them in piles for each room.

Willa opened her secret blog, wondering afresh if Hale cared. His absence screamed at her like a separation, like the one evidenced by the stark white paper splayed to her left. Black letters on white paper that said her mother didn't love Daddy. With Mother's mind so far gone, would she remember such a thing? Again Willa felt the tinge again that she should make a visit, realizing that Mother was a human being, needing forgiveness and grace—two things Willa lacked right now. It occurred to her that she'd visit Mother for selfish motives, to pry the unpriable from Mother's damaged mind. Had she, in her need to know the truth, turned into the selfish woman she feared?

Instead of combating her unforgiveness or overcoming her wrath, Willa rehearsed the justifications in her head, reminding herself that she didn't deserve all those words spoken over her. And then she wrote:

Blog title: Separation

It's such an ugly word, separation. Like soul separated from body in death. Or a child separated from her father at Target. Or parents calling it quits. What would have hap-

pened if my parents gave it up before I came into their lives? If they had taken the next step? Divorce? Would there be no more me? I guess I'm narcissistic enough to believe it's good that I'm here. I do have a primal urge to live.

But that's where it gets complicated for me, Hale. I don't want to just exist. I want to live. To be free. To experience the filling of the hole, the completion of the project that is me, the period at the end of my sentence. Is that too much to ask? How can it threaten anyone for me to know what happened? Who would be hurt? In the darkness, I hurt. In the shushing and secrets, I burn and ache and bleed. Doesn't anyone care about me?

I guess you don't intend to answer this, since you're probably not reading my diatribe. But in the off chance you are, please know that I'm happy you're pursuing your dream in New Orleans. I am. But I wish you could see what I'm doing in Rockwall as my pursuit of a dream. I'm rebuilding too. My soul, unanchored, needs a foundation as strong as the wall buried beneath this town. I pray you understand this.

Don't roll your eyes. Don't tell me again to trust God with the foundations of my life. Don't make fun of me for my lack of faith. Just listen.

But more likely you're not listening, and I'm typing these words to empty space.

She published the post, then readied herself for another mysterious day in Texas. She heard Genie bustling in the kitchen, so she went downstairs. As the old woman nodded Willa's way, the grandfather clock in the left parlor struck noon. Willa noticed the opened kitchen windows, the faint smell of honeysuckle wooing her to step outside. But first, a conversation.

Genie pushed and prodded a lump of dough through strong hands. "You have to beat it to death before it becomes a baby." She blew an errant short hair northward, but it fell again across her forehead. Had Willa possessed an ounce of compassion, she would've seen the nuisance as it was, understood the pestering of an interloping hair, and brushed it from Genie's forehead. But extravagance of that sort called for relationship, affection. Instead, she watched the hair, reveled in how it tormented a still-puffing Genie. And again she condemned herself.

She remembered Genie's baby words after her trip down Condemnation Lane. "What do you mean, baby?"

"Flour has gluten." She said it as if Willa had any hint of a brain, she would know this. "And gluten must be man-handled for several minutes before it stretches into the right consistency." She slapped the lump of dough. "See how smooth the dough is?"

"Yeah."

"Like a baby's bottom," Genie said. "And this convection oven bakes it to perfection."

A breeze flowed into the kitchen like a forgotten, but cherished, memory. It sweetened the room, framing the vista. Had Willa been a cinematographer, she'd have reveled in the light, how the dust danced between. She'd mount the camera in the upper left portion of the kitchen, surveying the idyllic scene: an older matriarchal woman expounding the virtues of bread making, her younger protégée taking mental notes—both of them smiling in the circle of intergenerational friendship. A scene absent discord, ill will, sour words.

But life seldom held on to its idealism.

Willa broke the scene in a thousand pieces with one decision. "Before I was born," she said, "Mother filed for a separation. I have the paper to prove it. Care to tell me about it?"

Genie continued to pummel the bread dough, spanking it into baby-bottom submission. The tickling hair played at her forehead, enough for the woman to let go of the flour-dusted lump and try again to push it away. This time, she unwrangled a bobby pin from the side of her head, anchoring the busy hair to her part. All this without speaking, without acknowledging Willa's caustic words. She resumed her pushing and pulling, this time with a dusting of flour on her forehead — a baker's Ash Wednesday.

"Did you hear me?" Willa said it louder this time.

"I hear a great deal."

"And you have nothing to say?" Willa threw her arms in the air. "What is it? Can't you stand to admit that Rockwall's perfect couple almost split? Or that your devotion to them is marred by their own humanness?" She felt bile rise up her throat, tasted the sting of stomach acid. She'd tried Miss Nice Girl. Now it was Miss Angry One, and neither seemed to work. Genie wouldn't crack, not for mock kindness, not for genuine wrath.

Genie stopped beating up the potential loaf. She turned to look at Willa, an undecipherable look in her eyes. Not pain, but something akin to it. "I will not be bullied, Willa Muir."

"Clearly."

Not known for relishing close proximity, Genie came nearer than she'd ever had — a mere foot of kitchen electrified between them. "You listen to me." She wagged an index finger in Willa's face. "I keep my promises. Unlike others I know, I have character. Grit. You're asking something I cannot answer. So kindly keep your pointed nose in your own business. Let the dead bury the dead. And the living live their lives in peace!"

Willa stepped back, pulling away from the words, the finger, the echo of Genie's yowl.

"Nothing you find will bring back your father, Willa."
Genie said this calmer, almost soothing.

"I do not want him back." The six words stifled between
them. Her next words should have been, "I want the truth," but
the starkness of the sentence, the untruth it conveyed, couldn't
be taken back. Tears moistened her eyelids, wet her cheeks. But
more than that, a cry pressed from her chest, a weight heavier
than sadness pushed it out of her. She ran from the kitchen,
up the back stairs, into her room where a pillow welcomed
her weeping. She clutched the percale to her face, groaning
but not wanting to. Heaving, but trying not to. Pulling in jag-
ged breaths, but not feeling the air. The crying stretched from
seconds to minutes.

How could she live without Daddy? She'd jutted her lip
forward, keeping the proverbial stiff upper lip when he passed
on, hardening her soul. But he always whispered to her, quietly,
in the times no one looked, as if to torture her of his loss. He
was there, but he wasn't. Always near, but completely separated.

Willa pulled the pillow from her face, breathed in the apple-
scented room, and told herself to calm her hyperventilation. For
a brief period of time, perfect peace replaced her raucous crying. Maybe that was it, she thought. Maybe all this struggle was
her way of bringing Daddy back, of grieving his loss. Maybe the
missing hole was a foil to bring her to this place. And maybe,
oddly, God — who often seemed capricious and distant — used
Genie Skye to point that out to her. Mother Teresa said Jesus
often came in the distressing disguise of the poor. Perhaps he
also came in the form of a bread-beating woman.

In the empty room, Willa longed for Hale in a way she
couldn't put words to. Any sentence she'd string together
couldn't convey the hunger she had, the thirst, the unquench-
able ache she felt for him in this discovery. She knew he should

be beside her, holding her, stroking her hair, rejoicing with her, soothing her Daddy wound.

"Jesus," she said. "The missing's too much. Why won't he call?" But Jesus stayed as silent as Hale in the staleness of her room.

She picked up her phone and called Hale, waiting to hear his voice, hoping he'd have a change of heart and pick up her call. But it went to voice mail. He'd never bothered to create his own personal message, so the best she'd get was his name stated plainly between an electronic female voice. She waited for it, endured the woman, then heard him say his name. She wanted it to be hers.

When the tone sounded, she hung up.

And felt as alone as a beaten loaf on the counter, waiting to rise.

nineteen

Willa heard footsteps. By now she'd memorized the tenor of Genie's soft-soled shoes on the landing. She waited for a knock, for an intrusion, but none came. Instead, a note flitted under the door, a simple sheet of lined paper lying prostrate on the dark wood floor. She left her bed, bent low, and picked it up.

It read: *Arbor House of Rockwall, Number 5. Ella Muir.*

"Mother," she said.

All the guilt for neglecting Mother the past five years pressed into her. Sure, Mother had told her to leave forever. That much was true. But what daughter would obey such a mandate? And with all her conniving and evasion, hadn't Genie made a practice of visiting Mrs. Ella Muir? If Genie could do such a thing, why couldn't Willa?

She stared at the paper again, wishing there'd been invisible ink she could decipher with heat, that the entire truth of her childhood would emerge, that every mystery would stare back at her. But no such cloak-and-dagger messages existed. Just a room number and the name of the one who'd forgotten every mystery.

Tomorrow, she told herself. The visit would come tomorrow.

Always tomorrow.

twenty

As the lyricists penned, tomorrow never came. At least it didn't
come the next day because Willa spent the day in bed, nursing what could only be explained as food poisoning purgatory.
She'd visited a fast food restaurant the night before, determined not to buy from Genie's pantry. The chicken patty tasted
weird on her tongue, felt different as she chewed it—a bit too
slimy, oddly sinewy. But she dismissed it, obeying her hunger
instead, and finished off the entire chicken sandwich, chasing it with practically a gallon of sweet tea and a large order
of fries. She smiled as she finished, remembering Hale's rage
against commercialized fast food. At least apart from him she'd
be free of organics.

At three o'clock in the morning, the angry chicken patty
enacted its vengeance, sending every ounce of food Willa'd
eaten the previous day northward. She quietly thanked God
for Genie's ingenious positioning of the bathroom in the closet,
very close to the bed. She spent hours worshiping the toilet
there, holding the cold, hard rim, cooling her head on the
subway-tiled floor. She said the name of Jesus as she shook,
then sweat, but he seemed so far away.

She remembered, in those delirious memories, how she'd
helped Daddy the last few months of his life. She flew from
Seattle to be at his side, missing the pomp and circumstance
of graduation in light of seeing his face, though nothing could
prepare her for the haggard way he looked, how his breaths
came in shallow gulps. He even lost the ability to urinate on his

own. The one who changed her diapers became the diapered. In that reversal, Willa found purpose nobler than herself. She found beauty in small things, in the hint of a smile, the weakly uttered thank you from dry lips. As if she'd been born to be a caretaker, Willa blessed Daddy those last few days with her service, her heart, her selflessness. A strange ending to her college career, but the right one.

But as she wallowed alone on the cold floor, she wondered who would feel the reversal with her. She had no husband, no children. No genuine friend to her name. If she choked on her vomit in the dark of the bathroom, who would miss her? Who would check on her?

She needed a Willa in her life. Someone who loved her, who felt privileged to bless her.

At dawn, she curled into a ball, covers over her head. She slept like death until midafternoon when a knock startled her awake. "Yes?"

Genie entered, carrying something on a wicker tray. "It's not like you to not stir until now. Is everything okay?"

Willa pulled herself up. "Food poisoning," she said through grimy teeth.

Genie placed the tray on the nightstand atop the magazines and catalogs. "I brought you some ginger ale."

How did Genie know that was exactly what her water-bereaved body craved?

With a strange motherly tenderness, Genie sat gently on the bed, then poured a glass of ginger ale. "I'll leave the container here," she said. "And Rheus found an extra dorm-sized fridge in one of his auctions. Said he thought you might want it. When you're up and about, I'll have him bring it up." She stood, smoothed the place where she sat, and padded out the door. She didn't slam it. It closed on creaky hinges as the clock downstairs chimed three.

An odd reversal, this life. Willa pondered Genie's kindness, wondering if she could treasure it in her heart the way the Virgin Mary did when Jesus did his amazing acts. She'd not been one to treasure, at least not since Daddy's death. Or Mother's great pushing away. She whispered a prayer after ginger ale soothed her throat. It came out in desperation, in hesitation, garbled by grief. It went something like, "Lord, help me."

twenty-one

Hale's letter came the next day. Willa brimmed excitement when she touched the inside-out envelope. The return address, sure enough, was New Orleans. Post-stamped yesterday. If only she could transport herself to Hale in such short manner. She practically danced up the stairway, feeling the smooth wood of the risers under bare, warm feet. Spring had bloomed now, in blatant fury, bringing with it nearly eighty-degree weather. In her room, the sun brightened her bed, made her smile. She found a warm hollow of sunshine, relishing its heat like a curled-up cat.

She didn't rip the envelope in haste. Instead, she cherished the opening like a present long anticipated. Careful not to tear Hale's handiwork, she slipped her finger under the flap and gently lifted it, retrieving the letter.

It didn't waft evergreen. Didn't have much of a smell at all. She opened the single white page whose back was a bank advertisement for the highest rate of savings and the lowest rate for credit. The numbers didn't match — were about as far away as Willa felt from Hale now.

Something about the letter distressed her, jumped her heart. She closed her eyes, hoping a bit of preparation prior to reading would steady her galloping heartbeat. But her heart cantered on in her chest.

Dear Willa, it said.

Not Wills?

I feel a deep kinship with Jesus down here in the muggy South, figuring I'll find him here amongst the ruins. The more I read about him, the more mysterious he is in the way he loves people. After careful study and reflection, I believe he is asking me to follow his ways in corresponding to you.

I met Reality today, and it wrecked me for the ordinary. I'm not going to be plain and straightforward about my encounter with Reality, except to say I believe Reality will change everything about me.

Jesus has given me dirty, painstaking work, and I'm forever grateful for it. It keeps my mind and heart where it should be, in weakness, in dependence on the One who is strong. I hope you've found what you're looking for, hope you're finding the perfect peg to fit into your round cavern of a hole. But as I think about it, Willa, I wonder if God would rather the hole be left unfilled for his sake. Something to ponder, anyway.

Oswald Chambers knocked my socks off the first time I read his book My Utmost for His Highest. My favorite quote comes into play in your quest. He writes, "Let the past sleep, but let it sleep on the bosom of Christ. And go into the irresistible future with Him."

I hope I'm in your irresistible future, though I'm no prophet. However, your hasty departure from my proposal seems to say otherwise. In that, I grieve. But my grief is something I won't burden you with here.

My letters may not come as often now that I'm busied with houseless folks. Their stories have a way of consuming me in the best possible way. In the meantime, rest in knowing I'm praying for you with every breath, and hoping someday you'll wear my ring.

Hale.

Another period, not the punctuation she wanted. And though she worried briefly that Hale was embracing some esoteric belief about Reality, the rest of the letter seemed Jesusy enough to refute such a thing. So now Hale would be cryptic. From here on out, he'd write parables to her, hiding his words behind symbolism, driving her near insane with the interpretation. She shook her head. "Hale," she exhaled to the room. "Confounding me like Jesus did his disciples."

Had she lost him forever? Just as the disciples thought they'd lost Jesus? Would there be a resurrection? Would the person who dared to love her ever come back? For years she embraced chaos, welcoming it as a trusted friend. Her world felt right when drama reigned, particularly when Blake enacted the drama, coddling it, encouraging the side of her that needed confusion.

But it had been Hale who pointed out her penchant for chaos — at the base of Mount Rainier as they picnicked on foccacia salmon sandwiches and fizzy, fruity drinks. A fly buzzed around them. Hale flicked it away, only to be pestered again. So, quick as a Venus flytrap, he captured it, cupped between two hands. She could hear its frantic buzzing as it collided with his finger prison.

"This is you," he said.

"I'm a fly?"

He laughed. "No, you're you. The fly is a crazy, painful life. It buzzes around you. You make a halfhearted effort to bat it away, but eventually you capture it to yourself."

"I don't follow you."

He kept the poor fly trapped. "Here's my First Theory of Willa Relativity. You grew up with chaos and pain, right?"

She nodded. The sunshine drifted behind a cloud, shivering her.

"That's your haven. What you grew accustomed to. It became your familiarity, your safe place."

"That makes no sense. Why would chaos be a safe place?"

"Because it's what's comfortable for you, what you know. What if God were calling you to something radically different? What if he wanted you to let go of the drama, to turn your back on it, and walk confidently in a new place?"

Willa let the words warm and chill her. Was it true? Had she made chaos her safe place? She remembered the panicked feeling she had when she moved to Seattle and everything in her life settled down into a strange, mundane Normal. Away from Blake's obsessive words, the way they waffled her affections. Away from the memories of parents screaming, Daddy dying, Mother banishing. "So you're saying that to live a normal life is a risk for me?"

"Touché!" He released the fly, let it buzz free. Only it hovered around him again. "And just like this fly, those tormenting voices from the past, how they lulled you into believing lies, will continue to buzz."

"Buzz," she said.

"Guess what, Willa?"

"What?"

"You have a choice. Chaos or wholeness. I know it sounds wacko, but your comfort zone is chaos. Take a risk for wholeness," he said.

Willa lifted her gaze from Hale's perfect sky eyes to see Mount Rainier looming behind him. Strong. Sturdy. Undisturbed. Rooted. She'd been a moving target for years, afraid to settle, afraid to be quiet enough to wrestle with the aching hole inside. Were Hale's words the truth? Could she feel safe only in chaos? In pain?

Hale tilted her chin to look at him. He placed his left hand on her cheek, bent near, and kissed her. "I'm here. Right now. And I consider it my privilege to help you be so enthralled with life today that the pain of the past becomes a fading dream. This is the reality of my love, Willa Muir. You can count on it, depend on it."

Sunshined on the bed, no longer sitting on a quilt under the watchful eye of Mount Rainier, Willa remembered Hale's use of the word *reality*, how he equated it with love. It stuck into her heart and mind in the mountaintop moment like a fly pestering and never leaving. Reality.

She'd grown more in that truth-filled talk with Hale than she had in a year's worth of counseling. Hale had plucked from her an essential truth: she thrived on pain, flew from normalcy.

She replayed the Café Oasis proposal in her mind, all the while clutching Hale's letter with such force, it wrinkled between her hands. She hadn't learned from his observations. Hadn't internalized his words.

No. She ran.

From home.

From Blake.

From Mother.

From Hale.

From reality.

On the nightstand, in the matchbox, sat proof of that reality: a ring. She smoothed the letter, re-positioned it back into the recycled envelope, and grabbed the box. She pulled out the ring, looked through its center, hoping to be transported into one of those alternative universes where love prospered and angelic beings sang joyful songs about beauty and freedom. But the ring's empty center only revealed her toes baptized by sun on a bed deep in the heart of Texas. It found her alone, with a future seeming less and less irresistible.

Willa placed the ring on her left palm, pressed it into her

skin until the circle made a pink mark. Her hole unfilled. She remembered Hale's handwriting, how he challenged her to deviate from the quest to fill her heart. She felt the weight of the ring, the weight of her past, the impatient wait that seemed like a lifetime all culminated in a simple gold ring. She fingered the ring in her right hand, looking through it briefly again, then filled its emptiness with her engagement finger.

"I will," she said to the quiet room. "I will find a way to the irresistible future."

twenty-two

Willa made herself do it. Made herself face one bit of reality from the past, slices of memory she shoved down deep ever since coming back to the Muir House.

Maybe the ring circling her finger gave her the power. She pulled on her Toms, scurried down the side stairs, and exited out the side door. She looked in the parking lot—Genie's car was gone. Good.

She stood behind the house in the back yard, facing the house's rear and the street beyond it. A sudden thought seized her with vengeance. *You could run flat out, past the house, and into the middle of Goliad and let the gods of traffic decide your fate.* It was the same voice that teased her from the observation deck of the Space Needle to jump. The same voice that told her she'd never find home. The same elusive and slick voice that berated her with her own unworthiness. She breathed in the spring air, squinting under the sun, and determined to disobey the voice. Instead, she walked to the left side of the house where the utility shelter stood.

Finally.

On seeing it, her pulse escalated. Just three walls of its own, borrowing the fourth from the funeral home. A makeshift door. A crooked window. Where the earth had been padded grassless before its entrance, weeds reached to the sky. Her place of refuge, now ramshackled and unkempt.

It seemed so small.

She felt like a giant.

When sheltered there, she fancied it a mansion, but now she had to duck to get through the doorway. Her makeshift napkin curtains hung askew, faded by years of sun damage. The electric meter whirred, its dials moving slowly to the rhythm of spring air conditioning. She smelled her anguish, felt a presence there of herself as a child, as if Old Willa and Young Willa shared a tea party in the cramped space. She sat inside, wrapping her arms around herself, wondering what the young Willa would say, whether she'd spill a secret in their fellowship of two. But she heard no voice except her own, clanking around her head. *This place means nothing. Get out.*

A pang of memory bulldozed her — of strong, sinewy arms pulling her from this place in the dead of night. Her — kicking, hollering, crying. She dug bare feet into the soil of the tiny vestibule, hoping the arms would let go, but they wouldn't. They pulled relentlessly while shouting erupted from outside. She grabbed the meter, her hands grasping as tightly as she could. She felt the pull outside stretch her hands, remembered how her fingernails scraped the gray meter's paint beneath chipped nails. She remembered the release, then a flashlight outside spotlighting her to the dirt. A slurred voice above in the darkness said, "Are you Willa?"

She didn't answer.

"Your eyes," the stranger said. He belched. Then shook his head, hollered, and turned away.

Hurried footsteps thudded the evening earth, leaving Willa breathless and gasping on her back, the flashlight gone, the stars standing in their place. They seemed to tease her there, showing just how small she was.

So the child Willa did speak after all, but she told such awful stories that Willa had to unfold herself from the shelter to see the sun again. She sat on the grass, telling her heart to settle itself, but it rumbled against her chest with fury. The photo-real memory stunned her, bludgeoning her resolve. Did she really want to know the truth? Of a drunken man commenting on her eyes? Of being pulled from her shelter, exposed to the night?

Willa picked at the grass around her, uprooting short tufts as she thought. She knew her next task: illustrate this flash-back. But she couldn't stand just yet. The weight of the memory covered her like a wet afghan, and though the sun winked warmth on her, she shivered on the earth. And then hollered. Something stung her ankle. And another something. And ten thousand others. She stood, noticing ants swarming above her left foot—fire ants, the ultimate ankle biters. She brushed them off in a frantic rush, yelping with the effort. Each sting felt like a bee's. For such little critters, they packed a mighty bite.

She ventured back into the house, ran upstairs, and threw off her clothes. The shower, warm and steamy, welcomed her. She washed her ankle with shampoo, trying to remember if she brought cortisone with her. She knew to pop a couple anti-histamines when she finished, but she also knew the sting would remain a bit longer, replaced by itching galore.

So much like the recovered memory—at first a surprising sting, then a pestering itch that reminded her of something she couldn't quite discern. While the shower water raced down her torso, she wondered at the teetering man. Who was he? Was he the man in her photo? With the flashlight beaming her face and his face shadowed, she would never be sure. But she was certain of one thing: it had been the right decision to return to Rockwall. All her years of investigating from a safe place had given her no such leads. Only on the fire-ant marching earth did the memories ignite.

She turned off the shower and stood dripping in its wake. She pulled a white fluffy towel around her, the smell of bleach so strong her eyes watered. Again, she shivered for no reason. And there, in the vulnerable place with an ankle blaring red and skin hatching goose bumps, Willa remembered Hale's words about risk on the mountain, how she favored chaos over normal. This was not normal, but it felt like the new memory led her toward normal. When she stepped through the threshold from the bathroom to her room, she knew her life would never be the same.

For Hale's sake, she would grow. She would learn. She would uncover, then heal. It was as simple as wanting it to be so.

twenty-three

Even with the cortisone cream dried flaky on her ankle, she still itched. After sketching the memory in her bedside notebook, Willa fought to create the final sketch for the Great Wall of China Room. She couldn't quite flesh it out, so she reached for her stack of magazines she bought half price at a local bookstore. She thumbed through, looking for patterns, fabrics. She cut out the perfect curtain material found on page 127 of *Better Homes and Gardens* when she spied a house drawing for a modern Craftsman bungalow with wide eaves, a deep porch, and double hung windows. Her fingers trembled a bit as she cut out the plans, then slipped them into the pages of her Bible. She set the needed-to-be-read book down while the fire ant's itchy gift persisted. She allowed herself a few scratches. Ah, bliss. But the next second, agony.

She drove to the library, hoping to catch Blake and ask him a few questions. Telling herself that she only desired his expertise. She kept the car's windows down, marveling at all the window-upped cars here and there, basking in stale air conditioning. Didn't people like fresh air?

She parked, then paused briefly behind the wheel. How long would she be here in Rockwall? Would she rent this car forever? Would she continue to search for the truth, or as Hale put it, for reality, until she flipped her age from twenty-six to sixty-two? Would she never resolve the empty memory and become one of those women married to four cats living in a tiny home, sipping tea, and embracing spinster ways? She glanced at Hale's ring. No, she would find the truth. It would set her free. To love, finally.

She left the car, locked it, and pushed through the two sets of doors into the library. A librarian sorting books at the counter nodded a hello. Willa ascended the cantilevered staircase, hoping to see Blake once she reached the summit. But his desk sat empty.

She ventured to the back corner of the library where a small section of Rockwall history books preened in a display. She lifted one, a book about First Baptist Rockwall, its first hundred years. She scanned through recipes, faces, histories. Someone touched her shoulder.

She jumped.

"Hey, it's only me." Blake kept his hand on her shoulder as she turned to face him.

"Is this your habit? Scaring patrons? Don't you know you've caused me to stumble?"

"Stumble?"

"You nearly made me holler. And we're in a library!"

Blake directed her to a grouping of comfortable chairs by the window. She sat. Beyond the freeway, Willa watched the blocks of retail strips, a church the size of Texas, and more cars darting here and there.

Blake leaned in close. She could smell his cologne. In Seattle, all scents had been banned from libraries. Too many sensitivities. She wondered if this was Rockwall's rule too, and if Blake rebelled because he could.

"So, what brings you here? Couldn't stay away from me, could you?"

"I guess you're right." She sat on her hands, remembering Hale's ring circling her finger. Did her new resolve mean commitment? Would indulging in flirtation be a betrayal? After all, Hale had no knowledge of her renewed hope for them.

Smelling Blake, remembering him, drowning in his eyes, weakened her. Though she knew better, she reached out, grabbed his hand. Held it. Held his eyes to hers. Tumults of guilt pestered her; she felt them not in her heart, but in the remembrance of a stung ankle. Her forwardness pushed her into fire ant territory. But she didn't care. Not this time. This lonely, longing placeholder.

"This is a surprise," he said.

Hearing his voice broke the spell. She half expected Hale's deep voice to resonate from his chest, but it was Blake's — higher, needier, less assured. She pulled her hand away, letting guilt pummel her. "I'm sorry. I shouldn't have."

"I liked it," he said. He sat back, smiled. "I knew it, you know."

"Knew what?" She kept her ring finger covered.

"Your feelings."

"It was a mistake."

"What are you referring to? Holding my hand just now, or leaving me behind?" He winked at her, kept her gaze, maddening her.

"I shouldn't have held your hand."

Blake shifted. Sat forward. "You know, in Africa, the men hold hands. In friendship."

Willa let out a sigh. "Friendship," she said.

"Hey, I'm as screwed up as I've always been. I won't lie to you, Willa. I like you. I love you."

She felt the "I love you" like a blow to the chest, held it to her, letting it steal her breath. But she said nothing.

Blake smiled. "Yeah, I figured you knew that. But as I said the other day, I can still help you, even if you walk away again. Maybe I've grown up a little bit. Or maybe I'm a glutton for punishment, to use a trite cliché."

"You've never been one for cliché."

"It fills the awkward spaces between us, wouldn't you say?"

Willa nodded. "Listen, I don't know what came over me."

"My irresistibleness, I'm thinking."

"It won't happen again." Willa looked beyond his gaze to the greening field beyond the library. She hoped her actions would obey her words.

"Really?" Blake stood.

Willa joined him, feeling the tension between them — a tightly wound coil of need, intrigue, and danger.

"Listen," Blake said. "I promised I'd help, so I will."

"Thanks."

He motioned for her to follow him to his desk. She did, smelling the trail of cologne. He sat, then shuffled through some papers. She stood like a patron, her left hand to her side, her right smoothing the surface of his desk.

"Did you know your paternal grandmother well?"

"Yes, why?" Willa believed his next words would mean something, would be a clue to unravel her terribly confused heart.

"Just curious. I uncovered something yesterday that I thought would interest you."

"What is it?" She kept her words to a whisper.

"How often did you see your grandparents on your dad's side?"

"Fairly often."

"And you knew your grandmother to be a good woman?"

"Blake, quit being elusive. Just tell me what you found." With this, she freed her left hand, gesturing to the window, to Blake, to the world.

"She's not your father's mother. At least not the woman you knew to be your grandmother."

"Yes she is. Daddy called her Mama, and Grandpa, well, he cherished her."

"No doubt. But from what I've gathered, your real grandmother left your grandfather when your dad was a toddler. Just up and left. Your grandfather hastily married the lady you knew as your grandmother."

"Did my dad know this?"

"It came out, eventually, right before he married your mother."

"You found this in the library?"

He shook his head. "I have my sources, but this one wasn't a book."

"From a person?" Willa fidgeted.

"Yes."

"Who?"

"You forget that my father and yours were friends."

"What else do you know?" Would this be the answer? Would he share everything he knew? That Blake's father knew?

"Nothing really beyond this."

"Oh come on!" She stood. "I'm getting closer, Blake. I need to know the truth!"

"Keep your voice down," he shushed.

"Sorry."

He stood. "It's okay. I know this is upsetting, but you have to realize that sticking your nose into things hurts people. You and I are of the tell-everything generation. But there's an entire generation of folks whose lives centered around dignity and secrecy."

She looked at the parking lot below where an older woman struggled to secure her book bag to a walker. A younger girl helped her with her things, patting the woman's back as she shuffled toward the library. Two generations. Two different ways of living. "I don't find secrecy dignifying. Especially from you."

"Ouch."

She looked at her shoes. "Secrets hurt."

"Don't you think I realize that, Willa? But I have to tell you — I also don't find tattling a virtue. Don't ask me to tell you more than this. Please." He looked at her as he had so many years ago, a desperate but strong longing in his eyes. He traced her face with his eyes, then picked up her left hand in his. His eyes rested on her ring finger.

She pulled her hand away.

"Engaged much?" His words sounded cramped.

She tried to twist off the ring, but like Hale's dogged persistence, it held. "It's not what you think," she said.

"Then why are you blushing?"

"I'm just warm." She backed away from him until her shoulders touched the windows, still trying to pry the ring from her finger. She wondered briefly if Hale tracked security cameras, if he could see her do such an angry thing to his ring. He'd surely dump her then and there. She would keep this a secret, and as she thought about that, she realized how convenient secrets could be. How very convenient.

"Listen, Willa. I'm trying desperately to be your friend. It's no secret that I'd like to be more. But if you're engaged, I'll shove my desire down. I'm not one to push into someone else's territory." He moved toward their two chairs again.

"I'm not territory."

"Well put." He sat on the side of the armchair she'd sat in, where she'd touched his hand, held it. "I know that. It's just that I understand your need to find out the truth. I get it. And I'll keep helping you. Though it's not easy for me."

She sat opposite him, on the other chair's arm. "You understand?"

"Sure. We all have things from our past that bewilder us.

Why do you think I became a research librarian? I had my own
past to figure out. I enjoyed it so much that I've spent my life
discovering other folks' pasts. You know what I do most of the
time here?"

Willa shook her head.

"Help folks create family trees. Do genealogical research. I
love making a difference."

"That's really great." She twisted the ring again, but it
remained in place.

"Don't worry about the engagement. Whoever he is, I wish
him the best. He's got the most beautiful girl in the world." The
last words he sang quietly, from an ancient song. He'd used to
sing it to her when they dated, and even then it was an oldie
by Charlie Rich.

Willa looked at her hands.

Blake leaned in near, so close she could smell his breath.
He touched her chin. "It's okay. I'm heartbroken again, but I
got over it last time—eventually. I'll get over it this time." He
kissed her cheek, lingering.

Chills rushed down her spine, tingling her toes.

An "ahem" sounded to her left. Blake stood. The librarian
who nodded a happy hello now stood above them, head shaking a decisive no. "Blake, may I talk to you?"

Blake said, "Yes, ma'am," and followed the woman. He
turned back and looked at her then, but she couldn't discern
his expression.

Back home, Willa spent an hour researching her grandmother, but could find nothing that would indicate she wasn't
Daddy's biological mama. She'd have to order Daddy's birth
certificate to confirm it, so she pulled up the State of Texas
vital statistics department. Thankfully, Daddy's birth fell
within the seventy-five years ago requirement, though since

she didn't truly reside in Texas, she couldn't expedite the process online. Instead, she downloaded the form, printed a copy with her portable copier, copied her Washington State driver's license, and mailed it.

When she returned from the mail slot, her blog beckoned.

Title of Post: Two Mysteries in One Day

Hale, if you're reading this, you'll be glad to know I'm getting closer to uncovering my past, though right now it feels more like I'm putting together a thousand-piece puzzle without the benefit of a picture. Somehow these things connect, but I'm not sure how yet.

I remembered a new memory, of me hiding in the utility shed at night. Must've been from the empty year. Someone pulled me out. Said something about my eyes, walked away.

Then I found out my grandmother is not Daddy's real mama. Which he never mentioned to me. But then again, he never didn't say anything either. Seems he kept the secret?

All this begs the question. What is this Reality with a capital R you are writing about? It seems cryptic. Not really like you. I know this will sound needy (and maybe you're smiling as you read this), but were you referring to our talk on Mount Rainier? I just had to ask.

Of course, I'm not sure if you're reading this, which actually makes me mad. I read your letters, Hale. Read them several times. Because I miss you. But you've given no indication that you're reading my words. You said you're taking a fast. I wish you weren't. Why? Because I'm wearing your ring as proof of my desire to get well. It circles my finger as I type this.

I miss you.

Wills

She grasped the ring. Though it clung to her at the library under Blake's broken gaze, it slid off easily now. She wondered if its release were a sign. Cross-legged on her bed, she noticed how the same shade of pink where the ring had been twisted matched the raised welts of fire ants scarring her ankle.

twenty-four

Rheus breezed into the middle of Willa's agenda the next day, as if he knew she needed him. She'd been feeling the pressure of finishing up all her pictures and design boards for Genie's approval. So many color swatches, so little time. Rheus knocked just as she decided on "Gray Day" as the Berlin Wall Room's main wall color.

"It's a spectacular morning, don't you think?" He wore a light blue jacket, torn at one sleeve, a pair of ancient Levis, worn out shoes, and a giant smile.

Willa glanced outside. Drizzled rain ran down the windows. "I guess so," she said.

"I figured you'd be thrilled."

"Why is that?"

He stayed anchored below the doorjamb. "It's your weather."

"My weather?" She shut her laptop and stood.

"Seattle!" He looked flustered, as if his joke hadn't landed its mark.

"Oh, right! Sorry."

"Well, I'm actually here to ask you a favor."

Secretly she rejoiced. Apparently Rheus wasn't one to hold a grudge. "What do you need?"

"Your car."

She laughed. "It's not exactly my car, and I can't let anyone but me drive it."

He leaned against the doorway. "I know. 1 was hoping

144 / MARY DeMUTH

you'd have time to take me to a sale. A big bank of storage units is going up for auction today south of here, and I'm itching to see what I can find."

"My car can't fit a storage unit in it."

"Oh, I know. If I buy a unit, I'll borrow a friend's flatbed. I just need to go and take a look-see, decide whether it's bid-worthy. But if you're busy, I—"

"It's really not a problem. I had some questions for you anyway. I'll give you a ride in exchange for information."

Rheus laughed. "Well, I'm not sure I have much of that, but I'll do my best."

Willa pulled into the Vault, just south of Interstate 30. A bee-hive of men and women clustered around a man under a tent. The man held a microphone tethered to a speaker.

"We're a little late." Rheus jumped out of the car.

She cut the engine and followed.

The man wore an orange rain parka and a smile as wide as his face. "We have five units to auction today," he said. "They're open, so feel free to take a look. For those of you who are new-bies, remember you can't go poking through stuff. It's what you see from the front without gerrymandering everything. It's a risk. You buy the whole thing, nothing left behind."

Rheus murmured several hellos to a grouping of people who bantered together. He pulled Willa in. "This is Willa," he said. Several hands shot forward. One woman wearing all black held a coffee thermos. "For a rainy day. It's hot chocolate," she said. "Would you like some?"

"That would be nice," Willa said.

She nursed the hot liquid in a two-deep paper cup while Rheus led her toward the units. "Folks got too much stuff is what it usually is, so they store it. If they don't pay their bills, it goes to auction. But sometimes it's not that they have too much stuff; it's that they fell on hard times. Some of these are life possessions. It breaks my heart."

"You really try to reunite memories with people?" Willa felt her hair limping in the mist, but tried not to care. What did it really matter, when folks would be losing so much that day? Even if the people weren't here to see their belongings auctioned to the highest bidder, Willa felt their haunting. Were they standing around, hoping for a savior, someone who would rescue their belongings?

"I try, but I'm not always able to."

They now stood in front of unit 10, its garage-like door up. A blond-haired doll had fallen from the top of the gigantic pile of stuff. Willa picked her up, dusted her off, then bent her legs to sit in front of the hodgepodge of stuff. A pathetic spokesperson, that doll.

"Some little girl may be missing her baby," Rheus said.

"How can you do this? How can you deal in people's bad luck like this?"

Rheus looked her straight in the eyes. "Because I understand."

She wanted to push further, but he pressed on to the next unit, more sparse. A rowboat tilted against the left wall. Power tools littered the floor. A life-size gorilla statue stood as sentry to the entire scene. "This one will go fast," Rheus said, though Willa had no idea why it would.

They viewed two more units, both full of what looked to be garbage from floor to ceiling. Rheus stopped in front of the last unit for sale, put his hands on his hips, then wiped his eyes with his left gloved hand. "This one," he said, "is from a family on the run." He shook his head, then turned away. "Let's go."

"Don't you want to bid on any of them?" She shivered as she said the words. The misty rain had now penetrated her sweater.

He said no as he walked to the car.

They drove on Goliad Street, flanked by businesses bustling with the day — such a contrast to overfilled storage units hawking themselves.

Willa cleared her throat to give the car's silence a rest. She turned right toward the library. "Is everything okay?"

Rheus let out a long breath. "When I was young, we moved around a lot."

She looked over at him, but he kept his eyes out the window.

"Mama, she promised me no matter what happened, we'd never lose my things. Said storage was temporary, and that I could visit when I wanted. Problem was, she and my stepdad loved popping pills more than they loved keeping promises. We moved from place to place, keeping my things in that unit outside of town. Mama let me visit. Once."

"What did you do? Did you take anything back?"

"Well, I ran into its belly, searching for my bear and just one Matchbox car. But she was impatient, tapping her feet, then flailing her arms, huffing here and there, telling me to hurry, to not be so stupid, to get my behind back to her. She had business, she said. No matter how much I rummaged, I couldn't find what I was looking for — it felt like one of those dreams where you're running from a stranger and you never get anywhere while he closes in. No matter how much I looked, I couldn't find my stuff."

"That's terrible!"

"But the worse was this: she made me leave. I left empty handed, looking back at that unit, memorizing the streets it took us to get there. Remembered it was number B – 308. The next time Mama and George were off on some pill-selling spree, I rode a borrowed bike to the unit. Took me a good two hours. I talked to the manager, explained who I was, but the manager just shook his head real sad-like. Told me he'd sold the whole lot three days prior. That my stuff was gone."

"Didn't he have records of who bought it?"

"Not at that time. He didn't do the auctioning."

"I'm so sorry."

"Thanks."

Willa turned left, passing the aquatic center on her right, nearing the county jail on her left, wondering if Rheus' parents spent time in a place like that. "So you buy folks' stuff and try to return it to them?"

"In a way." He exhaled a long, slow breath. "I do make a passable living at it. And I investigate to find out who the folks were who let their payments lapse. But I don't always do right by them. A few months ago, I scored a jackpot. Tucked in the way back of a small unit was a gold mine of LPs. I sold them on eBay, later finding out the woman who lost them all was a widow on a meager pension. I found her and gave her half my profits."

"That's amazing!"

"No, it was selfish. I should've given the whole lot to her. I held back."

Willa wound her way through the backside of downtown, eventually turning left toward the YMCA. A park flourished on the right, with trails beckoning bikers and runners. A small lake, with boats angled by the shore, looked dull under the gray day, as if it wept alongside Rheus' words, now silenced.

"Most people would've kept all the money," she said.

"But I'm not most people. I'm supposed to bring restoration. Hope."

"Hope's not an easy thing to manufacture." She turned her blinker on to turn left toward home, marveling that God turned on the sunshine, breaking it through the haze of the late morning, goldening the still-damp road. It stretched out like a shiny serpentine before them, their own yellow brick road. Only her home led to Louisiana, and Rheus' stayed locked somewhere in an empty storage unit.

She turned into the Muir House, wondering how many more days she'd be there, whether she'd up and leave to find Hale, or return to her fractured life in Seattle. She turned to Rheus. "Did you know my grandmother on my father's side was not my biological grandmother?"

"No," he said. "But does it matter?"

"Somehow, I think it does."

He looked at her, the sun touching the side of his worn, rough face. "Did she love you? Love your dad?"

"With everything inside her."

"Then I'd say she's as much your grandmother as someone who shared your blood. Sometimes folks with your blood do you wrong. Family's the people who love you well, who go out of their way to bless you."

"I doubt Genie is family, then." She knew once the words flitted from her lips that she shouldn't have said something so honest to a man she barely knew.

But he smiled. "She may just surprise you. You know the saying, right? Broken people break people? She's carrying her own broken heart, but deep down, she loves. She really loves."

Willa shook her head, wondering if such a miracle could be true of the stern-faced woman, hoping perhaps it would be true, but then chastising herself for wishing Genie to always be a nemesis. Didn't Hale say she preferred drama over peace? Did she need Genie to be painted only in black, with no white, not even a shade of gray? Or could she welcome a Genie who loved—the kind of woman who brought ginger ale and stilted compassion? Hard to say. She exited the car.

Rheus stood on the porch, hand poised at the door.

"No need to knock, you know. It'll soon be a public building," Willa said.

"But Genie's a private woman, and she deserves my knock."

Before he could rap a knuckle at the door or Willa could burst through like she owned the place, Genie Skye opened the left door. She smiled. Not a pasted on grin, but a real one. "It's so good to see you, Rheus. Why don't you come in?" She looked at Willa. "You can come and go as you please." A hint of sarcasm bled through Genie's words, but Willa chose to rest her mind on the smile. Maybe the old woman could soften. Maybe if she chose to believe that, Genie would let go of the stark exterior and start sharing the truth.

With Rheus now parked on the settee in the right-hand parlor and Genie sitting across from him, Willa mounted the stairs, wondering if love would flourish between the two of them. Rheus who loved restoring memories, and Genie who seemed to relish keeping them mysterious. Could two people so different find common ground?

twenty-five

While Rheus and Genie chatted below, Willa storyboarded the months she couldn't remember, piecing together fragments. In the quiet of her room, she drew little pictures, of the utility shed, the faceless man, the confusion on her face. She traced a line through the few memories, the photo, the swing in the back yard. She added the piece about her parents' apparent separation and her grandmother's strange identity. Nothing came together in her mind. Truth was, she felt as lost, as confused as she did when she watched her Seattle rental burn to the foundation. What if this trip only meant quadrupling the confusion, ripping away obvious answers from her? When she played it safe, relying on files in boxes, she had more purpose, more clinical objectivity. But here, sitting on her bed, preferring the method of pen to paper over finger to keyboard, she felt utterly empty, void of meaning.

"Jesus, help me," she said. But the ceiling said nothing in reply.

She was a detached observer, even with her fingers pressing in on the pen. Unconnected. But why?

"Love is a risk." Hale pointed to the sky while she shivered beneath it. "Like this. Coming to the top of my building isn't permissible, but I did it anyway, because I knew it would touch you."

She said nothing, her heart clenching her throat. He knew

her well, knew her desire for the wilderness, the great expanse
of sky, how that love got choked in the exhaust of the city.

Hale pulled her to himself, more brotherly than boy-
friendly, his arm pressing her upper arm — not too hard. With
his other hand, he pointed. "I'll name that one Willa," he said.

Her star.

Who cared if it anchored the Big Dipper and probably had
an appropriate astronomical name? This was Willa the star,
Stella Willa, the pointed out one. All her life she'd been jumping as high as she could to the sky, hoping to pull it down, to
touch the transcendent. Or maybe she leapt in hopes someone
would notice. *Look at me! Look at me*, her life screamed. And
here stood Hale, sheltering her beneath a warm beating heart,
pointing her out, simple as that. She didn't have to jump, didn't
have to holler. Just be.

She settled herself there, fantasizing about marriage and
a home in the country with chickens, a horse, a vegetable garden, a grove of fruit trees. Children scurrying outside, bringing in mud, her not caring about the mess. This was her dream.
She'd found the one man who noticed only her, who named
heavenly bodies after her, who knew her so perfectly it scared
her. It may not have been the thrill that Blake brought, but it
was stable. Right somehow.

In that flicker, she felt alive. Finally. Almost ready to risk
for love.

But under the winking stars on a forbidden city roof, the
peace dissipated. She tried to clutch it to herself as Hale kept
his words to himself. In his silence, her mind left its happy
place, traveling again down the road of empty memory. What
trauma had she endured? Was her lack of remembrance a ticking bomb? And when she knew the truth, what would Hale do?
Would he continue to surprise her with rooftop rendezvous,
or would he un-name the star and find a stable girl to name it

after? Would her secret devastate her? Make her an unfit wife? A mother like her own? So many thoughts tortured her.

She pulled away from Hale's shelter, said, "I'm tired," then left him standing alone while she descended the stairs inside. She risked him then. Risked his not understanding. Took advantage of his faithfulness. She'd make it as hard as she could to prove his love would endure her after the truth unraveled. If she could shun risk, push him away time after time, maybe she'd finally prove to herself that he would stay.

Her life, though, proved the opposite.

People didn't stay, at least not the ones you want to stay.

Some remained to taunt. The ones who soothed your soul up and disappeared.

Which was probably what would happen to Hale.

The rush of the rooftop memory pushed further into Willa. She could nearly smell Hale. Could hear the timbre of his voice in the crisp darkness. A saint that man was. And she threw it all away, exploiting his risk while forsaking her own. She twisted the ring on her finger. Round and round. Remembered his words about infinity, the nonsense of eternal love. The stark truth evaporated a permanence like that. Real life meant confusion. Doubt. Emptiness. Secrets. Deception. And love meant all those things too.

Willa felt the heaviness of everything, as if a rain-soaked cloud entered her room and showered her with doom. She placed her papers inside a file folder, walked down the side stairs, tiptoed through the side door so as not to rouse Genie's ire, and headed west on foot. She crossed Goliad, remembering the voice telling her to risk it all and walk into its middle. She fought to disobey, looking left then right. She turned left toward downtown, but didn't venture into its belly this afternoon. Instead she turned right by the police station and began the long descent toward Lake Ray Hubbard's shoreline. A boat launch loomed far ahead. So she walked, eyes intent on the shoreline while cars whizzed past. Halfway between downtown and the shiny lake under an afternoon sun, Willa knew why she'd left, knew why she had to leave the house today, knew why she headed this way. She stopped, looked across the six-lane road, and crossed to the other side where the divided cemetery loomed.

Daddy had a good view of the water. From where he slept, he must've watched the boat launch inaugurate, must've fretted over the downtown construction. Her feet took her through the metal-gated entrance to her left. Fake flowers, a staple of Texas cemeteries, stood in odd contrast to the stark grounds. At least fresh would fade with time, decompose. But plastic boasted an artificial life Willa could never reconcile.

She found him there, suddenly wondering why this hadn't been her first stop after she flew down here. Why didn't she pay homage to the man who deeply loved her? Instead, she'd ventured to an empty home, rich with memories, but devoid of her daddy's laughter. Willa sat before Daddy, smoothed away his marker. Read his gravestone. "Parker Hazleton Muir. Born September 12, 1943. Died October 15, 2005. Beloved husband, father, and civic leader. A man who kept his word."

She hadn't thought about the last sentence, not deeply at least. It'd been his wish to have it there, about him keeping his word, but somehow in the light of today, the words needled Willa. What did Daddy keep his word about? Everything? She remembered his promises, never empty, in childhood. If he said he'd give her a lollipop for cleaning her room, he'd give it to her — even if it meant an inconvenient trip to the store late at night. He promised to teach her to drive, which he performed in patient, heroic fashion. He promised to help pay for college — another kept word. Before his verbal ability left, Daddy's eyes moistened when he said, "I promised I'd walk you down the aisle. I can't do that, sweetie. Just can't make it … that far."

"You'll be there," she told him, willing herself not to choke on her grief. "You'll watch from heaven. I'll look up to make sure. And I won't walk until I see you wink."

He winked. Said, "You got yourself a promise, then. I'll walk beside you from glory." So many words said together wearied him. He shut his eyes and drifted off to sleep while Willa held his hand, wondering how long his warmth would touch her cold hand.

She pulled a few stickaburrs from his grave. They stung when they poked her flesh, drew blood. She thought of all the houses she cut from magazines, how she hoped finding the perfect home would make her feel life to the fullest, but nothing, certainly not four walls, enlivened her. Yet the blood on her fingers proved otherwise. She breathed on this hillside cemetery. Her heart pumped blood while her father's body decomposed beneath her. She was alive. She just didn't feel it.

Willa remembered how she'd hollered at God in the middle of broad daylight near her Green Lake home, but now, under the Texas sky, she was afraid to take the risk. No one lurked nearby. Other than cars whirring past, no voices interrupted. She sat before Daddy, and he had all the time in the world to listen. She kept her voice low under the humming of power lines above. "Daddy," she said. "I miss you."

At that, tears erupted. She held her head in both hands, sucking in air, choking back sobs. She felt the sun on her back as if it were patting her, saying there-there. But other than that, she cried to an empty amphitheater, no audience, not a soul to see her grief.

Daddy didn't see her college diploma. Didn't help her finally relocate to Seattle. Didn't applaud her very first interior decorator job. Didn't meet Hale. Didn't tell the final secrets.

Daddy didn't.

So she walked life solo.

"I wish you would've told me," she said, "that losing you would be like losing my life." She sniffled, wiping a hand under her runny nose. "I wish you would've promised me the impossible, that you wouldn't dare die on my watch. But that's one promise you knew you'd break."

She sat cross-legged, searching the area surrounding Daddy's grave for fire ant piles. She remembered their sting, then relived the sting of Mother's words. "Why did you love her, Daddy?"

A twin-engine plane, about as different from a Boeing jet as you could find, buzzed above, heading eastward, probably toward the Rockwall County Airport.

She realized Daddy wouldn't have answered that question if he were alive, preferring to elevate Mother even when she careened out of control. That man had the patience of Job. Willa cleared her throat, picked some grass, then settled herself there. "It's okay. You don't have to answer that. I am going to visit her, you know. Though she doesn't want me. I never thought she did. With as much as you loved me, she made up for it by hating me all the more. Couldn't even look me in the eye. Still hates me, I think."

Willa stood, dusted the ground from her jeans, and waved a feeble goodbye to the unspeaking headstone. *A man who kept his word* sounded through her as she walked back to the bed and breakfast. Daddy, captured in a half dozen words. It was Hale too. Nearing the house, she wondered if Hale had Daddy's heart and verve. If Daddy could tolerate and love Mother, would Hale dare to put up with her, as fragile as she'd become? She smelled springtime, hoping that Hale would return to her, hoping she'd smell his evergreen scent again, hold his hand, rest her head on his shoulder, be the object of his risk.

Would he stand beneath a Cajun sky tonight, calling on her star? Or would he turn away, abandon his word to love and pursue her, and follow after someone else? She'd left the house feeling empty, and as she mounted the stairs, she embodied neediness. When she opened the door, Rheus stood nearby, waving goodbye to a blushing Genie. He breezed past her while Genie left for the kitchen.

"Love," he said in passing, "is the most beautiful risk."

twenty-six

Rheus' words added to Willa's guilt. A strange sense of God's conviction led her to start her car, point it toward the assisted living center. She drove while her heart rapped against her chest. Dreaming of Hale just now, heart filling with longing, made her take the risk.

She sat in the parking lot a good long time, steadying her breathing, fretting about what would transpire. But no matter how many ways she could visualize their meeting, Willa couldn't predict the unknown. Mother swung on wild pendulums last she saw her, morphing from matter-of-fact to fiery wrath, then to blank nothingness. She tried to pray away her fear, realizing how her own on-again off-again relationship with God must've unnerved him. Full of prodigal tendencies, only to shoot prayers to the sky when her needs outweighed her abilities. But mostly, lately, she camped on silence.

Here she sat, unmoving, unwilling to open her car door.

The front door of the place opened, and Rebbie, wearing an apron and a smile, exited. Willa left the car. When Rebbie saw her, she squealed. "What are you doing here?"

"Maybe I should ask the same of you." Willa noticed her friend carrying a straw tote full of utensils. "What are you doing here?"

"I'm teaching a cooking class for the residents. We're having so much fun." She checked her watch. "Are you going to see your mom? She's such a dear."

A dear? Really? Her mother? "Yes," Willa said, but her voice carried no conviction.

"She would love to see you. I'm sure of it. She's one of my best bakers, and she always has a smile to give. 'Course, I have to coax it from her, but she gives it eventually."

"That's Mother," Willa said, trying to quell her sarcasm.

"Well, I best get going. I have a lunch I'm catering for a book club in the Shores. Making a fajita bar. Should be fun." She breezed by Willa, the latest fragrance from Bath and Body Works trailing behind.

Willa waved goodbye, but didn't move from her place under the portico. She stood equidistant from her car and the front door, held to the cement by dread. Her mother, smile? Maybe it was the fear of change, of not being able to handle good and normal and safe, that kept Willa in conflict. She'd spent her life with an angry, distant mother, a woman with a permanent scowl only for Willa. She'd grown deeply accustomed to the treatment, wearing Mother's disdain like a merit badge, as if she'd survived a hellish childhood and deserved reward. Her identity entangled itself with grief; this was true.

Several crepe myrtles flanked the front of the building, just barely leafing out. They would be the most prolific of the summer and fall flowers, dazzling the assisted living's entrance a good many months. But now it was simply too cool for the heat-loving shrub to birth its flowers. A little more warmth, a little more sun, and they'd give their gift.

Willa sighed. She used the crepe myrtles as her excuse as she pivoted back toward the car. Her heart hadn't been warmed sufficiently yet, hadn't felt shined upon. The ripening was there, deep inside her, but the willingness felt cold.

When she started the car, she found the word *Mother* escaping her lips. But no matter how many times she said the word in the quiet hum of the car, nothing could make her want to turn the car around.

twenty-seven

The next few spring days Willa spent mired in design. When she wasn't shopping for furniture, paint, and material, her mind bothered her, told her she was foolish to withhold a visit with Mother. But even more maddening was Hale's silence. No letters. Of course, no calls or texts. Though the ring stayed on her finger, her heart rested in reality. He must've meant it when he said he'd be too busy. She thought he'd break his word and send a few sentences her way. No. He kept his silence and distance.

Which is why she said yes to Blake's invitation for a Saturday night dinner at the Harbor. And when he drove up, she removed the ring, placed it back in the matchbox, determined to be done with Hale's silence. Perhaps the irresistible future meant fun and life and dates. Putting behind her past once and for all. She'd been old for far too long, and as she practically danced down the central stairway, she felt youth return. A date. A new life. A new her. Though Hale's ghost haunted her periphery, she shooed him away. Tonight would be fun. Like tasting freedom.

Blake opened the car door for her. She slipped into the Mini Cooper, welcomed by a catchy world-music tune. She pointed to the radio, but before she could say something, Blake answered.

"Aaron Spiro," he said. "An amazing songwriter. Heartfelt. Original."

"I know him!"

"You do?"

"Yeah, he played a lot in Seattle venues. Great on disk. Great live too."

Blake laughed. "I'm jealous." He pulled out of the driveway, then headed through downtown. She watched as the center square gave way to strips of businesses. Traffic lights stopped and started them until they reached Rockwall's preening glory, the Harbor, full of restaurants, some with live music, a dock, a fountain, a waterfall, and a multiplex. When they walked toward the complex, she smelled cigars.

"That's En Fuego's fault," he said. He pointed to a tobacco shop. "Good guys there."

"So you know them?"

"Yeah, but then again, I know most folks here. Rockwall's sprawled and grown and stretched, but it's still a small town if you get to the heart of things."

She nodded, wondering if she could trade the thrill of Seattle's flying fish and too-excellent coffee for the permanence of small town living. Hard to say.

They entered the water-facing restaurant, which, according to Blake, was his favorite. "You have to have the s'mores," he told her as they sat by a large window.

She noticed several sailboats moving slowly across Lake Ray Hubbard as the sun danced its descent. "Like the things you eat around a campfire?"

He took a drink. "Yeah, but these are amazing, with a homemade marshmallow on top. Trust me."

"I don't trust many people," she said.

"Way to over-deepen the conversation."

Had he not said it with a smile, she would've nursed an insecure anger, but his grin melted it.

"Your ring finger is naked, I see."

She looked at her hand. She'd grown accustomed to the

feel of the ring there, and it did feel naked, like it was missing its essence. "Yeah. Long story."

He waved his hand between them. "Perhaps another time. I'd actually like to get something off my chest that I can't seem to shake. One of those things I'm supposed to say, supposed to obey."

A waiter took their order in the awkward pause. Willa wondered what Blake would say. Chastise her for the way she handled their relationship's ending? Declare his love? Scorn her for her forwardness, then withdrawal? She got a sick feeling inside, wondering how she'd ever eat all the salad and pasta she ordered.

"Listen," he said. "It's just that you deserve to move on with your life knowing the truth. It's always better to know, right?"

She nodded, then noticed she hadn't placed her napkin on her lap. As she smoothed it, she said, "You sound like me, like my twin. I'm desperate for truth."

"Well, then you should enjoy our date."

"To our truth date!" They bumped glasses. She drank to it, but her stomach would not stop hiccupping inside.

The waiter brought a basket of bread with several different spreads—a homemade hummus, and a garlicky-herbed butter, at least that's how he described it. They ate in silence while the sun oranged and pinked and reddened over the surface of the lake. Finally, Blake said, "You don't have his eyes."

"What?"

"Your father's eyes. Not exactly."

What in the world was he saying?

He leaned closer, held her eyes, but his brimmed anguish. "Remember when we dated?"

She nodded.

"You used to tell me you had your father's eyes. And every time you did, I cringed. Because I knew something but I never told you." He looked toward the lake, keeping his eyes there for several seconds.

"Listen," she said. "I don't know what kind of story you have concocted here, but if you're saying I'm not my father's child, then you're wrong."

He turned back to her, eyes wet. "I'm not saying that."

"Then what are you saying?" She heard the desperation in her voice, how it lilted in a higher pitch than she'd prefer, but she couldn't prevent it.

"You're … " Blake took a sip of water, then looked into her eyes. "Adopted."

She pushed back from the table. "What?" Adopted? How in the world? She would've uncovered something so obvious in her years of box filing and investigation. Surely Blake was wrong, pulling something out of the air.

"It's true." He let out a long breath.

"It can't be."

"It is."

She tried to piece everything together, remembering the illustration back in her room. The separation. The non-grandmother grandmother, who, if this were true, would've never been her grandmother even if she were related. Adopted? Really? "How do you know this supposed information?"

He sat back, took another drink, looking like he needed more refreshment. "I've known a long time."

"Since when?"

"Since before we dated."

She felt the anger bite her. "Then why didn't you tell me?"

"They said it was for the best you didn't know."

"Who is they?"

"Your parents."

"Hmm, which ones, Blake?"

"Your adoptive parents, the Muirs."

"And they told you this, but you didn't bother to tell me? This makes no sense! Why would you know and I wouldn't? And to think I've spent years trying to figure out who I am, what I'm missing. And all along, Blake Alderman has known my secret. I suppose others know too?"

"I don't know."

"How convenient for you not to know." Rage settled into her, took up residence.

"Listen, I'm not trying to fool you. I'm just trying to tell you something for your own sake. Our fathers were friends."

She nodded, and as she did, their salads arrived. She speared some arugula on her fork, chewed, then swallowed. It tasted like dirt. "Yes, so what does that have to do with anything?"

"Please let me finish." He left his salad untouched. "I overheard them talking in my dad's office. Your dad was confiding something to mine, and his voice was quiet, so I snuck closer. I heard him say something about you, which piqued my interest, since I liked you even then."

"When was this?"

"The summer of our seventh grade year."

"So you were eavesdropping."

"Yes," Blake said. "So I heard him say something else, but it was muffled. Right about that time, I'd leaned so close that I tripped from my momentum and fell into the room."

"Graceful."

"Just listen, okay?"

"Fine." She speared more arugula. Chewed it. Swallowed. Winced.

"So your dad tells me this is the most important secret I'll ever keep. He asked me what I heard, but I hadn't heard much, just your name and some murmuring. He said, 'Son, Willa's adopted, and she doesn't know it. If she did, it would ruin her. She can't know, do you understand?' I nodded that I did, and since I respected your father and liked you, I figured it wouldn't hurt to keep the secret. My dad reinforced it later that night when he came into my room, sat on my bed, and said, 'It's important you respect Mr. Muir's wishes, son. He's an important man.' He seemed kind of spooked, if you ask me."

"My father wasn't an intimidating man."

"Maybe not to you, but to others — to me, to my father — he was."

Willa didn't know which news was more shocking — her apparent adoption or her father's intimidation. She finished her salad and pushed it to the center of the table. "I don't know what to say."

"I didn't expect you would. I know it must be shocking."

"Why didn't you tell me? I thought you loved me." Her words were more accusation than sadness.

"You weren't wrestling with your past then. And I figured, knowing you as a daddy's girl, that the news would crush you. I didn't want to hurt you. Plus, I'm a man of my word. I kept my promise."

A man of his word. Just like Daddy.

"So you kept quiet."

"Yes. I'm sorry. Had I known how important it was to you, I would've shared it. But let me ask you this. Would it have made a difference?"

"Blake, I'm not one for logical, coherent thoughts right now. I can't even entertain how my life would have been different in light of what you told me."

"I know, Willa. I'm sorry."

She stood. "I'll pay the bill, okay? Just tell the waiter to nix our dinner. I want you to take me home." At the word *home* Willa's heart collapsed on itself. She'd thought home was learning and knowing the truth, of discovering every little detail so she could move on. Only this rendition of truth and home careened into her safely constructed definitions. While Blake located the waiter, Willa left to stand outside in the portico between the bar and restaurant. The lake looked darker under a steadily dusking night, more sinister.

She remembered swimming in Lake Ray Hubbard with Blake once — where the rumor was you weren't supposed to swim there without a boat nearby, though she didn't know if it was because of snakes or amoebas. It had been a night like tonight, slightly chilly, but cautiously warmed by spring. The water slid over her in delicious sips, but she couldn't fight the titanic fear that just below her lurked water moccasins, slithering, stalking, preying on her. No matter how much Blake laughed and splashed, she kept her head above water, swimming as fast as she could, knowing that a killer snake would reach its slick head skyward, taste her flesh in a quick instant, then slither back to its murky lair, while the venom made its way through her body to paralyze, then drown her. And the snake would have its way once her body rested on the lake's silt bottom, feeding off her flesh.

She hugged herself watching the lake, wondering if the word *adopted* would be such a snake, and her search for home would find her lying dead in the muck.

twenty-eight

"I won't leave you," Daddy said. But kindergarten loomed, awful and loud, before her. Kids cried, carrying on about leaving their mamas. Teachers bending low, wiping tears. The smell of fresh crayons and finger paints. The indistinct smell of urine. Goldfish crackers in Dixie cups arranged on each desk. Carpet squares. All foreign to Willa. She clung to Daddy's leg, felt the muscled strength, wished she hadn't grown up so fast to merit such a separation.

Daddy bent low. Mussed her hair. Smiled with wet eyes. Touched her cheek. "You're my girl," he said. "And a Muir. And Muirs always act brave, even when they're scared. You understand?"

She nodded as if she understood, but the words didn't quite sit right. Pretend you're brave even when you're not?

"You love to play dollhouse, remember?" He pointed to a tall wooden dollhouse, handmade, sitting in the corner of Miss Elliot's room. "Let's take a look-see."

She took his hand, felt its heat. In that simple embrace of palms, bravery entered her. She could do this.

They sat cross-legged before the tall house — three stories of plywood, now decorated with old wallpaper scraps, snatches of carpet, fake wood floors.

"The colors are all wrong," she said.

Daddy laughed. Patted her on the head. "You'll be a decorator someday," he said. "I know it. You have a knack for this. How would you change it?"

"It wouldn't have an embalming room."

Daddy smiled. "No, I don't imagine it would."

"And one parlor is enough. The other one will be for tea parties exclusively."

"Where did you hear that word?"

"Parlor?"

"No, *exclusively.*"

"I don't know," she said. And that was the truth. Big words had a way of nesting in her head, but she seldom knew how they flew in.

Daddy stood.

"What are you doing?"

"I have to go, Willa Bean."

"But you said —"

He picked her up, held her close. "You're my sweet girl, always will be. You know that, right? God gave you to me in the most special way." He set her back on the carpet. Hollering kids continued their chaos, but Willa saw only Daddy. He fished something from his pocket, bent low, and put it over her head.

She felt the necklace's chain, how the metal strung cold around her neck.

"Look at the end," he said.

A locket.

"Open it."

The heart enclosure dangled long enough on the chain so she could open it and see what was inside. On the left heart smiled Daddy. On the other, her.

"I told you I wouldn't leave you," he said.

She gave him a desperate hug, fierce and clingy.

"I have to go, Willa Bean. It's time to start class, okay?" He peeled her arms from his legs, bent low, kissed his finger. He pressed it to her nose, then the locket. "Daddies don't leave their babies. Ever. You remember that, Willa. I'm as close as your heart." With that, he left the classroom. She stood amid the cacophony of children, clutching the promise low around her neck, pressing it to her heart. Believing every word.

twenty-nine

On Monday Willa hurried a new request to the Texas vital statistics department for her own birth certificate. Though she had a copy to obtain her license many years ago, the fire turned it to ash, and she hadn't yet replaced it. At the time she hadn't thought to scrutinize it, look for altering. In a few days, hopefully, she'd have Daddy's, hers, and a magnifying glass.

But she couldn't bring her heart to believe the word *adoption*. It made no sense. Parents who adopted loved their kids, cherished them. Not exactly Mother's attitude. Sure, Daddy cherished her. Stuck up for her. Loved her. Sheltered her. For every one of Mother's verbal lashings, Daddy had the antidote, but in extravagant measure. He knew the dynamics of a young girl's heart, that if she heard one disparaging comment, she'd need twenty to make up for it. So Daddy made it his mission to heap on one hundred. With him gone and Mother silenced to anger or gibberish, she missed the affirmation. And with Hale playing MIA in Louisiana hundreds of miles away, along with her ignoring Blake's calls and texts, Willa had only the five bedrooms screaming for renovation and her overactive mind to occupy her.

If she could think her way out of this, she would. Everything would make sense someday. The truth would emerge, and she could find home.

She drank a swig of water, hearing kitchen noises below — more than normal. She looked outside to see Rebbie's yellow vehicle. The house's front door opened and closed. Then

Rebbie flustered around the SUV's rear, bringing a tray of something through the parking lot, up the steps.

Willa made a quick decision. She left the comfort of a well-appointed bed for the scurrying below.

Genie eyed her up and down, disapproval on her face. But Willa internally shrugged it off. "Do you need any help?" she asked.

"The Friends of the Library board meeting is here today," Genie said. As if that would make everything clear.

Rebbie pushed through the doorway, carrying another tray. "Hey, Willa!"

"Do you need help?"

"Absolutely! I have a few more things in the car. Can you help grab what's left?"

Willa pulled two more trays from the back of the SUV, which had several baking racks built in. A clever use of space, she thought. Then she scolded herself for judging Rebbie's car. Once back in the kitchen, she asked, "How many are on the board? This looks like a giant feast."

Rebbie shook her head. "I'm the worst! I always over-estimate. Better to overshoot than underguess, though."

Genie busied herself in the kitchen, pulling out serving trays, rearranging tiny quiches, crudités, and stuffed mushrooms. "I need the tables set," she said.

"What tables?" Willa looked around the front parlor. No tables there.

"They're in the back storage room. Set up four, two in each room. We have folding chairs too. The linens for the tables and the chair slipcovers are in the closet at the top of the stairs," she said.

Willa located the tables, rolled them into place, set up chairs, then went in search of linens, trying to remember a closet upstairs.

Tucked into a corner, next to the Great Wall of China Room, stood a newly constructed closet she hadn't noticed before. She opened it to find white tablecloths stacked neatly. She pulled them down, upsetting a stack of papers beneath. They fluttered to the floor like snowflakes. She set the linens down, gathered the papers, then stopped. The paper on top was a letter addressed to her in unfamiliar script. She turned it over. Nothing. She scanned the bottom of the page looking for the writer's identity there. But it was simply signed "Me." She leafed through the rest of the papers, finding only pink construction receipts, photocopied bills, and legal papers belonging to Genie Skye. Feeling her heart in her throat, she heard voices downstairs. Then Genie's voice broke through. "Never mind, Willa. I'll get the linens." She heard Genie mount the wood stairs. In a flash, she returned the tablecloths to their place, replaced the papers except the letter, and tiptoed to her room, hoping she'd put everything back just so.

She stayed behind her door, listening for Genie. The closet door opened, then closed. Willa ran back to her bed, settling the letter under a pillow. A knock sounded, startling her.

"Come in."

Genie poked her head inside. "What are you doing in here?"

"I had to use the restroom."

"Oh."

"I'll be down in a second. I have to take care of something really quick."

Genie shut the door, but before she did, she flashed a strange smile Willa's way.

Willa retrieved the letter, then all at once felt like the house had eyes, and Genie knew her every move. She scanned the room for hidden cameras, at once chastising herself for her conspiratorial thinking, then wondering if her worries had merit. She crossed the room, locked the door, and returned to the letter, written in block print with no hint of gender in its script.

> *Willa,*
>
> *I'm not one for words, though you probably are. At least I hear you're artistic. I don't suppose you'll ever get this letter, and that's just fine by me. But putting words on paper addressed just to you seems the right thing to do, at least on my side of things. It's what I owe in small part.*
>
> *You grow up, strong, Willa. You make your way in the world. Don't take detours, angling down roads leading to destruction. That's me. That's my story. And, knowing my wayward ways, I'll end up destroyed, with nothing to make of myself, nothing to show for my name.*
>
> *You have the best possible name for success. Wear it proudly like a necklace. You deserve every happiness coming your way. Just wait and see.*
>
> *Me.*

Who was Me?

Time froze. Willa captured a memory, felt it enliven in the corner of her mind. The man, the ring, and something else. What was it? A clearing of the throat, a turning away, then nothing but black.

The flash didn't last long enough for her to capture it with pen and paper. But she wondered at the irony. Was this coughing man, Me? And if she were adopted, then was he her father?

No.

Willa saw her eyes in Daddy's. Blake might not, but she knew. The same shade, the same nearly black ring circling the irises. Everything in her screamed that Blake had been mistaken, that the conversation he overheard and the subsequent instructions had been marred somehow. Daddy was Daddy, plain and true.

And yet.

She shook her head. Read over the letter again.

What if Mother wasn't her mama? Perhaps Mother's words that opened up a vacancy in Willa's heart were hazed words, untrue. What if Mother regretted leaving Daddy, pined over it, then returned, only to find Daddy with another woman? What if this letter was from her real mama—Daddy's solace when Mother left? While clanking and rummaging bustled beneath her, Willa felt the pieces of her puzzled life fall into satisfied place, though with pain connected. Daddy—an affair? Perhaps during their time apart, to salve his pain over her absence. She could forgive such a thing in time. And if she were completely honest, she'd always found it easier to forgive men than women, always seemed to trust the intentions of older men more than mother figures. Came from growing up with her own mother, the way she scowled through life. But Daddy? Tender, sweet. No doubt he'd found a soul mate, but when Mother came back, he had no choice but to stay with Mother, adopt Willa from the woman, which, of course, would make Mother hate Willa to no end.

Or maybe not. Maybe her real mama died tragically in childbirth, and Willa'd been a ward of the state. Daddy found out somehow, and suggested the adoption. Even then, that would make Willa an interloper, an outsider.

Scene by scene of her childhood played out before her in cinematic tragedy. Mother moving away from her touch, recoiling when Willa tried to kiss her cheek. The look of disdain when she wore her first prom dress, how Mother said she looked trashy. Working in the kitchen while Willa asked a question, Mother pretending never to hear. She'd wash dishes, humming, but would not respond.

Of course.

She wasn't Mother's.

The revelation secured her somehow, tethered her to herself, her will, her desires for a normal, happy, home-blessed life. She folded the purloined letter, hid it within the pages of her unread Bible, and pulled her laptop onto her lap. She wrote:

Blog title: Hale, I'm ready.

You're going to think this surprising, but I'm okay now. Really. I've figured it all out. Those missing months are gone still, but I've uncovered something huge. And it all makes sense, Hale! Which is why I want to marry you. To say a big, happy yes! Can you come and see me?

Love,
Willa

She clicked *publish*, then wondered if he'd take the time to read it. Or heed it. Just in case, she broke his rules and texted him, letting him know. Surely he'd want to know this. Willa settled back on her bed while cars pulled into the parking lot below. Library people scurried up the house's front stairs, joined each other in both parlors, and chatted like birds. Though Willa mocked herself for not making good on her promise to help, she clicked through airlines sites, finding airfare for New Orleans, then Seattle. One way or another, she'd get to Hale, then home.

thirty

Hale's letter arrived on the heels of the library function. Willa watched the mail truck deliver a slew of pieces, and she knew. She *knew*. When she brought in the stack, sure enough Hale's handwriting appeared on yet another recycled envelope. She placed the rest of the mail in a new wire basket on the counter. Genie nodded, but said nothing, so much like Mother Willa shivered.

She trotted up the back stairs, then stole away to her room.

She ripped Hale's handiwork, revealing an envelope whose former life advertised an organic lawn service. Made sense.

Willa,

When I first relocated here, you were on my mind like a headache — a constant nagging. But as I settle into life in the Deep South, I find I'm losing you, the curve of your cheek, the spark in your eyes. I thought that loss would devastate me, but in looking back, I'm seeing it as a healthy thing. I loved you too much, Willa. Loved the idea of being in love with you more than I should have. I'm sorry.

He was sorry for loving her? Sorry for cherishing her? Willa felt the rejection with nearly the same intensity as her mother's disdain. How could he write such words? She thought about the careless things she wrote on the Internet, not thinking about what others praised as her raw authenticity, only to recant and repent. Perhaps this was like that. Maybe he felt emboldened to say whatever he felt without her in front of him.

Words written across a white page were far easier to deliver when they weren't spoken face-to-face. She continued to read.

I hope you can forgive me for making you into an idol, a false god. No human should fill a man as such, even one as beautiful as you. While designing, sweating, building, and loving the least of these, Jesus has brought all this to my mind. And as he has, he's redirected my affection toward Reality.

I hope to visit next week, if you'll have me. Mark your calendar for Monday, March 30. No need to pick me up. I'll make my way there; I have the address. I have some big things to tell you, important things, but I can't share them on the page. I am praying you'll be able to hear my words, receive them in the spirit I intend them. In the meantime, would you prepare your heart? Read the Gospels, think on Jesus, how he loved folks, went out of his way to touch the least of these. That's my onus for coming to you in the middle of my project.

Sorry for such a vague and perplexing letter. Everything will make sense in light of Reality.

Finding joy,
Hale.

Willa shook her head, said no to the empty room. What could this mean? What would Hale have to say? His words sounded ominous, almost schoolteacher-like. Would he reprimand her for some sort of relational infraction? Had saying no been the nail in the coffin of their relationship? Had Hale moved on to another woman? Willa forced herself to breathe. She held his ring between thumb and forefinger, looking through to the sky outside her window. No portal. No destination. Just Rockwall peeked through.

She told herself not to panic, not to think about Hale's

strange correspondence. She would spend the week finishing her work — at least in terms of giving all her designs to Genie, letting her make the purchases, hire the painters. Then she'd make reservations and quickly tie up relationships here. Maybe she'd even see her mother, right before she left Rockwall forever. All those tasks gave her enough to do, enough to occupy the seven days between Hale's letter and his appearance.

Read the Gospels? Maybe. Maybe not. Jesus hadn't done much to help her investigate the truth. She flew. She drove. She uncovered. She poked and prodded unwilling folks.

Willa shushed the voice inside, reminded of the well-laid clues, how God had led her gently to this place. Was that really true? Hadn't she handled it on her own?

She folded Hale's letter, married it to her real mother's letter, and reclosed the Bible, ironically, in Matthew.

And then she steeled herself to face down Genie.

thirty-one

Willa added money to the food fund while Genie cleaned the dishes from the meeting. She turned and said, "You don't have to pretend anymore."

"I'm not one for make believe." Genie washed another glass, carefully, methodically. She rinsed it, then set it on an Ikea wooden drying rack. She picked up another glass.

"I know the truth." Willa expected a reaction, but got none. Another glass washed, rinsed, and set.

"The truth is never so cut and dried, Willa Muir."

Willa moved closer, could see Genie's neck redden. "Are you angry?"

Genie turned toward her, face flushed. "It's called a hot flash. And they're not fun, I tell you."

Willa backed up. "Don't you want to know that I've discovered the precious secret?"

"You haven't."

"Try me." Willa crossed her arms over herself, a defensive position.

"You're not even close."

"How would you know?" Willa felt the urge to strangle enliven her fingers. If they could just reach up and circle Genie's neck. As soon as the thought crossed her consciousness, she recoiled inside herself. Who was she becoming? A twenty-something tyrant? A reality TV show star? She settled her hands into her pockets for safekeeping.

"I've kept my mouth shut for many years, and I don't intend to open it now."

"You don't need to." Willa measured her words as she would rat poison, particle by particle.

Genie turned her back on Willa, resuming her dishwashing. "Sometimes the most simplistic answer is no answer at all. Now, if you don't mind, I need to get back to my work."

No escalation tainted Genie's voice, just calm confidence. To that, Willa said, "She's not my mother, and you know it."

Genie sighed. "It's a child's obligation to take care of her parents in old age, and you've neglected your duty to your mother, leaving her care to me and the care center. Even Rebbie visits her, for crying out loud." She rinsed the last glass, then placed it on the rack to dry. "It's a shame and a disgrace. You should visit your mother. Whether you think otherwise, she is the only family you have on this earth."

Willa heard a crack in Genie's voice, noted a strange desperation in her eyes. She thought better of twisting the knife or pressing the issue. It was clear the woman knew she'd figured out the mystery, finally, and relied now on the old tools of shame and ridicule to deflect the fact that Willa knew the truth.

"Maybe I'll see her; maybe I won't."

"You should."

"Should."

"It's the truth."

Willa fumed. "The truth?"

"How are the designs coming along?"

"They're nearly done. You'll be happy to know that I'll be leaving in a week or so. Out of your hair. You can get back to being the caretaker of secrets, hosting civic groups." Willa's voice raised as high as the attic rafters, and she felt control slip easily away from her. She'd prided herself of late on her even-measured ways, rarely resorting to theatrics or mean words. Certainly not a raised voice. And here she stood, shaking, yelling, losing control. If Hale saw her now ...

Genie walked past Willa like she was an appliance and ventured into the parlor, stopping instead in front of a bookshelf. She knelt while Willa struggled to regain her composure. She pulled out an old brown photo album from the leaded glass bookcase. She walked it back to Willa, handed it to her, then said, "Maybe this will help clear up your obvious confusion."

She took the album, said nothing. Willa felt her insides quaver. Thinking murderous thoughts, wanting to strangle, losing her temper. All this investigation had uncovered a hideous monster who sucked in truth through a straw, then spewed it back out like venom. "I'm sorry," she said to Genie.

"Save your words. Keep them handy for your *mother.*" She turned, left through the kitchen, and walked back to the carriage house, shoulders stooped.

thirty-two

Willa spirited the album to her room, her strange, fleeting, now impermanent sanctuary, wondering why she'd not seen this album before. Inside she found pictures of her parents prior to her arrival. Some winsome, some somber, some smiling through faded color. When she saw her mother with fresh eyes, she saw herself. Not precisely, but the way she crooked a smile, how she carried her arms when she walked, the way she bent her head toward the sky when she laughed.

Odd, though. No pictures of her mother pregnant. Just Daddy and Mother living their lives as newlyweds in the funeral home, followed by dozens of pictures of her in a bassinet, preened and cooed over by every single relative, some she didn't recognize.

The picture that surprised her was one she hadn't seen at first glance. A frayed corner peeked out from underneath one of her swaddled in a pink crocheted blanket. She pulled away the photo-killing plastic, freed the snapshot, then felt her heartbeat in her throat. There stood Mother, arms behind her back, pressing her very pregnant belly outward toward a length of pasture. Mother scowled in a place she didn't recognize, under a grove of trees, the sun beating on her. She wore exasperation as an expression. No joy. Not laughter. No playful pointing at her belly. Just the same look she'd given Willa nearly every day of her life.

Willa traced her fingers around the photo's obviously

well-worn edge. Who had loved this photo? Who had touched it over and over? Was it placed in a wallet? Or neglected on purpose? She looked closer at the picture, trying to discern what it meant. If only she had ultrasound vision and could confirm it was her taking up unwanted space in Mother's uterus. But she had no such ability. All at once, in the strange magic of her room, a scene returned.

"Why don't I have a baby book?" Willa put her hands on her seven-year-old hips, trying to appear gruff.

Mother tended the muffin mix, beating it exactly two hundred strokes. Though Willa knew not to interrupt, she'd been so bothered, she chose to wade through the anger for the sake of a real answer. But Mother counted. "One hundred ninety-eight. One hundred ninety-nine. Two hundred." She looked at Willa. "Now what did you want?"

Willa shook her head. "Mary Alice has the most beautiful baby book with ribbons and lace and pink everywhere. Her mom made it for her. Why don't I have one?"

"People who forget things make books, Willa. But I won't forget you, so why would I need to make something to remind me?"

The words jumbled in Willa's mind while Mother scooped the bran muffin mixture into paper-lined muffin tins.

"It's not for you. It's for me. I want one," Willa said, her voice quiet.

"It's too long ago now." Another scoop into muffin hole number seven.

"But you said you remembered, so it shouldn't be hard—"

"You're disrespecting me. I said no."

So that was it. Willa thought a bit. "Can I make my own?"

Last muffin. "Suit yourself."

"Can I have some baby pictures?"

"Yes."

Willa ventured another question, wincing. "Can you get them for me?"

"I suppose." She placed the muffins in the oven, then twisted the timer. Twenty minutes. Its ticking reverberated through the kitchen, as if it counted down Mother's potential explosion. She wiped her hands on a towel adorned with roosters, then stormed to her bedroom. Willa followed, eyes to the floorboards. Opening the closet, Mother pushed Willa back with a strong arm. "You are not to come in here, you understand? Ever! And I mean never. This is my closet, my room."

"I know." Willa stepped way back, tiptoed to the doorjamb, and settled herself there. She leaned against it, feeling the strength of old, sturdy wood, wishing she'd always feel safe. But even wood as strong as oak couldn't prevent Mother from shaking the world in the wind of her anger. Willa suddenly couldn't remember why she asked for a baby book. Why should she have to create a book most Mothers labored over? Why was it up to her? The questions bounced through her head as Mother rummaged, swore under her breath, and finally pulled out a small box.

Enraged, she flung it her daughter's way. Willa ducked, scurried into the hallway.

"See what you made me do!" Mother's eyes became an untamed animal's then, full of yellow, then red fury. Willa looked behind her, wondering where Daddy had gone. She couldn't move, couldn't stoop to the ground and retrieve smiling baby pictures. Instead, against her will, she cried. Wet, sloppy tears fell down her face, dripping off her cheeks, chin. Why did Mother hate her? What had she done? She must've done something awful. But all she could think of as baby pictures scattered at her feet was that her crime had simply been this: she'd been born. And that sheer fact was enough to merit Mother's wrath.

Mother roared her way, but instead of slapping Willa, as was sometimes customary, she flung herself on the hardwood, placing all her efforts there. Willa backed to the end of the hallway while Mother grabbed at pictures, pulling some to herself and crying, throwing others.

"See what you made me do." She whispered the words, not to Willa, but to someone unnamed. Or was she scolding herself?

Willa shook. Her hands, though they should've been warmed by summer's heat, felt like ice on her shorts-clad legs. She slinked back to her room while Mother clutched and clawed and threw pictures into the shoebox, willy-nilly.

Willa wished for a lock on her door. Dreamed of it often. But when the knock came, she told herself that the proper amount of time had passed and that Mother would be in her right mind again. The gamble paid off. Mother stood in the doorway, eyes drawn, a thin-lipped pout. She held the box, unlidded. "I'm sorry. I shouldn't have yelled like that. Or thrown the box."

Willa lunged at Mother, grabbing her fiercely around the waist. "It's okay," she said. "I forgive you. I'm sorry I made you do it."

"You do push me, girl," Mother said. Her voice held a TV quality to it, detached.

Willa didn't dare ask Mother for a book to put her photos in. Instead she said, "What was my first word?"

Mother set the box on Willa's canopy bed, then smoothed the covers with white, long fingers. "So long ago," she said.

"You told me once it was Da-Da." Willa sat next to Mother, but not so close they'd be touching. She knew better than that.

"Yes, that's it. You were and are a daddy's girl. Started right off, the moment you could string a few syllables together."

"Would Daddy know when I rolled over? Mary Alice's mom wrote all that down. When she got her first tooth. She even cut a piece of her blond hair and put it in this tiny envelope. When you lift it, you see Mary Alice's curl. Do you have some of my hair?"

Mother stood. "I didn't have time to bother with little things like that."

"It's okay. I know you're busy."

"Someday, Willa, you will understand what it's like to be a grown-up. It's not easy."

"I'm sorry," Willa said.

"You have a lifetime to be sorry. It's good you're starting the habit now."

Willa didn't understand the words right then, but as she sat on her bed, no longer canopied with pink sheers, she understood them. She was sorry. For so many things. She spent her life feeling like God had marked her with an X, only she wasn't treasure to be found, but a marked girl who somehow escaped death by her own grit and determination. Sorry was a painful word to her, not the kind of word Hale used when he actually meant it. Not the kind of word that invited relationship. No, sorry, when wielded by Mother, or used in between them in the cadence of a painful relationship, was merely a commodity traded back and forth, symbolizing nothing. Willa was sorry for living. Mother was sorry Willa lived.

Sorry, sorry, sorry.

Willa fingered the picture of the woman with a swollen belly, sweaty from the heat. All her investigation led her to what she thought was a probable conclusion, something that made sense. But with Mother carrying a child, perhaps it all meant nothing. Perhaps there was no secret after all. Maybe Mother just didn't love her, regretted being with Daddy in such a way as to have her. Maybe the simple truth of the past was that Willa was unwanted by half of her parents. Nothing glamorous. No elaborate cover-up. No rumors.

Just plain, sorry truth.

Something poked at Willa, though. A terrible, frightening thought about Daddy. Could it be? No. No, Daddy loved her. He'd promised. And Daddy always kept his promises. Gravestones didn't lie.

thirty-three

With all the busyness that week of half-preparing to leave, half-wondering if she should stay, Willa felt like crane flies had taken a permanent home in her belly. Hale would be here today. Her Hale. She'd pushed him way back, banishing him to a dark corner of her heart, but in the anticipation of seeing him, smelling him, touching his face (if he'd let her), that dark, dank corner suddenly filled with light and a longing she'd forgotten about. Her fickle flirting with Blake now seemed like schoolgirl frolic. This was the real thing. Real life. A real man.

And though she didn't subscribe to the notion that men were shining knights and girls were princesses in towers in need of rescuing, after reliving the past to the point of pain wide and deep, she needed Hale to be knightly. And she pined for rescue as towered Rapunzel might've.

But first, she had to wrangle her own hair into submission. Of all days to have bad hair, this was the worst. The spring had come slowly by Texas standards, but now it strutted, with humidity as its crown. Which resulted in oddly curly hair, and not in the right places. In front of her tiny mirror, she straightened her brown hair, lamenting that it had so little shine of late.

But the sun shone through the windows of her room, and today she'd see Hale. He'd always been one to praise her beauty even when she pulled her hair into a ponytail, when she wore no makeup. He liked her that way, he said.

But those words meant nothing while flies flitted inside. She would make herself irresistible. Understated but flattering makeup. Her best jeans pulled over long legs. A layering of tanks and tees with earth-friendly and poverty-slinging slogans. Right up Hale's heart-for-the-world alley.

Hair wrestled. Jeans on. Shirts assembled, Willa waited. Picked at a hangnail until it struggled free, revealing pink, tender skin beneath. She checked her emails, double-checked her phone for any message from Hale. Nothing. She finished the Hadrian's Wall Room design, finally, preferring a subtle plaid in shades of brown and turquoise. She kept the ring on her finger, shined it with her spit and the corner of one of her shirts. All while the flies jitterbugged inside her.

When a car pulled up, she leapt to her feet. She spied Hale behind the wheel. He paused a long time, fishing around the car for something. He opened the door, shut it with determination, and looked up. Their eyes locked, she behind the warbled glass of her old room, him under the Texas sun, squinting.

She found herself running down the central stairway, through the hallway, past the bookcases, and through the house's right door. She clambered down the steps, then stood, facing Hale.

He didn't speak. His eyes said nothing, gave no indication of his feelings — so much like his vague letters that suddenly the flies died all at once in her stomach. Little corpses of hopelessness rested there.

thirty-four

"There's another girl."

Hale's words pierced into her, like nails to the cross, though his eyes met hers in the most sincere way, and his fingers touched the ring now engraving her finger. Between them stood two iced teas while patrons bustled behind and around them at Chiloso's, Rockwall's premier Mexican bistro. But it didn't feel so premier right now. Not after those words.

Willa couldn't breathe. She pulled her hand away, looked at the ring. The symbol of their love, the way to her heart now circled her hopes like a noose. How stupid she was. "I—"

But he shushed her next sentence, finger to lips. "It's not what you think."

"Then why on earth did you say it that way?" Her voice rose with the cacophony of the diners around her. Laughter, the sound of high schoolers bantering, the distant sizzle from behind the long food line—all these mixed together with her hyena words.

"I'm a jerk; that's why. Wanted to see how you'd react."

She sheltered her eyes in her hands. "Don't play games."

"I'm not. I'm telling the truth."

"New Orleans has changed you," Willa said.

"In the best possible way. But first, just listen, okay?"

She sat back, drank some tea, avoiding his eyes. "Go ahead."

"Reality," he said.

Willa swallowed. "Does this have to do with Egyptians?"

"Not at all. Reality happened to me."

190 / MARY DeMUTH

She turned away from him, watched a group of men enter the doors, Bibles in hand. "Vague, vague, vague," she said.

"I know. I'm sorry."

"You're sorry?"

An employee arrived then. "You both had the fish tacos, right?"

"Yes," Hale said. He nodded to the young man. His demeanor seemed so normal. Not pinched. Not anguished. They must've looked like an old married couple frequenting their neighborhood restaurant. The worker left them to deal with Hale's "sorry."

"You didn't interact with me for three weeks, Hale."

"I wrote letters."

"One-sided."

"I read your blog."

She looked at him then, seeing his face as if for the first time. Tiny lines etched his eyes. His goatee had been tamed and relegated to a simple square soul patch beneath his bottom lip. His unkempt hair seemed tamed. And his pale skin boasted a warmth she hadn't seen in Seattle, probably because the sun seldom decided to peer out in winter there. Not like the Great Warm South. "You read my blog," she finally said.

"Are you going to repeat my words?"

Willa took a bite of fish taco heaven. She smiled in spite of her mood. He'd cared enough to read her heart on the Web. It meant something. But what?

"I read it all, including the latest. I want to hear what you've found, want to discuss the ring on your finger, but first I need to tell you about Reality."

"You sound esoteric."

"I know."

"Just spill it."

He took a long drink of tea, then ahhhhed. "Reality is the name of a girl I met in New Orleans."

Bells ding-ding-dinged in her head. Hale wasn't writing about a state of being, but a person. A girl with a strange name. She felt her disappointment in a flood, choosing to mask what must've been a look of deep regret by taking her own long drink. "A girl," she finally said.

"She's seven, Willa."

"Seven? As in seven years old?"

Hale nodded. "Her mother died in Katrina. She's being cared for by an uncle. She has these big, needy eyes. And her hand fits perfectly in mine."

"What are you saying?"

"It's impossible, I know. But I'm wondering if God is prompting me to foster her, maybe adopt her."

Willa swallowed. Said nothing.

Hale pulled out his wallet and retrieved a picture. He slid it across the table to Willa. There stood Reality, devastation all around her. And next to her kneeled Hale, his arm around slender shoulders. Reality was black, with an open smile, cautious eyes, and a threadbare dress that looked to once have had vibrant flowers circling the hem. But they were as faded as the sky behind them—a whispery cloudy day that looked heavy and hot—if such things could be said about a sky. Willa fingered the photo, slid it closer to her. "She's—"

"Beautiful," Hale said. "And precious. And she's stolen my heart."

"But you can't just adopt a child. Aren't there rules? What about her relatives?"

Hale shook his head. "It's complicated. I don't know the answers. I've researched everything, but nothing is clear. I just can't get her out of my mind. Certainly not out of my heart."

"I can see that." She slid the photo back, daring herself not to care, not to think about the little haunted girl, about her future. But those eyes bored into her.

"I can't pursue us if you think this is a crazy idea."

Willa exhaled. "My head is way too crowded, I'm afraid. I'm still trying to process my own issues, let alone have this one introduced."

"I get that."

"Speaking of issues. How long are you going to be here? And where are you staying?"

"I'm off a week, then I need to go back. I'm staying in the old embalming room."

"What?"

"Seriously. I called Mrs. Skye and got permission. The price was right. We'll be neighbors."

"Don't you think that lacks propriety?"

"You sound like you're quoting Jane Austen."

"So what if I am?"

Hale ate half a fish taco in one bite, then finished it the next, while Willa made her way through the second one, bite by bite. As they caught up, Willa wondered if the man devouring tacos would be the man who shared her life. Could she say yes to Hale? Could she trust him? And what of Reality?

"Your mind is racing ahead, isn't it?" Hale swallowed another bite. Cilantro ranch dripped onto his bottom lip, obscuring a sliver of his soul patch.

She motioned for him to clean it up, but he didn't take the hint. So she dabbed it with her finger.

"You should lick it. It's rightfully yours. Finders keepers, as they say."

So she did, no doubt shocking Hale, and even scandalizing herself a little bit. Hale brought out the daring Willa, the happy

Willa. Maybe he'd entice the risk-taking Willa, long dormant, to come out and play.

"Tasty?" he asked.

"The best."

He reached across the table, held her hand. She felt its warmth while her stomach hiccupped inside her — a happy hiccup, the best possible one.

All would be well now. She knew it.

thirty-five

When they returned to the Muir House, Genie sat on the porch in the cool evening. Today in their absence, she'd populated the front porch with five forest green rockers, the kind you'd see in Savannah, looking out toward the sea. Only these rockers faced traffic.

She stood from rocking. "So this is my first non-family guest."

Hale thrust his hand her way. "Yes, I'm Hale. Nice to meet you, Mrs. Skye."

"Such nice manners. You two care to rock with me a spell?"

Before Willa could feign fatigue, Hale sat, then rocked to the rhythm of Willa's heart.

"So you know Willa from Seattle?"

Willa looked at Genie, rocking beyond Hale. How would she know this?

"Yes, but I'm in New Orleans now on a temporary assignment."

"You'd think it'd be pretty cleaned up by now. How many years has it been?"

"Four. But there are so many pockets of devastation still. For some folks, it still seems like 2005."

Willa kept to herself, concentrating on rocking to the opposite rhythm of Genie.

"But there are a lot of good folks doing great things. Houses going up. Neighborhoods too. People are starting to return. Many aren't, though."

"Home's a funny thing," Genie said. "Once it's destroyed, it's hard to come back to."

Willa wondered at her words. Was Genie trying to tell her something?

"But these folks are hardy, the ones who return. Even more so are the ones who stayed through it all. I can't imagine the horror they lived through. I heard far too many stories. Even now, years later."

Genie kept rocking while the night deepened to purple. All Willa wanted was to go inside, have a nice long talk with Hale, clarify things, sharing everything she learned, but he kept in rhythm with Genie, not getting up, not making motion that he would.

"Stories are hard in the telling, sometimes," Genie said.

"True." Hale tapped his feet to the rocker's rhythm. "Thanks for the nice company," he said. "And thanks for letting me stay here even when it's not finished. I'll keep you to our bargain."

Their bargain?

"I am a man of honor, and I know what it looks like for me to be sleeping under the same roof with Willa. You have permission, as I discussed on email, to interrupt us at will."

Willa expected Genie to laugh, or crack a mean joke, but she simply nodded. "It's getting late. Best you both turn in soon."

She left the porch by the left steps and disappeared into the night. Willa heard the carriage house's door open, then close. While crickets sang their night songs, Willa said, "So Genie's our chaperone now?"

"All in the name of personal propriety," he said.

"Now you're the one who sounds like Mr. Darcy."

"He was an honorable man."

"And he had ten thousand a year."

Hale laughed. "Not much by today's standards. Most folks I'm meeting in the Big Easy don't live on much more."

"Are you saying Mr. Darcy would be poor?"

"Yep."

"That's ironic," Willa said.

"Indeed."

Though she didn't intend such a thing, she found herself rocking to Hale's rhythm. The rocker rails creaked on the ancient porch while scattered cars whirred past, hurrying home, no doubt. She pictured a car pulling into a suburban driveway, the lights enlivening the home. The occupant opened the door to the vehicle, shut the garage door, and entered home. Laughter and firelight welcomed him. A table set for five boasted homemade rolls, a roast fresh from the crock pot, a pile of mashed potatoes, a simple green salad. The family shared their stories. Their conversation became a shelter from the harsh realities of life.

Reality.

Willa looked at Hale, who seemed to be detached from reality. Was he dreaming of that little girl, tucked safely into his wallet? Did he think of the future? Of a home? A family? A well-loved dinner table adorned with a feast?

He broke through, reaching his hand across the expanse between them. And as he did, he stopped rocking. He held her hand, squeezed it. "I missed you."

She felt the tears trickle her cheeks. She missed him too. But her words caught way down deep, as if they garbled and gurgled inside, not knowing how to erupt.

"You don't need to say a word," he said. "But I do have a favor to ask you."

"Anything," she finally said.

"Please take off the ring. At least for now."

She felt her heart sink into the seat of the rocking chair.

She wanted to ask why, wanted to explore what Hale meant. But instead, she sighed. She circled the ring around and around her finger until it wrestled free. She placed it on his open palm, which he'd extended as if he'd expected such a thing. The ring lay flat on his hand, lifeless. He closed his fingers around it. He said thanks, then stood. "I'm tired," he said. "I think I'll turn in. Let's catch breakfast in the morning, okay? Unless you have work to do."

"I can fit in breakfast," she said.

He left her there. He entered the right-hand door. It hollered when it opened and closed. And then, silence. No cars sped past toward home. Willa resumed her rocking. And thinking. And worrying. And wondering.

thirty-six

Willa wondered what Hale looked like when he slept. She'd wondered this before, but had never been so close to him, just a single wall of lathe and plaster between them — yet a lifetime away. She wondered if she pressed her ear to the wall if she'd hear the in and out of his breathing, or locate a viewfinder to his mind and spy on all his thoughts. Then again, maybe that wouldn't be so great. Knowing someone's every thought might not be the best idea.

Death greeted her in Hale's room, along with Daddy's all-out-there thoughts. At five, she lurked around the corner as Daddy put the finishing touches on a grandmother mannequin lying still on the cool metal table. She stood on her tiptoes to get a better look. She wasn't sure why she knew it then, but as Daddy fussed with the woman's starched neckline, as he fiddled with a golden necklace at her throat, Willa suddenly knew the old woman was once alive and now lived somewhere beyond life. That grandmother lying there had a granddaughter. Like her.

Her heart in her throat, her cry held in her chest, she listened as Daddy sang, "Ain't No Sunshine." His voice filtered slow and sweet, full of such agonizing soul that Willa wondered if he'd known the woman. He smoothed her hair, then stood back, silent.

"So you're keeping them for the afterlife," he said.

Willa kept her mouth shut, longing to hear her father talk,

yet terrified she'd be discovered and have to come face-to-face with Death.

"It's okay," he said. "I understand. I have mine aplenty. Wish I could whisper them to you so you could spirit them away to heaven for safekeeping. But you're gone already, and so are your secrets. Safe in the grave, as they say."

Willa wanted the woman to say a thing or two back, but she didn't move her mouth, didn't twitch a muscle, certainly didn't breathe the stale air of the embalming room. From her vantage point, Daddy kept it all in stride. He walked around toward the windows, placed his hand on hers, and lifted his head toward the bead board ceiling. "Lord," he prayed, "she's with you now. At least I hope so. She kept you to herself, is what I hear. But perhaps your mercy covers her silence. Perhaps the sunshine follows her. I hope so." He let go of the woman's hand. It thudded to the table.

In a photo-ready instant, he caught Willa's eyes. His widened. He didn't seem angry, just startled.

"Willa," he said.

"She's not a statue," Willa said.

"What?" He walked toward her, as she still crouched behind the door like a little mouse in hiding.

"She was a person like you, right?"

"I suppose she still is."

"She's cold, isn't she?"

"Yes, baby. She's cold."

"Is that what death means?"

Daddy placed both warm hands around her shoulders. She felt his strength, knew he'd be there to hold her up no matter what life threw her way. "Death is a long goodbye after a life well lived," he said. He sounded like the man he was — a funeral director — with perfectly scripted words.

"I don't want you to die." At this, she let the tears have their way.

"Baby, I won't die." He didn't look at her when he said it. He looked beyond her.

She turned to see what caught his attention. Mother.

"You filling her mind with fairy tales again?"

Daddy stood, took Willa's hand. From his pocket, he pulled out a soft white handkerchief and handed it to her. "Wipe your tears on this," he said.

"Not fairy tales," Willa whispered. She stood broad on her two feet, bracing herself for the words that might come. They came like thunderstorms in summer, ferocious and dark. "Don't kill the fairy tales."

Mother walked over to Willa, stooped to look her in the face. She didn't cradle her shoulders with warm hands. Didn't touch Willa's hand, her face. The distance between them seemed small, just a shoe size away, but the divide felt like a football field. "You listen to me."

"Ella," Daddy said. "This is not the time." He glanced behind him at the dead grandma, reprimanding Mother with a stern look.

Mother shook her head, as if she shook the rebuke clear to the heavens. "Willa, folks die. It's a fact of life. That lady was a strange woman, one who kept to herself at times. Told jokes. But she doesn't have a breath left in her to tell a joke. Not anymore. And that's the truth."

"I know that now," Willa said. She squeezed Daddy's hand, hoping he'd take the hint to walk her away from Mother, to take her in the great big outdoors to swing on a swing or race to the back of their property, arms and legs flying. She wanted, as much as a five-year-old could think such things, to be alive, free, flying, circling, dancing. Anything but stand between Mother who seemed to hate her and the woman on the table whose dreams died. Maybe they were the same, the dead grandmother and Mother. Maybe they both kept to themselves one day, told jokes the next. Maybe Mother had dreams that died. Hard to know.

Mother stood. Loomed, really. "We'll all die, Willa. Your father first, then me. That's the order of things. You'll be last to carry his name." She pointed at Daddy. "His precious Muir name. Let's just hope you're good enough to bear the weight of such a thing."

"Ella, that's enough!" Daddy's voice hollered clear to the rafters then bounced back down.

Willa felt her insides shiver, her heart start to quaver beneath Daddy's stern voice. The tears came again, not as a flood, but enough to wet her face. She didn't wipe them away. She looked into his sad eyes and said, "Daddy."

He squeezed her hand, then leveled a look Mother's way. "It's not right the way you talk to her. She's your—"

"Shut up, Parker!" Mother gestured in large, circular sweeps, her voice a force much broader and higher than Daddy's. "You fill her head with tales and fairies and nonsense. I'm simply telling her the truth about life. Don't interrupt me when I'm talking to my daughter!"

Now Willa felt her legs give in to the quivers. Her knees jellied. She wondered whether she'd become like the dead grandmother in the next room. Her breathing felt thin, like she sucked air through a too-small drink stirrer. The room that captured her parent's angry voices narrowed. Stars and flickers spun around her. She knew she'd fall on the hard wood floor, but didn't care. At least she'd be asleep to the fighting.

But Daddy caught her fall. He scooped her up like a little ball of ice cream and hurried her to her room. He placed her on the canopy bed just so, singing "Ain't No Sunshine" over her like a rope-skipping song. She wasn't sure where Mother went, but she heard the clack of heels on the central staircase. A front door opened, then shut with a slam, shaking the house with fury.

"It's okay," Daddy said. He stroked her hair, touched her cheek.

"Why doesn't Mother love me?" The blur around her vision opened up, light streaming in. The dizziness left like a mist.

"She loves you, Willa Bean. In her own way. But she's had a hard life, you understand?"

"No."

"I suppose not."

"I don't want you to die first."

Daddy laughed. "Don't fret about such things. We all have long lives."

"Like that grandmother in there?"

"Yes, like her."

"But you're so old."

Daddy laughed again.

She sat up. He propped pillows behind her. "You're older than all the other parents at my school."

"I know. You know why?"

"No."

He smoothed her hair behind her ears. "God saw fit to give me a full, but empty life for many, many years. I didn't think I'd ever have a little girl to love. But one day, you popped into this world, pink and screaming. And you made me young."

She thought about this a long time. Daddy's face had wrinkles. His hair was more silver than brown. But his eyes danced with life, and his smile was wide and welcoming. Like Grandfather's. Dusk settled into her room, darkening Daddy's face, smoothing away some of the years. Her eyes felt heavy, her heart too. She blinked, willing to stay awake, worried that if she slept, the fate of the dead grandmother would come to her, or worse, Daddy. "Don't leave," she said.

"I won't." He stroked her hair. "I'll stay right here until you fall asleep."

"How will you know if I'm asleep?"

"Daddies know these things. I'll run to the kitchen to get us some hot chocolate. You get on your pajamas, okay?"

She nodded. When the door shut, she listened for his footsteps in the hallway. In an instant, she tiptoed to the dead grandmother's side, then touched her hand. So cold. Like ice cubes. They made her shiver all over again. "I don't want Daddy to die," she told the woman in the quietest whisper. "So don't save him a place, okay?"

She padded back to her room, threw off her clothes, kicked them under her bed, then pulled on her pajamas. Daddy arrived with hot chocolate in matching mugs. He tucked her in bed, then lay on top of the quilt. They sipped hot chocolate while Daddy read *The Velveteen Rabbit*, her favorite. Her eyes felt warm, her lids heavier after so many tears.

"Daddy?"

"Yes."

"Am I real?"

"As real as this hot chocolate."

"Because the rabbit became real from love," she said.

"That's right. And I love you, so you're real. That's the reality of it."

The word *reality* came back to Willa, brought her back to her canopyless room. She remembered Daddy, how he petted her head until she fell asleep, or at least pretended to. One time she peeked out nearly opened eyes, obscured by eyelashes, to see if he was still there. He was. Slumped in her rocking chair, a gentle breeze of snore coming from his mouth. He'd kept his promise. He waited for her to fall asleep, then he stayed. When she woke up the next day, the sunshine had replaced him, but she noticed he walked a little funny after folding himself in that chair for so long.

thirty-seven

"I don't know who I am," she told Hale the next morning as they sipped coffee at Texas Roast. "I mean, I know on one level, but I feel like two people."

"How so?" Hale yawned, then said he was sorry. "I didn't sleep well. Must've been thinking about embalming or ghosts and such."

"I didn't know you were superstitious."

"Some things have to stay a mystery to keep me interesting."

Willa took a long drink of coffee, now cooled by the morning. "Nice."

He took her hand. "But you were sharing about your multiple personality disorder."

She looked at his hand on hers, so right, then wondered if it was pity or love that held hers. "It's not that. It's who I am, deep down. There's this broken girl from childhood who I feel I am right now. But all through my high school years, I seemed fine—perhaps because ignorance made it so. I feel like if I shared who I was right now, the mess that my head is, anyone who knew me then would think I made up my story."

"Have you shared what you're going through with anyone here?"

"A little, but not the whole story, not like I've shared with you. You must think I'm crazy."

"Willa, you're one person, not two. And you're not crazy. It's just that God has chosen to open up the wounds because you're now capable of looking at them and you're running after healing. Earlier, it wouldn't have worked."

"I suppose you'll say this is God's timing."

"I am saying that. But not in a platitude way. Don't you believe that he knows the best way to heal you? That he knows when you can stomach the truth?"

"I don't feel very capable right now." She lowered her eyes, looked at her untouched muffin, still preening on a plate.

"Wounds hurt when they're exposed. They divvy up a lot more pain as they get better. But eventually they heal over."

"How can you be so sure? How would you know something like that?"

"You're not the only one who has issues."

Willa finally touched the sugar-crusted blueberry muffin, breaking off a piece, chewing it slowly, just as she chewed on Hale's words. "But you're my rock, my stable ground."

"Everyone's on shifting sand some days, Wills."

Hearing her name as Wills stumbled her heart. Did he still care? "You think I'll be whole?"

"You said yourself that the hole in your memory is no longer an issue."

"How do you know that?"

"Remember, I read your blog."

"Right." Another bite. She offered a hunk to Hale. He took it, plopped it in his mouth, and smiled.

"So tell me why it doesn't matter anymore."

Willa looked at her hand, now free from Hale's. Without the ring it felt naked, and if she were honest, the hole still existed. In light of her mother's pictures and the strange return of memories, she needed to know everything. Still. But she kept that quiet. "Just trust me," she said. As if those words would calm the deluge inside.

"I'm trying."

She sat back. "What's that supposed to mean?" She noticed his distant look again, the same eyes she'd seen when he stepped out of the car.

"You said no the first time. Why would I trust your blog post? Have you really changed your mind? How can I be sure?"

"Doesn't my *no* in the Oasis make you trust me more? I told you the truth then."

"You spoke those words in fear, Wills. It may be the truth that you have this insatiable need to know the past. But you had a choice to give in to your heart. And you didn't. You betrayed what you really wanted in lieu of looking for something you may never find. I sat in front of you, like I'm sitting in front of you today, but you walked away." He rubbed his chin, then directed his attention out the window toward the old courthouse. A pair of doves cooed outside.

Willa said nothing at first. What could she say to something like that? Was it truth? Or was he trying to punish her because of a bruised ego? She decided to go for the latter. "You can't know what it's like to walk in my Toms."

"You forget I have my own pair." He lifted his right foot off the floor and placed it on the table.

"Hale!"

The waitress turned and gave Hale a look. He removed his foot with a stomp on the tiled floor.

He shook his head. "So I embarrass you now? Is that what it was at the Oasis? You were embarrassed, so you walked out?"

"You're changing the subject."

"What if I am? Did I hit on another sore spot?"

Willa ate another bite of muffin. This time it felt like wood shavings in her mouth. "Can't we just talk without conflict?"

"That's not real life, and you know it. If we are to spend our lives together—"

"Lives together? You took back the ring, last I saw. From my finger."

"You'll have to trust me. The timing is not right."

"I don't trust." She cringed inside, realizing her own hypocrisy. She expected to be trusted, but had her own hard time with living that word.

"Well put." Hale sat back, eyes to the ceiling.

The door behind their table squeaked open. Blake pushed through the door.

"Willa," he said.

She stood. "Blake. This is Hale, my—"

"Her friend from Seattle," Hale said. He extended his hand Blake's way. They held on longer than comfortable, at least in Willa's eyes, then let go.

"She's been missing home," Blake said, his voice flattened, emotionless.

Hale smiled. "Really? Well, that's interesting to hear."

"Nice to meet you. I'm off to get my morning fix. The coconut latte is calling my name." Blake nodded, then walked away.

"Your old boyfriend, right?" Hale's voice echoed off the high ceilings.

"He'll hear you."

"So what if he does. It's not like it's news or anything."

"You're acting strange."

"How long have you known me, Wills? When have I acted normal?"

She finished her muffin. "You have a point. It's just that I'm on overload right now. I can't process anything, it seems."

"So you take it out on me?"

"Hale, listen."

"I've been listening."

"Just hear me. You know I think the world of you, but—"

"But you want to be my good, good friend."

"No!" She grabbed his hand, though she knew it was terribly forward. "I just need to figure out a few things. Get my head on straight. That doesn't mean I just want to be friends."

Hale withdrew his hand. "Am I imagining things or is this the same conversation we've had one hundred times?"

Willa sunk into her chair. Blake walked past them and nodded his goodbye, his eyes settling into her heart. She wondered if he caught their terse words, if he relished them or dismissed them as insignificant. "Can we take a walk?"

Hale didn't answer, but he stood, then paid the bill.

They walked out the door facing the main square where springtime chose to boast. Bradford pears, fully enlivened, lined the street. "Do you have work to do — even here?" she asked.

"A little."

"There's a park down the road, but it's a good walk from here. If you'd rather drive there, I'd understand." Willa motioned past downtown.

"Let's drive."

"Really?"

"Yeah. I'm a little worn out. I'm afraid I'm not quite living up to my name today." He put his hands on her shoulders, looked into her eyes. "Wills, I'm sorry. I've been a pill. Can we have a do-over?"

She smiled under his gaze. "Every minute's new, as you've said."

"Let's make the next minute a good one." He held her hand, then walked her to the car, humming "Ain't No Sunshine."

thirty-eight

Hale listened while she poured out all her evidence. They circled Harry Myers Park twice, through a thicket of trees, around a play area and large pool, through picnicking areas, then walking around a small lake. It felt right unburdening herself while the birds sang and the grass, newly mowed, smelled sweet and alive. He held her hand the entire time, even when it grew sweaty. And he squeezed her palm when she needed his affection. The real Hale had returned under the sunshine, resurrected in a way. She could nearly remake the memory of jumping on his back for a rollicking piggyback ride. They may not run down a green-grassed incline toward the Puget Sound under the silent shadow of Gas Works Park, but she could picture the same momentum here, racing toward the shore of an unnamed lake. Perhaps love is what makes a place beautiful, after all.

They neared a picnic table. Hale stopped, then sat. She took the seat opposite him. The sun shot angles their way, elongating their shadows on the grass to their left. She didn't feel as tall as her shadow; she felt just right.

"Willa, I'm confused," he said between them.

"About what?"

"Your father."

"How so?"

"Something doesn't add up. You said he loved you. That he was a good man. All these years you've camped there. But I finally realized something. If he was so good, why did he treat your mom so poorly? You said they fought, right?"

Willa tasted her anger. "He treated her just fine! She was awful, just awful. He did his very best, considering."

"Yeah, but personally, I think a man's as good as he treats those he loves. He might've loved you well, but if he yelled at your mom, how can that be good?"

"He was taking up for me," she said, her voice low.

Hale sighed. "Listen, I'm not trying to mess with you, I want to understand. But I only have your side of the story. What about your mom? Why did she act the way she did?"

"How should I know? She didn't love me. You know that. I've shared enough of that story."

"She might not've known how to love you, but my hunch is that she did love you. She does love you. The question is, why didn't your father love her well?"

"Leave him out of this. He was a good man."

"Good men do bad things sometimes, Wills."

Willa shook her head. "What are you trying to tell me? That Daddy was awful? What if I admit that? I can't. If I admit it, then ..." She watched an ant march across the table. Tears filled her eyes.

"Then what?" Hale reached across the table and touched her shoulder, then withdrew.

"I can't. Daddy was gold for me. Everything."

"He was a man. He got angry, it sounds like. Treated your mom bad sometimes. That's the truth. Why hide from it? Didn't you come here to figure this out?"

"Yeah."

"And?"

"I need Daddy to love me."

"He did, so it sounds. So rest in that. But don't mourn a superhero. He was a man, plain and simple."

"Like you."

"Sure, like me," Hale said. "But here's hoping I'll make a better husband. At least that's my prayer for the future—to be a God-fearing husband and a doting, kindhearted father." He paused. "Which is why I have to get your take on Reality before we go any further."

"She's that important to you?" Willa flicked an errant leaf from the table's top. It floated, unanchored on a hesitant breeze, settling on Willa's shadow like it meant to.

"Yes. She's as important and real to me as my own flesh."

"Those are powerful words."

"I know."

"You want to meander through the Louisiana foster system?"

"I doubt you'd call it meandering. More like cutting through red tape." He kept his hands on the table. In the light between them she looked at his calluses. Worker hands. Hands that created homes where devastation once consumed. And now hands that wanted to embrace a child. Adopt, possibly.

As the thought of adoption filtered through her, she decided to give Hale the final piece of her puzzle. "I may be adopted," she said.

"That could be."

"You really think so? How does that make sense?"

"I don't know. Because usually adoptive mothers are in love with their kids—they don't act like your mother did."

Willa thought back to her friends who were adopted, how their mothers became room moms, baked cupcakes, attended every sporting event. None of those things defined Mother. "I don't know what to think. Her behavior is so confusing. Besides, I saw pictures of her pregnant."

Hale shook his head. "Strange. Wish I could help you there." He looked away, and as he did the sun brightened the left side of his face. "Though I will say I love adoption, the idea of it."

"Maybe for you, for Reality, but think about what uncovering the past means to me. That I was unwanted. Discarded."

"Willa, there are two ways of looking at things. I'm afraid you've spent so much time pining about the past and how awful it was with your mother that you've forgotten to find the good." Hale sat back, placed both hands behind his head, then let out a long sigh. "I hope you won't mind if I push you a bit on this feeling of being unwanted somehow. Instead of going there, why not see it instead as being wanted beyond belief? You don't know the story yet, so it's hard to say. But if you were adopted, consider that someone wanted you so much they jumped over huge hurdles to adopt you. They paid money. They pushed through the red tape I'm just beginning to battle. It takes guts and tenacity to adopt, and a whole lot of love. Would that be so bad?"

"I guess not." Would it?

Hale stood, then stepped onto the seat to the top of the table. A regular king of Harry Myers Park.

"What are you doing?"

He spread his arms wide. "I'm embracing the world."

She looked around, noticed a large black dog walking his master, pulling at the leash toward the water. Hale never cared what others thought. She wanted to scold him, but the day's halcyon mood prevented her. Plus she knew that a reprimand would only make him yell his world-embracing words louder. "And is the world embracing you back?"

He spun in circles, feet careful not to step off the tabletop. "Yes and no." He jumped off, landing with a thud on the grass. He pulled her up by the hand. "May I have this dance?"

She wanted to say no. Wanted to stop the man and the dog and explain Hale to him, but then thought better of it. She didn't have enough words to describe such an enigma. So she let him hum silly love songs and twirl her under the warmest sky. As they spun, she smelled his evergreen scent mingled with Texas springtime, and heard the sound of a happy dog breaking the water's surface. She laughed, abandoning herself to the ridiculousness of it all.

He stopped her.

"That's why I embrace it all, Wills. For this. For the sake of hearing you laugh."

"Really?"

"Really." He hugged her, strong arms around her fractured heart. He rested his chin on her head, humming. "The Egyptians believed—"

But before he could say another word, she covered his mouth with hers—the sweetest, slowest kiss. When she pulled away, she caught his gaze. She wanted to say the blog words she'd written out loud, for all of Rockwall to hear. She did love him. But something, a catch in the heart, kept her spoken words way deep inside.

thirty-nine

They spent the rest of the week with a ticking clock in the background, always counting down to the day Hale would leave again for Louisiana. It tocked and ticked and reminded, sickening Willa. The relational bomb would explode as he drove away, obliterating the fragile peace they'd forged in the in-between time. It made Willa jittery, fidgeting needlessly with her fingers as Hale tapped away on his computer. They sat on the porch as cars sped by and the spring sun highlighted newly alive mosquitoes, and greened trees housed chirping birds tweeting about nothing and everything.

She twitched and waited for the guests—Hale's communal idea. He pushed and prodded until she agreed to have a few of her "friends" over before he left. Said he wanted to know her through her community, which consisted of Rheus, Rebbie, Blake, and Genie. A strange mixture of humanity, but that's what Hale-the-relationship-mixologist thrived on. Willa? She wasn't up to hanging out with people right now. Particularly Blake.

But as Rebbie drove up in her mammoth car, and Hale suppressed a comment (oh how she could tell he was stifling his tongue), Willa smiled. It would make for interesting conversation, having Rebbie and her amazing food along. She bustled out of the car. Only then did Willa notice someone in the passenger's seat: Blake. Interesting. He opened, then shut the door, wearing a grin, khaki shorts, and a Tom Petty t-shirt. He waved before he helped Rebbie with the food in the vehicle's rear end. The roar of a motorcycle interrupted the birds' chirping. Rheus, helmeted and wearing long sleeves and old leather, roared in. He killed the motor, took off his helmet, and smiled. "I borrowed it from a friend," Rheus said.

Willa left the porch. Hale closed his laptop and followed. "This is Rheus," she told Hale.

Hale extended his hand. "Pleased to meet you."

Rheus just laughed. "You have your hands full with this one." He pointed at Willa. "But she's worth the pursuing and catching."

Hale didn't directly respond, which sent Willa's mind on a quick trajectory. Why wouldn't he simply agree?

They all gathered around the tailgate. "You've met Blake," Willa said to Hale. They nodded at each other. "And this is my friend Rebbie."

"I'd shake your hand, but it looks like you have your hands full. How can I help?"

"Grab that gallon jug," Rebbie said, angling a look at a lidded container of what looked like lemonade.

Genie stood on the porch in the same place she stood when Willa drove in, her hands resting on her hips, but her look softened. "Head out back, okay? I've set up the table out there."

The table, a long, broad wooden monstrosity, sported a blue and green flowered tablecloth, clipped at the corners with table weights. Mismatched chairs flanked it, six in all. As Willa watched everyone bustle, she realized folks from the outside might think this a Martha Stewart outdoor dinner of three happy couples. Photographers and food stylists would scurry around, making sure everything was just so, and the sun would happily cooperate. It shone its radiance in a dusking, golden light. Right then Willa felt nervously alive. The question poked her though: Would she participate in the meal? Would she enter the life, the conversation? Or would she stay as she was now, an observer standing back on the outskirts of life?

"Come and sit," Hale said, ushering her into his circle – one he hadn't even created. He had a wooing way about him, an invitational quality she adored sometimes, and despaired of at others. But right now, still cocooned in the shell of her own making, she actually felt thankful for the nudge.

"Rebbie, this looks fabulous," Hale said.

And it did. Already pressed and grilled eggplant and mozzarella panini, tomatoes stuffed with couscous, a fresh field green salad with caramelized pecans and shallots, homemade braided rosemary bread. They passed each dish with the appropriate oohs and ahs, plunking each item on porcelain white plates. Glasses clinked as Rebbie poured from-scratch lemonade for each guest. Willa nearly looked around for the photographers.

Rheus stood. "A toast," he said. He clinked Genie's glass. "To friendship, old and new. And to great food."

"Hear, hear," Hale said, loud enough for the doves to hear.

Though they didn't pray, Willa felt the prayer in their midst – the shared joy of great food around a large table. She unfolded her cloth napkin, remembering the linen closet upstairs, the letter, the mysteries yet unsolved. As she smoothed it on her lap, Genie said something, but Willa didn't quite catch the words.

Hale nudged her.

"I'm sorry, what did you say, Genie?" She looked at Rebbie, whose face seemed indiscernible.

"It's too bad your mother isn't here," Genie said.

The spring magic dissipated like a surprise rainstorm, dampening her heart. Willa felt the tears coming. Why now? Why say this?

"That's my fault," Hale said. "I didn't ask Willa to invite her. I hope you can forgive me."

Willa saw his response as unadulterated grace. She reached

her hand under the table, found Hale's, and squeezed her thanks.

"Don't bother Willa about her mother," Rheus said, his voice flat, not stern. "God has a way of timing things in unexpected ways."

"There is duty," Genie said.

Rheus placed a hand on Genie's arm, a gentle touch for a feather of a moment, then removed it. "Just let it be."

"This couscous is fabulous," Blake said. "Makes me think we're in Morocco."

"Have you been?" Hale pointed his fork Blake's way.

"No, but I've seen pictures."

Hale laughed. "Me too. Wish that counted. Maybe someday I'll make my way there. I always wanted to be one of those people who hiked Europe, then Northern Africa, maybe even the world. Though I have stayed in a hut in Kenya."

"Kenya? What was it like?" Rheus asked.

"Hot and beautiful and poor. But one of the richest experiences of my life," Hale said.

Willa chewed and swallowed a bite of Morocco. "Rebbie, I never would've guessed in high school that you'd be a caterer. Remember the spaghetti you used to make?"

"Oh, don't remind me." Rebbie looked at Genie. "You wouldn't think me a culinary genius by my high school standards. I overcooked spaghetti noodles until they mushed. Then I topped them with a hefty squirt of ketchup. Bon appétit!"

"I remember." Willa made a face.

"I've come a long way. And maybe someday," Rebbie said, "I'll have my own catering place."

Willa remembered the Methodist church, the longing in Rebbie's eyes, the excitement in her voice, and secretly wished she'd become a millionaire and grant the wish. On a night like this, Willa felt anything possible.

The conversation enlivened as the sun slowly crept to sleep. Willa could feel Hale's happiness, how made for people he was. He asked questions, engaging Genie, eliciting words and sentences from her Willa never bothered to want to know. She felt the sudden beauty of humanity, frail and terribly needy, looking for someone to listen, to really hear. Could that be the way into the woman's heart? Could she ask questions like Hale? Or had she traveled too long down the path of irking Genie?

Willa noticed Blake hadn't touched Rebbie, or shot a look her way. Nor did Rebbie send affection his way. They seemed comfortable friends, nothing more. But Rheus seemed to wear his heart on the exterior of himself, like naked skin under the fading sun. And Genie, cautiously, moved toward him, cocking her head when he spoke in low tones, laughing when he made a joke.

As they gathered dishes, Rheus sidled up next to Willa. "Forgive me for intruding," he said as he stacked plates next to the sink. She rinsed while Hale and the rest continued bringing in dishes and linens. As she put a plate in the dishwasher, he said, "Hello is a beautiful word, isn't it?"

Willa lifted her eyes, watching Hale as he hunted the grounds for bits of food, any kind of litter. He spoke with Genie as they scrounged together. "Yes, it is," she finally said. "It means a beginning."

He handed her a plate. "I'd hate for you to have goodbye be the final hello."

"What do you mean?"

"With your mother. You've said a goodbye, right?"

She rinsed, then placed the next plate parallel to the last, both clean, but unclean. "No, she said the goodbyes. And made it quite clear that she wanted no more hellos."

"Everyone needs relationship." He handed her another plate.

"And some people are unsafe. She's the one who drew the boundary, Rheus. Not me. Wouldn't it be going against her wishes to say 'hello' as you suggest?"

"Some folks close doors they wish they hadn't." At that the door opened, and Hale bounded in, fists tight.

"Where's the trash can?"

Willa pointed.

Hale deposited his small bits of garbage, then left the way he came, the door swinging open from his momentum.

Another plate, another rinse, another placement in the dishwasher.

"You don't want to live with regrets, do you?"

"You don't really know me," she told Rheus. "Don't know what I've been through."

"You're right." He handed her another plate. "But I know the pain of a final goodbye, and I wouldn't wish that on anyone."

They finished loading the dishwasher in silence, Rheus' goodbye words clanking around in her head.

She watched as Genie, Rebbie, and Blake stood outside, circling up in conversation. Hale returned, his face ruddy. He placed his hands on her shoulders, whispered a hello that sent shivers down her spine.

Rheus hummed. "I best be going," he said. "You'll say a hello yet. I'm counting on it." He left the house. His motorcycle roared, then dissipated in the distance. Willa wondered if he'd said goodbye to Genie.

Hale led her to the porch. They sat next to each other in the near darkness. She could hear the banter of the remaining three guests.

"Tomorrow is goodbye," Hale said.

She leaned her head against his shoulder. "Why does it have to be?"

"Because I have work to do. And you have a past to uncover. And Reality needs a home. That's why."

"When you say it that way, it seems simple. Is it okay to say I don't want you to leave?" Willa touched his hand, traced his veins with her finger. She wondered if Hale would re-pop the question. She prayed it would be so. He seemed nearer than her breath, and she wanted nothing more than to hear commitment drip from his mouth.

"Yeah, it's okay," he said. But he didn't pull her near him.

She hoped for words about Egyptians, about anything teasing and Hale-ish, but he kept quiet. The one who thrived in their ad-hoc community now forsook his words. Crickets filled in the gap, singing night songs between them while both rocked to the rhythm of a Texas evening.

She simply whispered, "hello," then kept the goodbye to herself.

forty

They replayed the scene the next morning, taking their appropriate places, her head against his shoulder while he said few words. "Keep me posted on Reality," she said. Willa tried to sound enthusiastic, as if she were really pulling for Hale's fostering and possible adoption, but even she knew she couldn't muster much vigor for his plans. Why try when Hale seemed distant again? Their kiss on the shores of Harry Myers' lake seemed to be a passing trifle, an anomaly tacked on to the rest of a visit that felt more pedestrian than romantic.

"My flight," he said.

"Don't go."

"I have to."

"You don't have to do anything you don't want to. I know you're a stubborn one."

"But I want to go. I can't explain it properly, and I'm afraid if I start, I won't make any sense. I'll just end up hurting you, and that's the last thing I want to do. Let's just say you still have some work to do here. And I'd like you to grant me the same space. I have a few things to figure out myself."

"You?"

He held her hand, then let it go. "Yep, me. I can be capricious — like when you kissed me. I gave myself over to that, but I shouldn't have."

She felt her heart untether, a ball at the end of a rope now flinging helter-skelter through the blue sky, only to thud on the porch and not bounce. Her dreams, though she pushed one away when Hale first gave her the ring, were usually close. She'd taken for granted Hale's reliability, his tenacity in loving her. Now her heart lay at his feet, but he didn't bother picking it up. Didn't say a word.

"When will I see you?" She told her voice not to waver, not to sound desperate, but the truth was, in more ways than she could quantify, Hale had become her home, her family, her friends, her community. He was everything. And he was leaving.

"I don't know," he said.

"Will you write?"

"Hard to say."

She wanted to dig her nails into his arms, clutch tightly, and not let him go. But she knew the clinging would only make him want to flee. She pulled in long breaths, still trying to steady her heart, her will. In desperation, she almost let the L word fly from her mouth, but she kept it inside, like the kind of guarded secret she'd been trying to uncover. She settled for sitting near, for hearing his breathing, for feeling his warmth. "I'll keep writing on my blog, if you want to check it out."

Hale stood. Looked down, an ache in his eyes. "I will miss you," he said. The words sounded final like he'd made a monumental decision and now delivered it to her. He turned, walked down the stairs, suitcase in hand. A dove cooed in the distance while the sun shone on his head as he walked. He placed the suitcase in the back seat, shut the door, walked to the other side of the car, then stood, shielding his eyes with his hand. He said nothing more. Just a ducking into the car's innards, the turning of the engine, a backing out, and a whirring away. In leaving, he didn't look her way, didn't bother waving.

But she waved back.

forty-one

A year after Daddy's death, Willa didn't know the Christmas visit with Mother would mean goodbye forever. Had she known, Willa would've inhaled the stale nursing home air like a kid gulping after drowning. She would've traced the lines of Mother's face, memorized the slight hint of smile that played on her lips. Would've consciously tried to piece together some happy memories, stitching them into her mind before Mother's words unthreaded them.

Willa sat, then, in a recliner near the twin-sized adjustable bed. A cup of water with a long bendable straw sat on the nightstand between them. A rerun of *The Waltons* played on the wall-mounted TV. A vase of dying red mums mixed with fake holly limped next to the water. Mother sat up in bed, her covers neatly pulled over a thin lap. "Well, what do you want?" she asked.

Why did Willa feel like a two-year-old under the woman's gaze? Maybe because she was in many ways. One year of work finished, eager to conquer the world like a toddler poised to wreak havoc on the contents of lower cabinets, Willa felt the surge of new life, new possibilities. She could practice sharing her Seattle life with Mother. Maybe.

"It's been awhile, hasn't it?" Mother's words sounded ethereal, not connected to the scene in front of her.

"Yes."

"Well, sit yourself down."

Willa obeyed.

"Catherine, tell me about yourself these days."

"Mother, it's Willa. Who is Catherine?"

She shook her head, an attempt to clear confusion. "You are. Always have been. Little Catherine."

Willa wished she could download Mother's brain into a supercomputer, unscramble the mounting confusion, and spit out a coherent document about her own life, complete with missing hole filled. But that would not happen. The time for that had passed with the summer when Genie called Willa in a panic, saying Mother had burned fried chicken on the stove. And if you knew Mother, you knew this to be a Southern aberration.

"Mother, I'm Willa. Your daughter."

She smiled, then frowned. "Of all the people who could come around, it would have to be you. Where's your father?"

"Daddy's in heaven. You know that. You stood next to me when he died. You spoke at his funeral."

"You are a foolish, stupid girl." Mother's voice took its edge and held on.

Willa looked around the room for a panic button, but saw none. This wasn't an insane asylum, was it? But her heart raced and her worry mounted. She told herself not to overreact. She closed her eyes and steadied her breath.

"If you speak that way to me, I'll leave." There, she said it. The dreaded standing up to Mother speech she rehearsed in her mind with a therapist. It always started with those words, and the threat of leaving. But there were so many more words to be said.

"Leaving is what cowards do. What insipid, idiotic babies do. So it doesn't surprise me that you're threatening such a thing."

"Mother, please—"

"Quit using that word."

"Please?"

"No. Mother. You of all people don't deserve to use such a word." Her eyes pierced Willa's. Only pure, hot hatred boiled there. Disdain.

All the feelings she had as a child, feeling in the way, unworthy, a nuisance, bubbled to Willa's surface. She stood, her arms and hands shaking. "Fine. I don't need to call you that. It's not like you've been a good mother anyway."

Mother shrieked. A nursing home worker hurried into the room. "Is everything okay?"

"Kindly escort this stranger from my room. She's bothering me."

"Mrs. Muir, this is your daughter. Remember? Willa? The one you're so proud of?"

Willa looked over at the staff worker, a woman about fifty, with short, cropped hair and a wide, kind face. Was she telling the truth? Had mother been proud?

"She's disturbing me," Mother yelled.

"Now calm down. Just you rest. Willa came all the way from Seattle to see you."

How did the aide know this?

"Seattle? From up north? I don't know anyone from Seattle."

"Maybe I should go," Willa said.

The worker pulled her aside, whispering as she did. "I know it seems like she's angry, but it's the Alzheimer's. I see it all the time. Even between what used to be sweet married couples. Something misfires in the brain, and it scrambles emotions, particularly anger."

Willa looked over at Mother, whose face erased its anger to blank. "I'm agitating her."

"Your visit is for you. Just say what you'd like to say, give her a kiss, and leave. You'll regret it if you storm out now. Trust me."

Willa wondered how she could trust a person she'd just met, but chose to believe the worker's words. As the woman left the room, keeping the door open a crack, Willa settled back into the chair, determined to say her words.

"Mother, I just need you to listen to me. I don't expect you to understand, just listen. Can you do that?"

Mother nodded slightly.

"I do love you. You know that, right?"

No nod this time, just a vacant look at the TV.

"It's just, I had a hard time knowing you loved me, Mother. I knew Daddy did, but you?"

" 'I'm in the mood for love simply because you're near me,' " Mother sang. " 'Funny, but when you're near me, I'm in the mood for love.' "

"I'm being serious and you're singing."

" 'Sing, sing a song,' " she sang.

"Stop it. Please."

"You're trying to tell me how awful I am. Go ahead, get back to it."

Willa put her face in her hands. This was not how she'd planned to say these things. "That's not what I meant. I'm trying to tell you how I feel. How your treatment of me has hurt me."

Mother smoothed over the already-smooth covers on her bed. "You choose your own hurt, girl. You absorb it. That's what my father taught me. It's your choice as to what you'll feel, and if you feel awful it's because you want to feel that way."

"You sound like my counselor."

"I am no such thing."

"I know."

"Are you finished? It's almost time for *The Newlywed Game*."

Willa told herself to do it. To touch her mother. But her hand's journey from her lap to her mother's clutches felt like the distance between them — a wide, impassable gulf. Still, she forced such a thing. Touched her. Felt her cold skin. Squeezed, hoping Mother would return the favor. She didn't. But she didn't throw her hands off in a huff either. For an eternal moment, Willa looked at their hands, so alike. Veins ribbed through Mother's slender, pink hands, making Willa wonder when hers would look as old someday. Mother's skin, translucent, bore no age spots, nor did her finger hold a wedding ring. Seemed her marital sentiment died with Daddy.

"Mother? I love you. And if there's anything I've done to hurt you, please tell me."

"You were born."

The words caused an involuntary withdrawal of Willa's hand. An instant feel of nausea in the pit of her gut. Willa thought she had prepared for anything, even entertaining the possibility that Mother would say words like these, but no amount of rehearsed words could've made her able to hear the devastating sentence. Unwanted. She told herself to speak, to keep her voice steady and not hysterical. "What do you mean? Didn't you want me?"

"There were other means," Mother said. "Other ways."

The Newlywed Game announced itself with fanfare while Willa said nothing, trying to make sense of Mother's words.

"It's called abortion." Mother stared at the TV, a straight line for a smile. "And I wanted to. Oh, how I wanted to. But you know how I hate procedures. How much I hate shots and the like. But I should've been brave. Should've just waltzed myself down to the clinic, signed my name, and been done with it. My biggest regret."

"Your biggest —"

"You should be thankful. Grateful. You're alive because of my fear."

"Why would you say something like that?" Willa stood, tears releasing, her voice warbling.

"You've been searching for truth, I hear."

Willa stood at the foot of Mother's bed. Turned around and shut off the TV.

"Hey, I was watching that!"

"I don't care."

"All the proof I need. This confirms your worthlessness." Mother sat up, wiped a sleeve across her face. It looked blotchier, as if anger reddened her face.

Willa moved until she stood next to the bed. She bent near Mother until she smelled Doritos on her breath. "I'll leave you soon. But before I do, why not just get everything out? What happened to me when I was four? I can't remember, but you must know."

She flitted Willa away, brushing her face with clipped nails. "I can't be bothered by this right now."

Willa kept her eyes looking steadily into Mother's. "Just tell me."

"I … you … your father … we … Catherine, why don't you just sit a spell and brush my hair?"

Willa put her hands on Mother's shoulders. She shook her gently. "I have to know! Find it in your mind. Find the empty place!" She was crying again, but Mother had no such tears.

Mother took a deep breath, igniting her voice. "I never want to see you again, you hear me? Leave me!" She took another breath. "You are worthless and ugly and stupid and not my child!"

Willa let go of the shoulders, forsook the eyes, turned from the strange smile. She walked away from Mother, not looking back.

"Goodbye!" Mother's scream followed her down the echoing hallway, strewn with Christmas decorations and lights. Though tempted to scream her own goodbye, she couldn't bring herself to do it.

forty-two

They arrived. On the same day, two pieces of paper in different envelopes on the same day. Daddy's birth certificate. Hers.

Daddy's proved Blake's words to be true. The woman she believed to be her paternal grandmother wasn't. Sequestered in her room, blankets over her clothed body, Willa rethought her childhood. Her visits with Nana. Daddy's affection for her. Her grandfather's secret. Why would he keep a secret like that? And where was Daddy's real mother?

But the second birth certificate proved more confusing.

Her mother was listed as she should be. And so was Daddy. Nice and neat. No discernable changes. Just black and white ink belying what she'd heard otherwise. Daddy was Daddy. Mother was Mother. And she was she.

Willa pulled out the letter from the stranger, wondering how his or her words tied into the birth certificate. She felt like a sleuth, finding clues, searching her mind for connections. She grabbed the timeline and pictures she'd drawn, trying to overlap everything she knew up until this point. She could now confirm Daddy's strange parentage. But their supposed separation? No. Her birth mystery? No. The four-year-old lost memory? No.

What did it all mean? Why were revealed secrets important? With Hale gone, did it really matter? In a bout of agonizing loneliness, Willa texted Blake, asked him what he was doing tonight, then regretted her neediness. In an instant,

"Nothing," answered back, then a second, "I'll be right over," as if he knew she needed him.

Blake stood beside his car, shielding his eyes as he looked up toward her window, he an unlikely Romeo, she a distraught, clingy Juliette. His eyes held more anticipation than Hale showed during his entire visit. She stood upstairs in her room, watching him, keeping his eyes, pouring her longing his way. She couldn't pull herself away from his gaze, but she made herself leave the room, hoping the spell between them wouldn't break in the few seconds it took her to dive down the stairs, rush out the door, and hop into the Mini Cooper.

Blake shut the door behind her. Hesitated before he opened his door. When he sat, he placed both hands on the steering wheel, gripped it tight. "It feels like a date," he said. The magic? Still there.

Reckless as her emotions were, as untamed, she kept her words mysterious. "Perhaps," she said.

"I have the perfect place." He wheeled out of the lot, headed toward the glistening-slick waters of Lake Ray Hubbard, toward the new boat launch. A gazebo perched on the water's edge; this she could see. He told her to wait as he ran around to grab her door, then her hand. "It's a long way up," he said.

Double entendré words, those. A long way up from the pit she'd been scaffolding, trying to scrape around and figure out the hole before climbing out to see the light of day. A long way up from leaving Blake behind. But now that she was momentarily dismissed by Hale, a very real and present Blake kept her hand, leading her toward the water's edge, a laugh on the curve of his smile.

She kept his hand, squeezed it, feeling the deliciousness

of teenage love swirl around her like a Nicholas Sparks book while the sun slid horizonward, warming their faces. Fishermen scattered here and there hurled long poles toward murky green waters, but Blake didn't seem to be curious about bass or crappie. He grabbed Willa's free hand, her left, kissed her empty finger, and caught her to him. She felt his chest, felt the heaving in and out, couldn't discern her heartbeat for his.

They remained on the shore, embracing. Willa restrained a thousand words she couldn't say. Blake kept the same verbal withdrawal, instead smelling, then stroking her hair. When Hale proclaimed himself to be Willa's home, maybe his words were preparing her for this home, this safe place in the arms of the first boy to love her — a rekindled fierce sort of love, better now because they'd both grown up. An agonizingly sweet compassion.

She pulled away, lost herself in Blake's crocodile-green eyes, letting the desire inside snap her into now. So fully alive, they were. Every piece of paper, every birth certificate, every angry maternal declaration faded as the sun retreated beneath the belly of the earth. She willed it to rise again so she could hold his gaze longer, but it disobeyed love tonight, preferring to rise on someone else's affection on the other side of the world. Still, she held Blake's steady look.

Blake pushed her hair from her face. "You have no idea how long I've envisioned this kind of reunion." His smile quirked as he said it, his teeth as white as the moon that would soon make its appearance.

She looked down at his wrists, then slid away, embracing them. "What do your tattoos mean?" she asked.

"Walk with me," Blake said. He led her to the gazebo where children chased each other in circles, Liesl and Rolf-style, then past that to a hidden path to the other side of Highway 66. "They're commitments," he said.

"For what?"

He pulled her to a bench. Her thighs touched his, sending shivers through her.

"It will sound a bit esoteric, I'm guessing."

"Esoteric is my middle name." Willa felt the weight of his arm around her.

"Nah, it's Harper, if I remember correctly."

She nodded. But as she heard it, she wondered afresh what it meant. Why Harper? She'd found no such name in her past search for family, for holes. Perhaps her mother loved Harper Lee?

Blake overturned his wrists. At first she winced, wondering if her sudden departure from his life meant he tried to take his. But no such scars marred the white flesh. Instead, blue-black ink circled both, covering up no such anguish. "Hebrew and Greek," he said.

"Really?"

Blake laughed into the air while cars sped by. "Why? Don't I strike you as an ancient language kind of guy?"

"I suppose, with all that research you're always doing. It just strikes me as strange."

"In college, while I pined away for you, I dove into all sorts of things. Philosophies. Religions. Partying. Girls. Some of it I'm proud of—the intellectual pursuits, sure. But not the rest." He turned his hands over, revealing more script. "I finally decided to make a commitment, once and for all, to the one philosophy that kept making sense, the wooing of Jesus, his radical, overflowing ways. And then I fell in love with Paul."

"Paul?" Was Blake gay?

"As in the apostle."

Willa let out her breath.

"And I particularly loved Philippians. Read it over and over again. It helped me make sense of my life. Of us. Or lack of us. Of my direction. Of how your leaving ripped apart my world. My passion to help others uncover things. All that."

"I never said I was sorry," she said. "For leaving."

"No, you didn't."

The quiet between them intensified, punctuated by a quack here, a speeding car there.

"I'm sorry," she said.

"I know."

He took her left hand in both of his. "Grace and peace," he said to the darkening air.

"Good words. I need both."

"I know."

"So what's on your wrists?"

"Just what I said. Grace in Greek. Peace in Hebrew. Ever notice how Paul starts Philippians? With grace and peace?"

"Sure, I suppose." Willa felt the moment slipping away, in light of staid theology. Hale would be happy, she supposed. On several levels.

"Grace is a Greek word, *charis*. And peace is *shalom*, Hebrew. Paul was sharing his heart for community, to bring Greek and Hebrew believers together by saying both words together like that. It was as if he said, '*Bonjour*, y'all' to a group of French people mingling with Texans."

Community. Hale's domain. Hearing the words from Blake's mouth sounded wrong. Blake's arm around her felt heavy, out of place. She shrunk away, feeling self-conscious and stupid.

Blake stood. "What's wrong? What did I say?"

Willa shook her head. "I can't do this," she said.

"Do what? Grace and peace?"

"No." She stood. Put her hand on his, then withdrew. "I don't want to use you because I'm lonely."

"You already have."

"I'm sorry." She walked toward the gazebo, a clip faster than her heartbeat.

"Wait." Blake caught up with her, grabbed the corner of her shirt, pulled her to him. For a second she let him bewitch her. "You're beautiful," he said. "I've known it all these years while I waited for you to come back to me."

"If you waited, then why didn't you find me? Call me?"

"I always knew exactly where you were, Willa. Knew every address, every roommate you had. Every phone number, email address, profile. I knew what you read on Good Reads, what you bought on Amazon. There's a deliciousness in knowing everything about a girl, yet not making a move, wouldn't you say?"

Willa remembered the old Blake, his words unlocking every memory of suffocation. He'd changed and grown up, yes, but the seeds of his neediness still sprouted. And while she still struggled to find herself, to know herself, in that moment she knew she wasn't that girl anymore—the girl who needed to be needed that way. That kind of protection meant isolation and myopia, not freedom. Still, the intoxication lingered.

Blake leaned in close to kiss her. In that space she almost closed the gap, but then reminded herself of who she was becoming and let the gap widen.

"Take me home," she said.

forty-three

But home meant more suffocation. Willa felt the need to roam, to walk, to think. She drove to Harry Myers Park, then walked its serpentine trails, all the while scolding herself for her crazy schizophrenic heart. What was it about her that needed a man so much? In Hale, she found the gentleness of her father's eyes, the staid confidence of a grown, confident man, the promise of home.

But Blake sparked a latent passion, something she'd forgotten about until his own pair of eyes captured her, wooed her to remember the part of herself that once felt deliciously, wickedly alive.

She tried to pray, but the words felt like gravel in her mouth, her heart. She knew she didn't deserve an answer from the heavens, not with her fickle heart swaying this way and that like a porch swing in a Texas storm. Sway it did. Creak too.

Willa tried to believe all her flirtation was a grand cover-up to quell the pain in her heart, the wound left by a vacant memory. But as she watched the sky tease the hillsides of the park, she wondered if she held some sort of permanent flaw in her soul. Maybe she was the kind of girl who couldn't hold mystery well. Others seemed perfectly fine. After all, Mother forgot most things in the dawn, then dusk of Alzheimer's, and she moved on. Why couldn't Willa, who remembered nearly everything? Was having a full memory without gaps really the key to sanity? Or was it better to sweep much of life under a giant rug for safekeeping?

"Something has to give," she finally said to Jesus, though she looked around, made sure no one was looking. "Anything. A glimpse of the truth, perhaps?"

Heaven kept its silence close to its chest.

Perhaps it was time to solidify her plans for a new life. Seattle seemed farther away now, and Texas no longer felt like home. She could travel, maybe find herself on the rustic roads of Tuscany. Or throw herself into missions, though she thought God would have a hearty laugh at that one.

As she neared the parking lot, no decisions came. Nothing focused. The blurry, hazy world obscured all the more. A voice inside rumbled a cautionary, "Stay." Then, "Mother."

forty-four

That night she dreamt of Mother, but no truth came forth. When Willa woke up, she knew she needed to see Mother in flesh and blood—not in memories, dreams, recollections. So she drove through Rockwall, stopped her car, told her heart to stop its careening, and walked into the building that might just change everything.

The hallways smelled as Willa remembered them the last time she saw Mother, a mixture of stale corn chips, urine, and antiseptic, all mixing together to rumble her stomach. She'd checked in at the front desk, not recognizing any faces. A lot can happen in three years, including employee turnover. She'd hoped to find the kind-faced nurse, the one who helped her with Mother before, but no face looked familiar. As Willa slowed her gait to a nursing home shuffle, she passed a man slumped in his wheel chair, mumbling something about Cheerios and toast. He seemed intent on viewing his knees, and as she peered down, she saw a smile on his face.

Blissfully unaware.

She wanted that. Could God simply erase her entire childhood, except for the good parts? She'd smile then, wouldn't she?

Halfway toward her mother's door, though, Willa stopped. Couldn't move. Her heart careened into her sternum, threatening an escape. Her hands slicked wet. Her eyes watered. Fully enraged panic coursed through her. "I can't do this," she said.

But no one heard her. And what if one had? Even then, it would be a stranger bringing her courage or verve, not a friend. In the middle of the hallway, Willa saw the sorry state of her life. No friends, really. No family except a no-longer-there Mother who wanted nothing to do with her. Two boyfriends she'd shunned. Not even a cat. Even the sadness of being forever single seemed impossible.

Willa leaned against the windowed wall, telling herself to move — go forward, retreat, anything. But her feet wouldn't obey.

"Can I help you?" an elderly man said. "You look a little lost. I'm the chaplain here."

"I'm okay. Just heading to my mother's room."

The man held her elbow. "I'll take you there. What's her name?"

"Ella Muir."

"A delightful woman. You're Willa?"

Willa turned to look at the man who, she found, possessed clear blue eyes like Daddy. "I am, but how would you know?"

"Her chart. And I was told by the staff to watch out for you. Apparently before Mrs. Muir slid away from us, she asked for you quite a bit. Not now, I'm afraid. And someone let us know you were in town. In a way, I think she's been waiting for you."

"She's —"

"Dying," he said. "I'm sorry."

Willa couldn't speak in the wake of death thrown into the conversation so casually. Sure, it might be commonplace here, and it had been pedestrian at the funeral home, but right now Willa felt the word tear into her heart. Death. Mother. Willa an orphan. Why hadn't Genie told her this?

"You came at a good time. She's more alert in the mornings." Before she could protest, they stood at Mother's door. No longer in one of the center's apartments, Mother had been shifted to her final home. A door with a number. Lacking the splendor of the bed and breakfast.

The man knocked, but no one answered. He turned the knob. "Would you like me to stay with you?"

"No, it's okay," Willa heard herself say. She nearly added, "I need to do this ..." but couldn't bear to utter the word *alone* to the world. Not right now.

When the door closed behind her, the world collapsed on itself. There lay Mother, her eyes half shut, an IV poked into the crook of her arm. Her hair, once brilliantly brown and groomed, lay in gray thinness across her pillow. Her breaths, shallow. Her mouth moving slightly.

It was easy to vilify someone from afar. Simple to calculate a nemesis several states away. But seeing her mother like this, curled like a child on a too-big bed, erased the nemesis. Here lay her mother.

She spoke the word to the room. "Mother."

But she didn't stir. Not even an eyelid fluttered. Willa remembered touching that dead grandmother at five, how cold the woman's hand was, and wondered if Mother had the same ice filling her veins. A gap roared between them, a half a room of space that seemed impassable. Though she knew she should reach out and touch her mother, Willa stood there, paralyzed.

So this is why Genie berated Willa. Because Mother slept on the line between life and death, steadily breathing earth's air. Pulling it in with light rasps.

Still immobilized, Willa realized she didn't hate Mother as she thought. Didn't wish her ill. She pitied her. One step, then another brought her closer to the woman who had pushed her away. Several seconds later, she stood above Mother who curled in on herself, eyes half-mast.

"Mother," she said.

Eyes fluttered, but no words.

Willa knelt beside her, put her face even with Mother's. "It's me. Willa."

Eyes wide open now, Willa tried to find her own there. Brown as tree bark, yet hollowed now. Mother licked dry lips. Tried to say something, but couldn't. Her eyes looked beyond Willa to the nightstand. Having helped Daddy convalesce, Willa knew she wanted water. So she grabbed the lidded cup with an articulated straw and bent it toward Mother's lips. In doing this, the immobilizing fear of minutes and lifetimes ago slipped away. Mother secreted a bit of liquid into her mouth. Only a small rivulet trickled out. Willa found a hand towel, also on the nightstand, and wiped her mouth.

Mother blinked.

Willa blinked back tears, tried to speak, but couldn't.

"Catherine," Mother whispered.

"No, it's Willa. I don't know who Catherine is." Willa exhaled, then sat on the chair next to the bed, pulling it to face her.

"You," Mother said.

Willa pointed to herself. "Willa."

Mother shook her head. The familiar fire, the squinting of anger, returned.

Willa sat back. Felt Mother's disdain move from her heart to her unsettled stomach. So this was how it would be.

"I'm sorry, Mother. I should've visited sooner." It felt good to get the *sorry* out there, to let it take flight in the stale air of the room. Nearly liberating.

Mother shook her head, slightly.

Willa inhaled another yawning breath. "I know you're not one to give your secrets, but if you know anything about my missing memory, I'm inviting you to share it now. Please."

She hated the desperation in her voice. Despised her neediness. Here was Mother, about to exhale all of the stale air, and all she wanted was to suck secrets from her, all because she had to know the truth. Willa reached out and touched Mother's hand. Cold, but not ice. Lord knew how long she had left, how long Willa had to reconcile a broken relationship, find the secrets, and move on. And yet, holding her mother's hand felt right. She held a connection to the old Willa, the pigtailed girl yearning for affirmation. Holding Mother's hand meant holding onto what Willa still wanted, still needed.

You never outgrow the need for a mother, she thought. She didn't say the words out loud. Not now. Probably never. Because when death haunted, it was best to let things rest. She hollered at herself for asking for secrets, for pushing Mother toward eternity. Instead, now, she rested right there, cradling a wrinkled hand, connected to an arm, a shoulder, a neck, a mind. A mind that paid no attention to her, but a mind nonetheless. A heart that still pumped blood, but had forgotten how to love. Like it or not, this was the woman God placed in Willa's life, named her Mother, and would now take away, orphaning Willa.

She let the tears weep out, didn't hold them in anymore. Her cries echoed off light green walls, the industrial tiled floor. And still she held on to Mother's hand.

"I do love you," she said. "And for what it's worth, I forgive you too."

At that Mother roused, pursed her lips, and said, "Speck."

Willa looked into Mother's eyes, expecting she had a speck there needing attending to, but saw nothing but milky irises. "Do you have a speck in your eye? Which one? Wink it at me."

But Mother didn't wink or blink. Instead, she took a long, pallid breath and said, "Speck!" enough to do her own echoing.

The chaplain returned.

"What does she mean? Do you know?"

The chaplain stood by Mother, his hand on her shoulder.

"She's said that word a lot — *speck*. No one knows what she means. Says Catherine too."

Willa kept Mother's hand. "I've upset her."

"It's how all our Alzheimer's patients are toward the end. Sometimes combative. Often not making much sense. Some can sing entire hymns, even the third verses everyone ignores. It's like their minds revert back to what they can remember from decades before."

Willa looked at the gray-haired man. "So Catherine and speck have something to do with my mother's past?"

"Possibly."

Mother's eyes closed then, her hand releasing its tension. Willa panicked. "Is she dying? Now?"

The man shook his head. "No, but in the next few weeks, she'll head to glory. At least that's my estimation," he whispered.

"I should've visited her sooner."

"You're here now." He backed away, leaning now against Mother's closet door. "The time for now and the future has come. No use living in the land of regret."

"Did you learn that in seminary?" Willa let go of Mother's hand and stood.

"No, in life. It's no use hanging on to what should've been. Does a body no good, if you ask me."

"I'm trying." In the circle of three, Willa yearned for a friend like the kindly chaplain. An older person who took time to care, to share wisdom. With Daddy gone, that hole opened up inside her, but she hadn't found a proper substitute. And she'd been looking into the eyes of men to fill that need. There were spurts of begging Jesus to fill them, in the vim and vigor of her high school and college Jesus days, but the pursuit fell short in light of new eyes to gaze into, new trinkets of pleasure that satisfied for a thrilling moment, fell short the next.

The man didn't throw words into the silence of the room,

something Willa thanked him for with a nod of the head. It was enough to hear Mother's breathing, to feel the sacredness of that time, though Willa's heart felt emptied.

The chaplain cleared his throat, easing away from the closet door. "I'll leave you two alone," he said.

"Thank you," she finally said.

He stood in the doorway now. "You should say your good-byes every time you see her. Best to say all the words you want. Life has a way of slipping from folks really fast."

She nodded.

But instead of saying words upon words of regret and anger and emptiness, Willa counted to one hundred in the quiet of the room, then slipped out without saying goodbye.

forty-five

Floundering was the appropriate word for Willa's life and soul. Flapping like a bass on the deck of a boat before it'd been thrown back into Lake Ray Hubbard's gut. Hale hadn't written. Life hadn't progressed. And she felt stuck, stuck, stuck within the walls of her "home."

The poetic invitation of Rheus to climb aboard what he called the SS *Mystery* felt apropos. Only she didn't realize this was the kind of boat needing the power of her arms, not an outboard.

The boat was a friend's, he said. Docked temporarily. "All we need to do is get there, and I'll take care of the rest."

So they drove in her Prius through the streets of Rockwall's center. She turned right at 66, heading lakeward.

They embarked on the two-person kayak at the boat landing below Daddy's grave while Lake Ray Hubbard stretched lazy before them in the morning sunlight. Ripples of excitement poured through her. Something about the quiet of the morning, the smell of the lake, the hope of sleeking through the water kept her in that anticipatory place. With the world falling around her, she'd thrown a prayer to the Texas sky the night before asking for a sign—anything that would ground her here once and for all, or give her flight. Rheus answered her prayer, thankfully. Or maybe it had been the Good Lord dressed in Rheus' clothing.

He had few words for her, as if he knew her need for solitude. Just a couple instructions about the paddle, the way she sat, her lifejacket. He led; she followed as the sun spread a pathway before them. Morning commuters, oblivious to her plight, raced their way down the Highway 66 bridge toward Dallas, whooshing with each pass. But even their mechanical intrusion lessened as Willa put oar to lake.

She'd kayaked before, on Lake Union, Lake Washington, and Lake Sammamish with Hale. She could picture his face, how he looked when he put on his teacher hat, eyes centered, mouth pressed into a determined thin line. Oh, how she missed him. He'd taught her balance, showed her what to do if waves capsized her on Lake Union. Sidled up next to her and kissed her. Kept her safe. But there was no need for safety habits, really, drifting on this lake. Like every other lake in Texas except for one, Ray Hubbard's roots were grounded in technology. Bulldozers, not nature, hewed out its belly. Nonetheless, the lake teemed with fish now and became a hotspot for jet skis, fishing boats, ski boats, and sailors. Thank God the morning didn't welcome any of them.

"You are and you aren't," Rheus said in front of her, the sun silhouetting him large and luminous before them.

At first Willa puzzled over the words, having no context but the lake and the two of them skimming its surface. But since Rheus said no more, the quiet made the connection for her. She knew. But she pulled the paddle through, left, right. Left, right, hoping the rhythm would calm the racing of her heart.

She was and she wasn't.

The picture formed slowly as her oar quivered the waters. She felt the sun at her back, felt it heat her neck as the memory returned. Oh dear God, how it returned. Like a tidal wave. An angry ocean. A torrent.

forty-six

The embalming room. The smell of chemicals. The hiding place.

Willa crouched. Huddled in the room's closet, away from eyes and ears, while her parents ripped each other to tatters with words, so many words. She felt the shiver reach through her, grabbing her throat, constricting her airway. The sliver of life shown through the thin line where the door barely opened. Daddy's suit, dark grey, rumpled and moved before her. Mama's flowery dress, pink and white and green, danced in anger. Though she saw only a slice, it was enough.

"Why do you keep acting as if she's yours?"

What was Mother saying?

"She *is* mine," Daddy measured his words, seeming to hiss through teeth.

Mother leaned against the back wall, the flowers of her dress touching the green of the walls. "Say it one thousand times, but it doesn't change the truth."

"The truth," Daddy spat.

Willa kept her eye on the room, her parents, while her heart leaped inside. Not the good kind where you're anticipating the ice cream man. No. The bad kind when you know punishment is coming and you're waiting in your room for it.

"The High and Mighty One," Mother said, "can't stand that he's got an illegitimate child." Though across the room from the closet, Willa could see Mother's eyes turn cold stone gray.

What did that big, long word mean?

"Don't start," Daddy said.

"Why not? Can't you handle my words? Since I don't fit in the right box? Don't adhere to your ridiculous standards? Well, you know what? The sexual revolution freed me, last I heard, and I have a voice. I have my own way of doing things. Unfortunately, I married you with your staunch, controlling ways."

"You loved me!" Daddy's voice sounded needy just then. He slumped in a metal chair, facing the embalming table.

"Once, yes. So long ago." Mother kept her leaning. She folded slim arms across her chest.

"You left," Daddy said.

"I needed some space, away from your suffocation." Mother's voice sounded hollow now, and her eyes lightened to the color of clouds.

"So you left my family."

Mother walked from her wall, stood over Daddy, pointing a finger. "Yes, the precious Muir family. Is that a crime?"

Daddy said nothing. Willa felt her heart beat in her fingers, her neck, her gut.

"Your mama was right to walk away."

Slap! Daddy open-handed Mother's face. "You will not talk about this!"

Willa shook. She hugged herself but couldn't still the shivers.

Mother didn't look angry, or even hurt. She held the side of her face. "Maybe she loved someone else," she whispered.

"I will not be mocked!" Daddy moved closer to Mother, his arms clenched around her shoulders.

"Don't touch me."

"You're my wife. I can touch you when I please."

Willa wanted to holler a "Daddy, no," but the words stuck deep inside, held captive by the horrible made-for-TV movie playing in front of her. She hoped it was a bad dream, an illusion. But the smell of Mother's perfume mixed with the scent of Daddy's rage kept her there. In the great Right Now.

"But you couldn't produce an heir. Even after all those years."

"Shut up!" Daddy's rage purpled his face, raised his neck veins.

Mother backed away. "And it kills you that she isn't yours. Not really."

"My name's on her birth certificate. Legally, she's mine."

"But not physically. Willa is my Catherine. No matter what you name the child, she's my child. Has my stature. Has none of you whatsoever."

Willa's eyes got wet. She felt welts rising inside her throat, choking her. What did Mother mean?

"Speck!" Daddy paced the room. "He's got a hold of you still."

"Lovers seldom forget each other," Mother said. At this, she erupted in tears, her hands holding her face, tears leaking through. This was a mother Willa never knew—a broken mama. She wanted to push the door open, run to hug her, but the rest of Mother's words kept her closeted.

Daddy sat again on the chair, elbows to knees. He looked up at Mother, his eyes holding something undetectable. "She must never know of Speck Taylor," Daddy said. "And you must never speak of him again. Not in this house. Under my roof. You forget. You've exchanged your lover for affluence. For stability. While Speck runs around as a no-good drifter, you are here. With me. With Willa."

"Her name is Catherine."

Daddy said nothing. The room screamed silence. Willa could hear her breathing, and wondered if Mother and Daddy heard her thoughts. *I am Catherine. Daddy's not my daddy. And even Mother doesn't want me.*

She closed her eyes, scrunched them very tight, then told herself to believe that every word screamed and whispered in the room never existed. She shook her head of the words, now scrambled. But Daddy refocused her.

"Willa will never know her true identity. Speck Taylor will never grace this house, never set foot in these four walls. You will love her, bless her, give her the life she deserves—the life a Muir deserves." Daddy cleared his head. "Do you hear me?" His voice echoed off the embalming room's walls, ricocheting into Willa's head.

She pressed her hands to her ears. Even so, she heard Mother's voice.

"I hear you." Mother smoothed her dress on her legs, then wrung her hands. "I will speak of Speck and Catherine no more." She looked at her shoes, then up at Daddy. "Are you satisfied?"

Daddy said nothing. He nodded.

Mother left the room, her heels clacking at the floor. She didn't bother shutting the door, but Willa couldn't smell her perfume anymore. The scent of chemicals overpowered her. And just then, Daddy looked at the closet.

She felt a hiccup coming.

It came.

He walked to the door, footsteps thick on the floor.

Her knees weakened, gave way beneath her.

Her mind lolled away, but before it left completely, she heard Daddy say, "Willa."

forty-seven

The memory invigorated her arms as they neared shore. Rheus said I'm sorry, but Willa wasn't sure why. Did he see her memory? Know it already? He who was in the business of restoring memories, did he possess a magical power to see pictures, hear voices, or plant scenes into someone's head?

She felt strangely calmed, oddly assured, as they re-moored the boat. And when she dropped off Rheus at his home, she suddenly felt hungry, particularly when she smelled beef grilling from Boots Burgers a block away. She parked her car on the side of the road, not bothering that it angled toward the ditch. "A double double," she said. The man encased a hamburger in paper and threw it hastily into a white bag. She brought it home with her, ran up the stairs before it lost its heat, and devoured it while juices sluiced down her wrists, staining the comforter. What did a stain matter anyway?

She wiped her hands on a bath towel, greasing it, then stood inside the embalming room. The closet still stood there, door ajar. The bed, stripped and waiting for clean linens, couldn't cover up the room's haunted past. Willa snuck behind the closet door, letting it open just an inch. She kneeled there, mimicking her four-year-old self, watching again the bully memory.

Daddy the Valiant One morphed into the Violent One before her eyes. She pulled the locket from her neck, examining the pictures inside. Her smiling. Daddy smiling. She was his princess, and yet everything she knew about him wiped away in the closet memory. And everything she knew about Mother reoriented. Why had Willa taken so long to remember this conversation? Wouldn't it have preserved her to know the truth? Why did she block it from her mind?

She slid down the wall of the closet, locket in hand, tears in her eyes. She needed Daddy to be the hero. Needed Mother to be the villain. Her life made sense that way—her normal. If Daddy was such a man, maybe Mother broke under his control. Maybe his words made Mother hate Willa. This revelation also meant Mother loved another man and that man wasn't the best of men. Her lineage traced its DNA to a scoundrel and an adulteress.

No wonder she couldn't commit to Hale. Maybe down deep she feared she'd turn into her mother, a wild, wayward heart chasing after what wasn't good for her. Ending up with an unsatisfied, stifled life, playacting on the stage of Rockwall's elite. Mother exchanged passion for security—in some ways good in that it provided Willa with a father and a mother, a home, a place. But she wondered what Mother felt about it all, particularly if the names *Speck* and *Catherine* leaked out as death neared. Those two people she loved, even if one was gone and the other an illusion.

Willa embraced her legs, pulling arms around them as Mother would do when she stared at the wall, reclined on her bed. A simple action proving again that she was Mother's and that she'd be as capricious. If she had a mirror in the closet, she'd examine herself, noting how her hair color mirrored Mother's, but her eyes didn't match either Mother or Daddy's. Perhaps Speck had the same tonal quality her green possessed. Maybe it was his eye she saw through the ring in her nightmare.

Life reworked itself in that tiny room, through a new paradigm of her parentage. Suddenly Mother's actions made sense. Willa was the reminder of her wanderings, a token of her entrapment. Even her name, every day said out loud in the four walls of the home, declared who ruled the house. And Daddy, though obviously able to overcome loving some other man's child, iron-fisted his rule out of Willa's sight. The town. His reputation. Mother's whispers. All under his control.

It reminded Willa of Hitler, in a way. How he doted on certain people, loved his dogs, pursued affection with a select few. To them he was the most beautiful, kindhearted man they knew. But to millions of others …

Could Willa bear a dethroned, despotic father? Could her history be remade? And would it make any difference? She couldn't confront the man. Not now. Couldn't resolve what she knew now. Couldn't figure out why Daddy never mentioned their closet encounter. Never brought up her fainting other than to say, as she remembered now, "You were sick, dear one. And your mind played tricks on you. Now rest." He smoothed covers over her, wiped her forehead. Though he didn't threaten or cajole, he did make it clear in unspoken ways that this memory should be closeted.

Willa overturned the locket in her hand. She felt its smooth back, the shape of a heart opened in two. How appropriate, she thought in the dusking light of the closet. In a quick move, she bent the heart on itself until the hinge broke. She gouged out Daddy's picture with sharp nails, picking at his eyes first, then severing his face from the back of the broken heart. Glue hung on. She licked it, piercing bits of photo paper with her nails until any shred of Daddy and his coaxing eyes had disappeared completely.

And when she looked at herself, she didn't smile.

"Why didn't you tell me?" she asked herself.

But the smiling picture said nothing, still obeying Daddy's mandate. So she tore at herself, freeing her face from the gold.

She came out more easily than Daddy, peeling clear free. She held her heart-shaped self, wondered at the girl who knew so little, who knew too much. She tried to make herself have empathy for the little girl, but that was as hard as offering grace to her grown-up self—something elusive she hadn't captured. So she crumpled herself in her hand, dropped the necklace to the ground. She stood, then pressed the broken locket into the floor boards with the bottom of her Toms.

She left the embalming room, left the necklace, left her heart. Flint-faced, she left the house and drove to Mother.

forty-eight

Mother lay in the exact same position, curled in on herself. Her breaths came in shallow bursts, her eyes open. Willa pulled a chair close. Put her hand on Mother's vein-roped hand. "It's Catherine," she said.

Mother stirred. A hint of memory seemed to knife through her. She scrunched her eyes as if in concentration. "Catherine?" she wheezed.

"I know. It's okay. I know about Speck Taylor. My daddy."

Mother said nothing. The moment of recognition ebbed from her.

"Where is he, Mother? If he's my father, I need to know where he is." She tried to engage Mother's eyes, but she'd vacated her mind. She said nothing.

So Willa sat there, holding her mother's limp hand. In the dim light of the room with monitors buzzing and curtains drawn, she retold her story, only this time with truth as a backdrop. How Daddy and Mother separated, how Mother fell in love with a man named Speck, then carried his child. How Daddy took Mother back, made a home for them. How he named her Willa, protected her. How Mother saw Willa every day, a reminder of her adultery, her love now lost. How Willa eventually learned to forgive Mother and Daddy for secrets, for hidden things. She told of the time she met Speck in the little house, how fleeting it was. And the picture. She pulled it from her purse, placed it in front of Mother's eyes, but again saw no recognition. "That was my Daddy, under the pecan tree, wasn't it?"

She spoke of the one she thought was Daddy, how he loved her, protected her, cushioned her from the truth and Mother's anger. She tried to make a villain out of Daddy as she'd made of Mother all those years, but couldn't bring herself to do such a thing. Could everyone have hero and villain lurking inside? If she were honest, she'd admit such things about herself.

"We're all broken," she told the dying woman. "I am. I ran from Hale, using my mysterious past as an excuse. But you know what? Now that I know the truth, know my real story, I still have to move on. I guess I hoped in finding it, I'd be okay. Magically. Only now it's worse. Now I know far too much, and have much more to forgive. I can't blame my own actions on not knowing now. I can only choose."

Mother licked her lips, tried to speak. "Forgive," she whispered.

"I forgive you," she said. "And I'm so sorry. I didn't know the whole story." Willa felt her heart enliven at her own words, as if God had been waiting all this time to turn on the switch. All her odd distance with him now felt ridiculous. All those walls she'd built now wobbled like they'd met a Seattle earthquake. Would they crash down?

Mother blinked. Another tear traveled out the corner of her eye. She squeezed Willa's hand, then let go, drifting off to sleep.

Willa held her hand several minutes, counting Mother's breaths. She sighed, then stood. She crossed the floor, opened the drapes, and let the sun filter in. This was a day of light. Of truth. And it deserved to have the sun dance upon it.

forty-nine

Genie rocked on the front porch of the Muir House when Willa pulled up. Best get it over with, she decided. She mounted the stairway, felt each squeak beneath her feet. She sat next to Genie, the same spot Hale took when he visited, a position Willa never bothered to duplicate in Hale's absence. She and Genie weren't exactly companions.

"I know," Willa said. She could've elaborated, stringing together sentences of discovery, but fatigue got the best of her. It felt as if she'd been playing the longest game of Monopoly, only to end it all by mortgaging her hotels and getting out. Way too much time had passed.

Genie didn't look her way. "We know a good many things. Doesn't make them true." Genie rocked. In the spring breeze that scurried through the porch and beyond the house, her hair didn't move.

"My father's name is Speck Taylor."

Genie said nothing in the silence that followed. She played with her hands on her lap, overlapping fingers, lacing and unlacing them.

"And Mother is still my mother."

More rocking. Time to sell everything, Willa told herself, to exit this game. "So I must have a daddy somewhere. Do you happen to know Speck's whereabouts?"

"A sister knows these things," is all Genie said before she gathered her hands, her self, and her words and left the porch.

fifty

Blog Title: I need you.

Hale, I feel like I'm lost in that U2 song about still not finding what I'm looking for. I know the truth now, ugly as it is. And in some ways it has set me free, but in other ways I'm stuck. It would take too long to explain here, especially as stark words on a screen. Would you please call me? Or text? I need to talk to you. Need to hear your voice. I suppose I don't deserve any of those things. Not now, anyhow.

Remember that locket my daddy gave me? With him and me smiling inside? I broke it. Intentionally. Ripped us both out of there forever. That's the gravity of how I feel. Ripped away. As if I'd never been born.

If it's any consolation, you were right. Even if I didn't know the whole truth, I needed to live life in light of what I knew. To jump into the irresistible future with both feet, eager to risk. I'm telling you, I'm fragile, nearly broken. My walls have been toppled, but I'm not sure I'm ready to let someone storm on in. Even myself.

Though I can't put words to the journey, God is helping me make sense of it all. That would thrill you, wouldn't it?

I feel as if I've been watching me live my life. I'm above it, calling the shots, but can't seem to connect to my soul. Can't connect my heart to my actions somehow. Does that make any sense? Probably not. Which is why I need you to call me. Please.

Love, Willa …

She hit *publish*, then waited in her room. She looked through the back windows toward the carriage house, wondering if Genie stalked back and forth there, cursing under her breath at her failure to keep her brother's secret.

Willa realized this made Genie her aunt. How could that possibly be? Way too much truth roared into Willa's mind then — she had an aunt, a living father, an entirely different identity. If things had happened according to Mother's will, she'd be signing her checks Catherine Taylor. Would that Catherine have dated Blake? Escaped to Seattle? Met Hale? What would her life have looked like in that dynamic?

A hodgepodge of vistas, memories, thoughts mixed together like an unlikely stew in her mind. They dizzied her, making no sense.

Her cell buzzed. She checked it — a text! Willa exhaled, then scrolled down to find Hale's message. Only it wasn't Hale. It was Blake, asking to see her. Of course, he'd want to know what she uncovered — for research purposes. It wouldn't hurt to see him, right? So she texted an invitation to meet at Harry Myers. He said yes.

Blake wove her through the Frisbee golf course, around brambles and wilds, preferring cover to open fields. It suited Willa fine, this camouflage. Her words came in halts, similar to their zigzagging trajectory. She emptied herself of the new story, leaving nothing out, feeling all at once alive in letting someone other than Mother or Genie, or even Rheus in his own way, in on the reality of her situation.

"Wow," Blake said. "That's a lot."

On the edge of the course, a picnic table stood. Blake sat on top. Willa did too. "I know. I felt like I would burst with the news. Sorry to verbally vomit on you."

"It's okay. I get it."

Willa felt suddenly aware of their surroundings, isolated, sitting on a lone picnic table while the sun filtered through too-tall trees. Though the air neared eighty degrees, she shivered. Something about Blake's tone of voice made her self-conscious, but she preferred silence to voicing her concerns.

He put his arm around her shoulders, then scooted next to her. Their thighs touched. The verbal vomit she'd hurled stung her throat now.

"I'm so glad you've trusted me with this," he said.

"I—"

He held his finger to her mouth. Shushed her as he did before. So much like Daddy's interaction with Mother, it took her breath away. *Get out of here*, she told herself, but her legs wouldn't move. In fact the only thing pummeling her, the only active part, was her heart thumping her chest.

"No need to talk," Blake said. His words sounded snake-like, almost. Had all his niceties been a façade, just waiting to reveal his real self? "I know you. I've loved you for a long time. I've seldom given other women a thought. I saw you first, you know. Then noticed you afresh in the back of art class, the way your hair played across your face, how you hid beneath it. I loved you then. And soon you loved me too. Once."

"I can't talk about this right now." She felt revulsion and intrigue as strange twin emotions. The smell of Blake, his captivating dedication intermingled with his forward, nearly insistent words knotted her insides.

"Talking's not what I had in mind. We've done enough of that." He bent near her, his lips nearly brushing hers. She tried to focus, to understand, but his lips covered hers then. Hungry lips, they were. Nearly angry in their ferocity, like they were ripping away her soul with each touch. She'd nearly forgotten passion, other than the last time she'd been in this park, stealing a kiss from Hale. Had he felt what she felt right now? A mixture of enticement and dread? Willa pulled away.

"What's wrong?"

"I don't know. It's Hale. He's — "

"Not here. Not the first to hear your story. Not the first to shoulder your burdens. Not the first to steal a kiss."

"*Stolen* is the appropriate word." Willa scooted from under his arm, then stood opposite him. Blake's eyes hungered for her. She felt what she'd been feeling all along with him but couldn't identify — that awful trap of commodity. She was a thing to be had. A possession to be paid for by Blake's proximity. She owed him because he listened to her sorry story, and he would take her.

Blake put his hands in the air, as if pushing her away. "Listen, I wouldn't have tried anything had you not sent me a thousand clues about your attraction."

Willa looked at her feet, then kicked the dust beneath. An infantry of fire ants roared to life. She jumped away, brushing her shoes free of them. Once safe, she looked at Blake, found his green, green eyes. "You're right," she said. "I shouldn't have indulged. Shouldn't have flirted. Not with my inside world so crazy. I don't think I should trust any man right now. Not after Daddy becoming a different man after his death. Not after Hale left me here and stopped communicating. Not after you just kissed me, trying to rekindle something long over."

"It's not over."

Willa sat on the far end of the picnic table, away from Blake's reach, his eyes. "You like the idea of me."

"I love you."

She felt the words bite her heart for the longest second, felt their teeth. Smarting like a fire ant attack only to itch later. She wanted to be loved, longed to be wanted. But not in this way. Not with this man. "I'm sorry," she said. "For so many things."

She looked at her hands. "How can I thank you for all your help? Support?"

"By saying yes to me. By making right what you did years ago. You left me, Willa. It was you who walked away. It took years to forgive and get my heart screwed on straight. I'm fine now. In my right heart. And I've forgiven."

"I had to go away."

"I understand that now. Everyone has to leave home, find themselves. I did that in college. But I came home. And now you have too."

Home weaseled through her. She remembered Hale's words about him being home. She thought of her home in Seattle, now ashen fertilizer. She thought of Genie's rocking on the porch of her home, scowling. Where was home? After the marathon of thoughts that stretched the silence between them, Willa said, "I'm not sure what home is."

Blake reached his hand across the expanse of wood between them. He touched the top of her hand, then withdrew. "I'll make you a home. I promise. Just give me a chance."

She shifted in her seat to face him. "No," she simply said.

Blake stood. "No?"

She nodded.

He shook his head, then leveled green-eyed anger her way. "You're a tease, Willa Muir."

"You're probably right. And I'm also a big, fat cry-fest right now. The only thing *home* means to me is chaos and confusion. You're better off without me."

Blake opened his mouth, looked as if he were about to speak, but he simply turned away, slump shouldered. He padded down the course, never looking back, while Willa counted each step a painful victory.

And yet each step he took, she felt all the more alone.

fifty-one

"Hale." She said his name to the treetops, but he didn't answer back.

"Jesus, then." He didn't seem to answer back either. She'd played his game on the streets and back alleys of Rockwall, said the prayers, memorized her verses to get gold stars, yet she felt strangely distant from Jesus in this place. Even covered by his creation here, she wondered if he would love her now. She who flirted then flung, who felt the sting of being unwanted by her real father, her mother. She'd let herself become fascinated again when Hale translated Jesus for her. His counterintuitive ways, the manner in which he wooed widows and bleeding women, his invitation to a sincere, loving life. Under Hale's gentle tutelage, Jesus resurrected for her.

A warm April wind blew around her, disturbing fall's left-over leaves. Several minutes had passed since Blake's departure. In the stillness, Willa pondered her walls, her fortresses, her control. With everything up in the air, she felt unsettled. Which is why she pled for an anchor in Hale, in Jesus.

The strange prophecy returned. Then magically lengthened.

You'll find home one day, sure as sweet tea on a hot afternoon. And when you solve its mystery, get yourself to a rocker to catch your fall.

The rocker, in this instance, was a picnic table. She had no sweet tea, though the thought of it thirsted her. She'd found the truth, but not home. She found the hole, but not the substance filling it.

She wished Hale were here to help her sort everything out, but then again, what would he say? Under another set of trees, sitting on two boulders perched above a trickling stream, Willa remembered Hale's answer.

"Just tell me how to believe, what to believe." Willa's voice wasn't much louder than the stream's steady flowing.

"I can't do that, Wills."

"But you're so assured of your belief! Me? I'm a doubter."

"Doubters — that's all of us. You're in good company." Hale reached down, grabbed a smooth stone, and pitched it across the creek. It hit a tree, then thudded on the bracken below.

"You're not going to help me?"

"I can ask you questions. Will that help?"

Willa grabbed her own rock, flung it heavenward, only to see it hit nothing and disappear into the woods. "Yes, I guess so."

"What are your three favorite movies? Quick now, you can't think about it. Just list them."

Willa flustered, tried to think.

"Don't think. Just tell me. What are they?"

About a Boy, *The Sound of Music*, and *The Princess Bride*."

Hale laughed. "Interesting."

"Is there a point to this?"

"Yes. I want you to think about the common thread between the three."

Willa tried to make the connections between a quirky British drama, a musical with Nazi overtones, and a silly farce. What could possibly connect them all? "I have no idea," she said.

"Think about it, Willa. All three of the main characters are orphaned in a way. The boy's mom in *About a Boy* is crazy and distant. Maria doesn't have parents, it seems, and Buttercup is the same. All characters are trying to find meaning in family. That's you."

The sun, which had been fickle, dashing in and out of gray clouds, came out to play now, shining brilliantly on the two of them, rockbound. It almost felt as if God put an exclamation mark on Hale's sentence. "That's insightful," she finally said. "I don't have a family anymore."

"But you're looking, searching, longing. Right?"

She nodded.

"What if that's what Jesus is all about? About helping you find your family in him? Maybe your quest is everyone's quest. And your answer is everyone's answer."

"What if? You have a lot of questions."

"I'm great at asking questions. You've told me that before. Might as well major on my majors!"

Willa let Hale's questions meander through her. Let them soak into her marrow, her heart. "You're into quests, aren't you?"

"In every way. Take *The Princess Bride*. It's a story of questing."

"True."

"Think of God as the Dread Pirate Roberts, if you can. Only on a bigger scale."

"God is not a pirate."

Hale winked at her. "In a way, he is. He searches for us like treasure, boards our hearts, then captures them."

"I guess so," Willa said.

"You guess so? Think of it as the greatest love story. The story that frames every story, even yours shrouded in mystery. God lost his bride, then took extraordinary means to find her. He, as king, becomes pauper to better find her, to understand her world. He finds her captured by an evil dominator, risking his life to free her from his grip. In the quest, he considers her freedom more important than his romance, so he willingly offers his life in exchange for hers. And unlike the ending of Romeo and Juliet, when all is darkest and dreary, she finds the king now alive, radiant. He sweeps her into his arms, brings her to his castle, and showers her with devotion. This is *the* story, Wills."

"But my story's so different. What if I don't feel God pursuing me in that way?"

"What you feel isn't the same as what is true."

Willa shook her head. Maddening, maddening Hale. Did he always have to be so secure? So logical? "Well, I have to say, I like feeling things, Hale. Feelings aren't all that bad. You should try them once in a while."

"I have them plenty. I just choose not to show them to the world."

"How convenient!" Willa laughed. "So are you saying me showing my feelings is wrong?"

"No, just different. Which is why I love you." He stepped over to her boulder, his left foot splashing into the water as he did.

She smiled. "You say that a lot."

"You need it a lot."

"True."

He kissed her on the cheek, his arm lanky over her shoulders. She rested her head on his torso, blinking under the still-happy sun.

"I make a poor Jesus," he told her. "I'm not the best at the quest."

"Stop this rhyming and I mean it!"

"Anybody want a peanut?" Lines from *The Princess Bride* jockeyed back and forth between them until they both laughed and held their bellies.

They stood together, picked their way through the protruding rocks on the stream, inhaling evergreen. They held hands. Willa felt the familiarity of Hale then, loving how their hands felt right clasped like that. Almost like God had intertwined them to fit. That day, she believed in Jesus.

fifty-two

But as Willa walked through Harry Myers' woods, she felt no hand in hers, and the loneliness suffocated her afresh. Maybe she needed the last piece of her story to find home. Maybe locating and meeting Speck would quilt her heart into something cohesive. The final square of fabric, perhaps.

An all-at-once purpling cloud dumped shovelfuls of rain on her car as she drove home. All that water from such an angry sky reminded Willa of her own untapped reserves of anger and sadness. Would she break, finally, as every new discovery settled into her? She'd read about trauma, how folks endured it valiantly, only to fall apart when everything settled. While the windshield wipers tried in vain to push away sheets of rain, she knew it was only a matter of time before the water—and her grief—prevailed.

She parked in front of the Muir House. Something seemed odd as she dashed through the rain to the cover of the front porch. She tried the door. Locked. Tried the other door. Same thing. So she ventured to the left side of the house, its third door. No good. Genie's car sat in the back part of the property, her apartment above the carriage house blazing light, a beacon in the darkness, though the last thing Willa wanted to do was to knock on Genie's life.

But, unless she wanted to live in her car or take up residence at the library and face Blake, she had to. Trudging through the backyard while mud slicked under her shoes, she picked her way to the carriage house door. It gave, thankfully.

She wiped her feet on the welcome mat, then mounted the narrow steps, trying to rehearse her words, but before she could, Genie stood mid-stairs, blocking her way.

"What do you want?"

"I'm locked out of the big house." Willa brushed away wet strands of hair from her face. "Can I please have the key?"

Genie shook her head, her face unregistering any emotion. She mounted the rest of the stairs, opened her door.

Willa followed, then shut the door. She pulled off her jacket, folded it inside out so as not to drip, then sat on one of Genie's feather-fluffed chairs, though the invitation to sit never came.

"I suppose you found what you're looking for." Genie shifted things in the kitchen, clanking pots and pans, clinking glasses.

"I don't know. You tell me," Willa said. No use in playing things nice. A fatigue deeper than a mono-induced sleep settled on her. In the coolness of the air conditioning, she felt hot.

"A good many things are settled in your mind, but they're not in mine."

"Care to elaborate?" Willa found lip balm in her purse, then applied it liberally.

Genie walked toward Willa and sat in the opposite chair. In typical fashion, she crossed her arms over herself like armor.

"Please. I need a key. And for the icing on the cake, I'd love to know where your brother, my father, is."

"You ask a lot."

"I deserve a response."

The silence between them grew. The ticking clock pounded now. Or was that Willa's heart?

Genie sighed. She looked to her right, staring through the bank of windows, past the pecan tree, toward the house. "This has been my life."

270 / MARY DeMUTH

"I thought it had been mine. Now none of it's true."

"You were loved."

Willa threw her hands skyward. "Really? Because I'm having a hard time seeing that so-called love. My daddy who adored me silenced my mother. I was more a pawn in his little game of control than a daughter apparently. And my mother? She couldn't stand looking at me. I must have been a walking billboard for her transgression and her affection for your brother. You love me? Hardly. And Blake, who I thought was my friend, really only wanted me as a thing to have, not a person to love—which I knew all along, but conveniently forgot. So you tell me, Genie Skye. Exactly how was I loved?" Willa felt the anger storm through her. Wet eyes proved the waterworks would come. She pulled in a few breaths, told herself not to fall apart here.

"No need to raise your voice." Genie looked into her eyes then, a mixture of anger and something else living there.

"If you'd had the days I've had, you wouldn't tell me to calm down."

"I imagine it's hard. But you got what you came for, right? Shouldn't you be celebrating? Hasn't the truth set you free?"

Determined not to cry, Willa pulled a mirror from her purse. She checked her eyes which still looked like they'd burst. Instead she ran a finger under her eyes where the eyeliner had smudged, as if doing something so rudimentary would change the sadness, would stop the eruption. She placed the mirror back in her purse, then looked at Genie. "I'm glad in some ways. I'm thankful to finally know everything." In the split second after she said *everything*, Willa remembered. The plastic flower. The woman. This room. "I stayed with you?"

"Beg your pardon?"

"Right here. I stayed here. In the carriage house."

Genie said nothing, but her face drained white.

"I must've been four years old, during the dark year. When did I live here?"

Shaking her head, Genie let out a sigh. "Mr. Muir asked me to keep you a spell."

"How long is a spell?" Willa's stomach hiccupped, sending bile up her throat. She swallowed.

"A few months while he and your mother worked things out. You still slept in your own bed, but I kept you during the days."

"Plastic flowers," Willa whispered.

"What?"

"It doesn't matter." The memory took complete shape now. The flower. Genie. Her harsh words. Proof that Willa was unwanted. "Is that when I saw Speck?"

"Only a few times. It was a risk, you know. He used to color with you. Do you remember?"

Willa shook her head, hoping to unscramble the memory further, but no recollection of Speck came to her. Only the memory of him talking about her eyes and walking away. And the strange letter about her artistic bent. Only that. "I was in the way," she said.

"I thought so at the time." A hitch unhinged in Genie's voice. "But it was me who was in the way. Me with my own opinions and prejudices, protecting Speck. I only thought of him, of me."

The weight of it all. The words. The memories. Heaviness crashed into her soul. Did no one really care for her? Every thread of stability wove itself into a rag rug like the one beneath Willa's feet, around and around itself, only to have it pulled out from underneath her.

Genie fidgeted, as if she understood the calamity pounding in Willa's heart.

Willa hardened herself. Took a breath. She looked at Genie.

"I would think you'd be relieved to have all this truth out in the open, but you seem more agitated."

"I am protecting him."

"Who?"

"My brother Speck."

"My father!"

"It's not a good time to visit."

Willa felt her resolve elongate, strengthen. "If I stay and try to see my biological father, I'm meddling. If I leave, I'm fulfilling some strange destiny you've decided for me."

"That's what you're saying."

Willa shook her head. "Why is it so wrong to want some closure? To see the man who gave me up?"

"My brother," she said, "cannot see you. Not now. Probably never!" Her voice shook as she delivered the last bit of pronouncement, as if she meant it with every sinew in her tightly wound soul. She strode toward the windows with bleak determination. Back turned to Willa, her shoulders heaved.

"He is my father." The only one left, she almost said.

Genie turned, red-faced. "But I have taken care of him, worried about him, provided for him most of his life, you understand?"

"What?" Willa stood. "So you deserve him? Like he's yours? You may share his DNA, but I do too in the most intimate way. I'm his child, for crying out loud!" But even as she said it, she wondered if she could handle seeing Speck. What if he turned away, indifferent? Like he did in the middle of the night, his flashlight bobbing as he left. Did she really want to risk a visit?

Genie sat. "Sit down, please." Her voice sounded otherworldly, like it disconnected from her when she settled into the chair.

Willa sat again, her shoes touching the rag rug beneath. "We've been here before."

"I know. Just listen."

"Apparently my time is running short."

Genie put her head in her hands, making Willa regret her snappy comment. Genie removed her hands, then ruffled her hair between searching fingers. "I'm sorry," she said. "I was the one who brought your parents together. I shouldn't have."

Willa let the words sift through her. "You introduced them?"

"Yes."

"Then why would Daddy keep you caretaking the place?"

"He didn't want it, exactly, but he's dead now, and your mother's alive. She kept me near to keep an eye on Speck. To report on him. As if there were anything to report."

"Then why don't you have the same last name as Speck?"

"I was married once—to a man like your father. Controlling. Confusing. An enigma. I kept his name, but left him behind."

"I'm sorry," was all Willa could say.

"Don't be. I'm meant to be single. It suits me."

Perhaps it suited Willa too. With Hale not talking or texting or writing and Blake out of the picture, Willa wondered if she could be whole without a love interest. "I'd really like to see my father," she said. Did she mean it?

"I know. It's just—"

"Complicated? Why did I know that? Searching for secrets has been like catching a giant octopus, with tentacles everywhere. Just when I grab one, it slimes away from me."

"In this case, the octopus is dying." Genie said her sentence steady, but her eyes shimmered.

"What?"

"My brother. Your father. Dying."

"How? Where?"

"He's not far. In Dallas. But he's nearing death. I'm just not sure he'd be able to take a visit from you."

"Please, Genie." Willa felt the dam behind her eyes give way, as if it had been held up with sticks and tiny rocks, not cement walls. She let out the grief, the stress, the bewilderment all at once. Or rather, it burst through her, not bothering to ask permission. Sobs bent her over. Oxygen felt scarce. A headache roared. Tears flew. Grief strangled. Her world narrowed to a tiny pinprick on the floor. She stared at it while her body convulsed. She felt a hand on her shoulder, a warm hand, but she didn't bat it away. No energy to. "I can't," she said, "breathe."

"You can and you will." Genie sat on the arm of the chair, placed her arm around Willa's heaving shoulders. "Take in a breath. There. Now let it out."

Willa obeyed. She had to.

"Another breath."

The pinprick widened. She saw the rug beneath her feet. Inhaled again.

"Easy. In and out."

Willa felt a snatch of connection, as if God came near in her weeping. Genie, the cold one, touched her as a mother should, spoke soothing words over her — a thing she longed for all her life. Didn't realize until now how much a mother's touch meant, how she craved it, deadened the longing, then buried it forever. Only now, under Genie's touch, the desire unburied. And her need for motherly affection resurrected.

"There you go. Keep breathing."

Willa melted into the down cushions, finally sitting back. Her face felt hot and sticky, and her eyes burned from the explosion of tears.

Genie left, then returned with some toilet paper. "I don't use Kleenex," she said. "This'll do."

Willa blew her nose, wiped her face, crumpled the wad, and set it on the table next to her. Genie picked it up and threw it away.

"I had no idea," Genie said, "that when I introduced Speck to your mother that they'd fly into each other's arms. Nor did I think she'd get pregnant after all those years your father and mother tried. There was no mistaking, at least in my eyes, that the baby wasn't Mr. Muir's."

"Then why the deception?" Willa hugged herself. Shivers erupted again and again.

"For reputation, I suppose. And fear too. You've heard about his mother leaving, right?"

Willa nodded.

"I think it bothered him more than he let on. Like it stooped his soul a bit. We all could see it, but he tried to cover his need for his real mother way deep. Funny how others can see your pain before you see it."

Willa thought of Hale again. Missed him even more.

"So he must've made a vow that he would not be part of a family where the mother walked away. Oh, your mother wanted to, but just not enough. She gave up when he wouldn't hear of it. Which is why he forbade Speck to see you."

"I don't remember coloring, but I do remember seeing him at least twice."

"You do?"

Willa fished through her purse, found the photo, and showed it to Genie. "This is him, isn't it?"

Genie nodded. "That's Speck."

"I don't know when it was taken. I must've been three or four."

"Looks that way. Under the pecan."

"And then I saw him late one night when I was hiding in the utility shed. He didn't say much, though."

"Let me tell you a little secret."

Willa sighed. "No secret is little, as far as I can tell."

"Speck loved you."

276 / MARY DeMUTH

The words had no life, no connection to history. They simply were, as if Genie had said, "Ronald Regan was an actor turned president." History might prove her right, but that didn't make it real to someone who'd never met the man. "What does it matter?" she finally asked.

"He wanted to be your father. He gave you your first name."

"Catherine," Willa said.

"Yes."

"If he was so interested in being my daddy, why didn't he fight?"

"Because it's hard to fight a hero like your dad. And my brother wasn't exactly a focused man. He drifted, chasing after schemes and such. And he dabbled in drink and drugs. But I will tell you this: he tried when he found out your mother was pregnant. For him, it was the most valiant effort, but even that meant nothing to your father."

"You make Daddy sound like a tyrant."

"He was a good many things, your father. Stubbornness was his strongest suit, and often it trumped any other trait. He wanted you. He wanted a family. So he made it happen."

Willa shifted in her chair. An echo of birds chattered outside the window reminding her of springtime, of life outside the walls of the carriage house. She'd have to leave here, eventually. "Yes," she said. "He made it happen. So what did Speck do then?"

The lines around Genie's eyes softened. The hands-on-hips tyrant who met her halfway up the stairs had curled into a strange kindness. "He did what Speck's always done — exited. He went to find himself. Only problem was, trouble had a keen way of finding him. Drugs, theft, homelessness, to name a few."

"Homeless?" With all her obsession with home and magazines and clipping pictures, how could someone who fathered her be houseless? Her father, a man not unlike the men Hale helped.

"Afraid so. I spent several years looking for him, searching here and there, culling the Internet. I finally found him in Northern California in some sort of tent community by the beach. He'd borrowed someone's computer to write short stories. They actually were quite good, but they always involved a man losing something—a diamond worth everything, a prized racehorse stolen, a castle besieged. He was writing about you, Willa."

Willa felt paralysis in her hands, as if they could only stay folded on her lap. Her body couldn't respond to this news, couldn't indulge the story in her head.

"Do you need more toilet paper?" Genie looked behind her toward the bathroom.

"No, I'll be okay."

"So I found him. Paid for a ticket to fly out there, hoping to locate him. I went from tent to tent showing folks pictures of Speck. They'd seen him all right, but he'd just left."

"When was this?"

"About seven years ago when you were in college."

The same time Willa realized the hole. "I need to go," she said. A hurricane swirled in her stomach, nauseating her. "Now." Before Genie could protest, Willa ran out the door, down the stairs, and sprinted toward the house. She tripped over one of the pecan's roots and flew toward earth, splatting in the mud. She tried to get up, but vomit exploded through her. Over and over again, waves of pain vomited on the clay-sloppy earth. She felt Genie's hand again, but didn't hear her voice. The unleashing of tears minutes before had opened up the very worst of Willa, every fear, every pain, every dashed hope. She hurled her sadness all over the grass—an illegitimate girl, unloved. And now completely, utterly alone—save for the cold hand of her aunt on her shoulder.

fifty-three

The bed softened beneath her as if it'd been made of feathers. The sheets, like silk, cocooned her. While Willa fought sleep-drunk dreams, memories invaded. Pictures of Daddy hollering at Mother, of Speck standing under the pecan, of Willa in a strange tug-of-war between the three, pulled in every direction. Who was she? Why was she? And who really loved her?

The green-eyed man from her dreams, the ring circling his eye, returned now. He didn't smile, didn't frown either. He simply beckoned with his hand, inviting her to come. But she couldn't move.

She wrestled awake, again feeling the sheets. Next to her bed stood a tall glass of ginger ale, and in the chair opposite her, slumped Genie, asleep. Willa tried to get up, but her head roared, and the resulting dizziness kept her bedbound. Genie stirred, opened tired-looking eyes. "What time is it?" she asked.

Genie fumbled in the darkness, found her watch. "Five-thirty in the morning."

Willa remembered the locked doors. The tree. The vomit. "How did I get up here?"

"It wasn't easy, but I called Rheus. He helped me."

"He's a good man."

"The best, actually."

Willa closed her eyes, then opened them. "You should marry him."

Genie cleared her throat. "It's always easier to tell someone she should marry than to actually be the someone considering it."

Willa let those words inch through her aching head. True, so true. She pictured Hale extending the ring her way, the Oasis Café, the longing he held in his eyes for Willa to say yes, and Willa's flight away toward a burning house. From the promise of a new life to a devastation of the current one. She thought of Speck's flight too, and made connections—like father, like daughter. "Speck, you must've found him?"

"You ran clear out of the place before I could tell you the end of the story." Genie opened the plantation shutters, then pushed open a window. "It's stuffy in here." The light, just a graying pink, edged its way into the room.

"Did you find him in California?"

"No, I found him here."

"In Rockwall?"

"On the stoop of the carriage house, years—a lifetime—later. He slept there—to me, the most beautiful person on the earth. I reckon that's what mothers feel when they see their babies sleep after a long, trying day of screaming and carrying on. He seemed so peaceful there."

"When was this?" Willa sat herself up, but the nausea continued, so she curled back down under the sheets, keeping her head pointed Genie's way.

"The same day as your house fire in Seattle."

Willa let the words travel through her. "So when I contacted you about coming to stay, you'd already found him?"

"Yes. He was sick, though."

"I'm sorry."

Genie said nothing for a long time. Willa couldn't add words either. She rested in the palpable stillness, oddly comfortable.

"Does he have cancer?" Willa felt *cancer* in her gut, worried about it, hated the word.

"No."

"What then?"

Genie sighed. "He's HIV positive, Willa."

Willa felt the need to cry, but her eyes were as dry as a dusty shelf. "Oh."

"Rheus tells me you should see him, that it would be a good bookend for him."

"I want to see him," Willa said.

"I know. But now it's time to rest. I need to get back to my place, take a shower."

"What can I do?" Willa asked.

"Just rest."

Genie left the room. Willa took a sip of ginger ale. She nearly opened her laptop, almost checked her phone for a message from Hale, but instead let both rest as well. The thought of not seeing words from Hale sickened her more than the already-boiling battle in her stomach.

No, she would rest, and in the meantime, try to conjure up the strength to see Speck so she could close this chapter on her life and move on.

fifty-four

With Genie bustling around downstairs readying it for a small party of guests, Willa grounded herself by cutting pictures of houses — a white Victorian, a cedar-sided cabin, an ultra-modern cement monstrosity, a low-slung throwback to Frank Lloyd Wright, a children's playhouse with clapboard siding. She slid them into her Bible, then thought it best to read the words. Jesus spoke about worry, about birds of the air, about his father taking care of us. "I'm sorry," she said to the red words on the page. "I've neglected you."

Rebbie stopped by and played Scrabble with Willa in her room, filling in the day of recovery, while Willa regrouped, healed, and tried not to worry about the future. Rebbie kept topics light, thankfully, but her nearness proved a deepening friendship.

"How in the world did you ever get so many points from the word *filament?*" Rebbie scowled, but it didn't last long. She laughed in the next second as if fate told her a joke.

"Triple word score, plus multiple completions of horizontal words." Willa pointed out how she completed two other words with *filament.* Hale would call her genius, she knew. He'd taught her the technique at the beach one summer while they played travel Scrabble on a large flattened driftwood disc. Memories of Hale seemed to intensify now, ever since she received his text yesterday. "I'm letting go, Wills," it said. But she couldn't let go.

"Blake's sad, you know." Rebbie burst through Willa's trip down memory lane.

"What is this? Junior high? How do you know?"

"We're friends," Rebbie said. "He talks to me."

"Is he okay?"

"He will be." Rebbie pushed away a long strand of hair from her face. "He feels kind of stupid that he took the bait and pursued you again. Said he should've known better with your fiancé and all."

Willa looked at her oh-so-empty ring finger. "He's not my fiancé anymore."

"What?"

"He's letting go. Moving on."

"What about Blake, then?"

"We're not meant for each other. That's clear to me now."

Rebbie played the word *scurry* for a good many points, inching nearer to Willa's score. "I'm sorry, on all accounts. What are you going to do now?"

"I don't know."

"You can stay with me. It's been so long since I've had a roommate. Oh we could have so much fun, running around at night, hanging out for lunch, making dinner for each other. What do you say?"

Willa held up her hands. "Hold your horses! I'll probably go back to Seattle once I see Speck and settle things up here."

"But Seattle's not your home. Rockwall is."

"To tell you the truth, I have no idea where home is. I've found the truth, just as I searched for it, and now I haven't a clue what to do, or where my real home is."

"Home is people, Willa."

"You sound like Hale."

"Well, if I sound like him, that's probably a compliment. Anyone who would want to marry you has great taste, I would say."

"Thanks, except that I ran away from him."

"Running away is normal. Lord knows I've done plenty of sprinting in my time. It's natural."

"Yeah, but when it marks your whole life and it's a pattern passed down from father to daughter, you tend to think it's a huge problem."

"So what's the big deal?"

Willa exhaled, then placed *quince* on the board, widening the Scrabble score gap for good. "The big deal is that I am destined to be alone."

"Says who?"

Willa wondered at Rebbie's words. They echoed Hale's about today's choices in light of the past. "I do, I guess."

"Well, then, change."

"You make it sound easy."

"Isn't making one choice easy?"

"I suppose."

Rebbie took the Scrabble board, bent it in half, and poured the balsa tiles into the box.

"Hey, we weren't done!"

"Well, I was. I could see the end. So I made a choice. I ended the game. Seems you could do the same. Make a choice to end the running game. Don't let life happen to you. Make life happen."

"You sound like a motivational speaker."

Rebbie stood, then laughed. Her blonde hair caught the sun in that second, dancing golden. "Lord willing, I'll be one someday. But first I have to build my catering business into something big."

"If anyone can, it's you." It felt good to shed the moping Willa, to think beyond herself, her dreams, and cheer another's.

"Thanks," Rebbie said. She spied the ring on Willa's nightstand. Picked it up. "And if I were you, I'd start pursuing the man who gave you this ring. Don't take his moving on as a permanent no."

fifty-five

Rheus and Genie sat next to Willa as she brushed Mother's hair straight. It splayed dry against the white cotton pillowcase, but its shimmer had waned. Rheus helped secure permission to move Mother home yesterday, and Genie found Ellen, a hospice nurse, to stay with Mother as her breaths came in ragged spurts. Ellen told them this morning that most likely it'd be Mother's last day on earth.

Last day. What would Willa do if she knew it was her last day? The answer came quicker than she thought, almost reflexively. She'd follow Rebbie's advice and find Hale.

But that quest would have to wait. Willa tried not to let her emotions get the best of her, but with each thin breath Mother breathed, she felt her own resolve weaken. So much mourning filled her heart — of a mother who never quite loved her, of regrets of her own bitterness and unforgiveness, of losing her family. She looked up at Genie, catching grief in her eyes too. Was Speck this close to death?

Willa felt the song come upon her. She took a deep breath, then sang out, "Ain't no sunshine when she's gone" into the room. Daddy's song for her, sung over a mother who felt trapped, who now struggled against death in the haze of the room. The sun filtered through the gauzy drapes of the embalming room, lighting on Mother as if to say it would hold on until she let go. The four-poster bed loomed large in the room while Mother seemed to shrink.

Rheus cleared his throat. "Should I be here? In this holy moment?"

Willa almost said stay, but Genie answered by grabbing Rheus' hand. Genie led him toward the door, hand in hand, then looked at Willa. "I know you've had your rough patches, but it's time to make peace. And only you two can resolve that now." Her voice bereft of empathy, Genie did hold a look of concern in her eyes.

"Thanks," Willa said.

She scooted in close so she could speak softly in Mother's ear. She tried to say something, but as the word *Mother* came from her mouth, grief overflowed. She shifted away, cradling her head in her hands, weeping. She tried to stifle her sobs, but couldn't. Still, Genie must've known she needed this time alone. No one opened the embalming room door.

She steadied herself, looked down at Mother who still pulled in earth's air, then noticed the opened closet. There, still on the floor, lay the broken locket — a talisman for a time such as this. She left Mother's side to pick up the pieces. Daddy no longer stared at her from one half. She'd been erased too, by her own hand. What was left was gold, broken at that.

She remembered the Sunday school verse about each person's work being burned up at the end of time, how some would have their works burned like hay and stubble, where others would have a pile of gold after the scorching fire. Seeing her home in Seattle buckle and succumb to flames reminded her of dust. When it breathed its last, no gold remained. Only empty memories and the smell of smoke.

Would Mother walk on streets of gold? Would God pardon her anger beautifully? Would her works burn into nothingness? Willa regretted, again, obeying Mother's mandate to leave her alone. She should've been a tenacious daughter, doting on Mother as Daddy had doted on her. She'd returned her affection to Daddy in like kind. Unfortunately, though, she'd returned Mother's neglect in the exact manner. Kindness for kindness. Neglect for neglect.

She tried to repair the locket, but when she ripped it apart, the hinge broke in several places. So much like her heart. Would it ever be whole again? Would God see fit to grace her with kindness? Or would she roam the earth as a vagabond, broken and world weary? Like Mother, would she travel her last years alone?

Willa stuffed the broken locket into her jeans pocket, then held Mother's frail hand, her skin, papery, cold to the touch, as if no blood pumped through her veins and capillaries anymore. She looked at Mother's face, tortured yet serene. Fighting death yet longing for it, she seemed.

"Mother, it's Catherine."

Mother stirred, opened her opaque eyes, then closed them.

"I miss you. I know I haven't always told you that, especially not when I moved to Seattle. We've traded plenty of words to the contrary, wouldn't you say?"

Mother said nothing.

"I don't expect you to speak. Let's just assume we're on the same page here, okay? Let's both say we have regrets listed aplenty. Can't we just erase them right now? Get things right?"

Mother's grip tensed a bit, then let go. Perhaps she understood.

"I know you've had a hard life. I know you said those things because you were broken yourself. I wish I had understood that as a kid. Wish I'd given more grace. But I can't remake me then. And you can't redo you. We're old rooms in need of decorating, but neither of us has the will. Certainly not now."

Willa steadied herself. She felt a choke of tears coming, but she knew her eyes had expended all of them already. Dry heaving would not help her sentences come out, so she told herself to relax, to say the words needing said. "I love you, Mother."

Mother opened her eyes again. She licked dry lips. Sucked in another wheezing breath. "Willa."

Her name. Her mother's love. Spilled out on death. "Oh, God," she prayed. Such a gift. She laid her head on Mother's hand, feeling Mother's warm breath against her skin.

Rheus had called this a holy moment. How could death be holy? Especially since love had finally been exchanged? Still, Genie's words proved correct. This short time was a gift, her time to finally make peace. Mother's too.

"You have to shake hands with the past, Wills," Hale had said when she wept over a memory. They sat at the Oasis Café, this time outside under the awning in tiny café chairs, nursing coffees on a rickety table covered with checkered oilcloth.

"I can't."

"It's what happened. Just be honest about it."

"I'd rather forget Mother's words."

"I know this sounds crazy," Hale said, "but her words don't define you. You're not a wasted life." He grabbed her hand. "But you will be if you don't make peace with her words."

"How can I make peace with her saying I'm worthless?"

Hale squeezed her hand, then let go. He nursed his coffee while a stiff wind curled around them. "You have to find your worth somewhere else. Where her words sound like echoes, but don't resound anymore."

"You sound like a counselor," she said.

Hale laughed. "I'm just a man who loves a woman, who hates to see her beat herself up with ancient words that aren't true. You know what I think?"

"No, I seldom do."

"I think you're repeating your past."

Willa felt his words in her stomach, then all over her body in what only could be described as pent-up rage. She would not turn out like Mother. She wouldn't. "How can you say that?"

"Because it's true."

"Exactly how is it true?"

"Your mother spoke awful words over you, right?"

Willa nodded.

"And she neglected you."

"Yes."

"And she was hard on you."

Willa rolled her eyes. "Why are you reminding me of this?"

"Just stay with me here."

"I'm trying."

"I know," Hale said. "You grew so accustomed to being treated that way that it became your normal. And now that you're safe, far away from Rockwall, from the memories, from your mother, you've taken her place. You're just as awful to yourself as she was to you."

Willa let his words mingle inside her mind.

"Listen, if I treated you the way you treated yourself, you'd leave me. If you ask me, it's time you left that Willa behind. Quit abusing yourself. Would you treat a friend the way you yell at yourself inside?"

"What's that have to do with shaking hands with my past?"

"Everything. A handshake is a recognition of someone's presence. Shake hands. Say it happened. Then let go of the handshake and walk away."

"You make it sound easy."

"It's the easiest, yet hardest thing you'll ever do. It involves faith. It means you'll have to view yourself not as a victim or as worthless, but as a dearly loved child of God."

"I can say those words about God loving me, but I've never felt them. Never really believed them."

"My guess is that you're so used to believing the crap in your life that you've crowded out the beauty." Hale took another drink.

Willa let her coffee cool, wondering if she should drink it tepid.

Hale leaned back, grabbing his unruly hair in both hands. His eyes danced. He had a way of disseminating truth, really hard truth, with a wink—his own spoonful of sugar, she supposed. "I love you," he said. "And it kills me to see you hate yourself, abuse yourself, carrying on the pain your mother gave you. Can't you let it go? Don't I make up for her words?"

"Yes," she said. She took a drink of her coffee, winced, then looked into Hale's Daddy-blue eyes. "But I've been this way since … forever."

"That's just the beginning of your story, Wills. I'm privileged to come in as you enter the stage of today. It's time to start living life. With me." He held her hand in his, not squeezing, but not letting go either. Not unlike the way Willa held Mother's hand just now.

She was shaking hands with her past.

fifty-six

But it was Mother who let go first.

"No," Willa wailed.

Rheus and Genie entered the room, both putting hands on Willa's shaking shoulders.

"She's gone," Willa cried.

A hospice nurse checked her pulse, then shut her eyes. "Yes."

Genie sat down next to her with a thud. Rested her head in opened palms. She didn't cry, but the anguish leaked out.

Willa felt death swirl around them all.

Rheus hummed "Great Is Thy Faithfulness" into the death-stale air.

"I suppose we'll bury her next to Daddy, then." Willa broke through the hum.

"Those were her wishes," Genie said. "Odd as it may sound. And she wanted the memorial service here, downstairs."

"You two need time to let this sink in," Rheus said, "and I need to do everything I can to release your memories."

Willa didn't know what Rheus meant, but waved him away. She stood, lifted Genie to her feet, then embraced the woman who she'd hated then grown to love. In that strange circle of two, they wept while Mother slept with Daddy, both dying under the eaves and eyes of the big, white house.

fifty-seven

Rebbie catered Mother's memorial service. Trays of food, glasses of fresh lemonade, and sweet tea lined tables along the back of the left parlor. Chairs crowded in and through both parlors. Rheus stood at a podium, a screen behind him near the fireplace. He opened the service in prayer, then nodded to Willa.

"Thank you for coming today. I'm thankful." She scanned the crowd, landing on Blake's eyes. She tried to clear her mind, to prepare herself for the words that needed to be said. Blake didn't glower back, thankfully, so she proceeded.

"Mother and Daddy loved Rockwall. And they gently and kindly helped bury many citizens. And now we're here to lay their legacy to rest." So much was meant in those words: legacy, rest. Would she ever find rest? Would she exceed her legacy? Or even have one? She felt tears coming, but instead of fighting them, she let them have their way. "Mother would be pleased to see so many of you here. It seems appropriate that in the place where death reigned, food and hospitality have replaced it."

Willa shared a few well-chosen words about Mother, keeping them true and respectful. When she sat down, Rheus stood. He said, "I've spent some time digging up memories, finding little scraps of history. I pray this helps you remember Mrs. Muir well." He started the presentation flashing on the screen behind him. Classical music played in the backdrop as old pictures, faded in shades of gray and charcoal, brought Mother to life. Each photo, in subsequent ages, took Willa's breath. She'd never seen these before. Mother as a crying baby, a toddler with pudgy chocolate-stained hands. She saw her own eyes there, the shape of her face, the slight wave of her hair. Mother preening in her back to school dress, dancing in the sprinklers, grinning with a lost tooth. Mother was a child once, with a past, with memories, hopes, dreams. The smile remained wide throughout all of school, culminating in her high school graduation photo, capped and tasseled.

The shift came nearly imperceptibly when Daddy intruded on the pictures. When Willa first saw him there, she longed again for his embrace, his words of life spoken over her, the feel of his hand in hers. How do you mourn a man who was two men? Because the sunshine that was Daddy was the blackest night when he took on the role of Husband.

She noticed how Daddy's arm around Mother looked awkward, forced. She saw Mother's thin-lipped smile, the slant of her eyes toward the ground. She wondered if the whole room saw the change in Mother, if they knew the sadness behind the couple. She looked around. Only glistening eyes met hers. They were grieving, nothing more.

Willa gasped, then covered her mouth, when she saw Mother pregnant. Why would Rheus include this? The next picture seemed to stay on the screen the longest. Mother bent over Willa who squirmed in an infant bathtub. Daddy held a sponge over Willa's pink frame, water baptizing her belly. Daddy laughed, but Mother's face turned from the camera.

Willa let her tears run their course while flashes of her childhood, now in full Technicolor, assaulted her. Were there happy memories? The pictures seemed to say so. Had she been blind to them? She remembered her counselor saying that once you've grieved the pain of the past, you can finally see the joy. Perhaps she hadn't grieved enough, because these pictures seemed fake to her — taken of another Willa, in another family.

The last picture stole Willa's breath. Rheus or Genie must've snapped it the last day of Mother's life and rendered it in black and white. From the doorway of the embalming room, you could see Mother reclining on the bed, still curling around herself, while Willa's head covered Mother's hand. It looked as if Willa were praying there. A touching photo, if it were the truth. But Willa simply grieved. Her prayers had dried up into short staccato bursts to the heavens.

Genie concluded the service with a prayer, which initiated a social hour where Willa would have to shake hands, accept condolences, and avoid Blake. But he stood behind her when she turned around. "Blake," she said.

"I'm sorry for your loss," he said. His eyes held nothing— no affection, but no hatred either.

"Thank you for coming," she said.

He nodded and walked away. Part of her wanted to follow him out to his car, to smooth over the end of their relationship, to make amends somehow. But a line of folks blocked her way. His sudden absence ignited the deepest loneliness in her, not just for Blake and what they'd been together, but for Hale, for his absence. She'd told him on a message that Mother had died, but he hadn't bothered to come.

She smiled, frowned, nodded, talked, patted backs while the loneliness seeped into her. The old house absorbed it too, as if the walls knew its owners left earth. Where home usually grounded Willa, today it felt empty, echoing. Even with the chatter of Rockwall natives and the beautiful food Rebbie prepared, the whole scene lacked community. At least for her.

All that cutting, all those clippings of home and hearth, all that pining for strong walls, both figurative and literal, burned up in a giant pile in her mind. Wood, hay, stubble igniting. No gold remaining. Her search for home, for memories, for truth had ended, and now she stood in a crowd, utterly alone.

When everyone cleared out, the house would be empty. A select few would venture to the graveside, placing Mother permanently beside the man who forced his hand. And she'd stand above them both, knowing every secret, but being none the wiser.

fifty-eight

The sky obeyed the words of "Ain't No Sunshine," graying itself for the burial. A few head-lighted cars drove the scant mile, winding through downtown Rockwall, where the flag flew at half-mast from the art-deco courthouse. The town mourned too, it seemed.

When Willa parked at the cemetery, she sat several minutes, gathering herself. Would she have sunshine again after death? Would she meet her biological father before he met the afterlife? And what of her? What did her life mean? Why was she put here? To live; to die; to ache in the middle?

The ache felt heavy, like a backpack too heavy to heft. It settled in on her, blanketing her with lead.

You will always be alone, her head said to her in a monotone, matter-of-fact way.

She didn't fight against the words; she accepted them. She deserved them. All that pining for a daddy who wasn't who he said he was. All that hating of a mother tortured. Running away from Blake's suffocation. Confounding Hale who loved her. She'd been either a turncoat or a defector all her life. Never discerning situations accurately, then overreacting and fleeing.

"Dear Lord," she prayed, "save me from myself."

She gathered her things, opened the car door, and trudged through the misty day where the earth opened itself up. A scraggle of people murmured there, but she stood aloof.

She could smell the ground. Pure, dark clay. She remembered digging in it as a child, hoping to plant a two-by-two garden in the back next to the carriage house, but the digging wore her out. Daddy'd said she could use the clay to make pots, which she did, but they never dried quite right in the Texas sun—just crumbled into brittle chunks. He'd bought her dirt as a surprise, filling the vacant hole in the ground with potting soil. When her seeds didn't sprout, Daddy filled the gaps with nursery plants. He'd planted her garden for her, much like he planned Mother's life. And now he could do neither.

The earth opened below the casket, its mouth ready to swallow Mother whole. The casket matched the color of the sky, gunmetal gray, with silver handles. A pastor Willa didn't know said words upon words about life, death, afterlife. He prayed prayers. He asked if anyone wanted to speak. She knew she should, but her words stifled inside her. A faint hum of a motor purred behind her, but she didn't turn. She kept her eyes on the coffin that sealed her orphanhood and wondered how much of herself would be buried today. Would Catherine leave forever? And what of Willa would remain?

The pastor threw a handful of store-bought dirt onto the coffin. Willa knew this from past funerals. Throwing clumps of clay didn't have the same effect when saying the words, "dust to dust." The song "Dust in the Wind" filtered through her mind as the wind picked up and scattered the dust away, as if the heavens were saying, "Don't bury her yet."

The tiny congregation sang a hymn, Mother's favorite: "O the Deep, Deep Love of Jesus."

O the deep, deep love of Jesus, vast, unmeasured, boundless, free!
Rolling as a mighty ocean in its fullness over me!

She'd known this was Mother's favorite only because

Mother said so. She rarely sang it, rarely sang anything. And the words sounded strained under the heaviness of gray, as if each person singing it wished it were true but wasn't entirely convinced. So much like Mother, it made Willa cry. The wishing, the longing, the never quite knowing.

Underneath me, all around me, is the current of Thy love
Leading onward, leading homeward to Thy glorious rest above!

Would Mother finally rest in heaven? Would the tortured part of her be renewed into something beautiful, like Willa's clay giving way to fresh, green plants? Is that what God did, exactly? Would Mother finally be home?

As men with strong arms waited to lower Mother next to Daddy, Willa's heart sunk with her. In the great burial of her family, would she ever know resurrection? Would she ever feel at home?

A hand touched her shoulder. She reeled around to see Hale, eyes bluer than the sky should've been, a face wet with tears. He engulfed her in strong arms. She felt his strength, melted into it. Cried into his jacket. Smelled evergreen.

fifty-nine

Genie and Rheus shook Hale's hand, asking him back to the house. Rebbie gave him an effusive hug. Willa smiled, an odd thing for such a sad, overcast day. Hale had returned, just when she needed him. When she needed home.

He followed her back to the house, and when they exited their cars, she expected an explanation. But none came. He fell strangely silent, mounting the creaking stairway, sitting in the parlor in one of the many folding chairs. Head in hands, he wept, his strong body, now tanned from the kiss of Louisiana's ardent sun, heaved and bucked. Willa sat next to him, feeling the energy of his grief. The others stayed to the kitchen, cleaning up, the clank of plates intermittent to Hale's cries.

"I've made my peace," she finally said. "With Mother. I'm okay, I think."

He sat back, wiped his wet hands on ripped jeans. "I'm not."

"What's wrong?"

He wept afresh, loud and deep.

She stroked his shoulder, feeling helpless. She had known Hale to be emotional, particularly when he saw injustice he couldn't right, but never to this degree. He heaved in a few more gulps, blowing his breath out in a steady stream. He pulled a handkerchief from his back pocket and wiped his face with it. "I'm sorry."

"What's wrong?"

"Reality's dead."

"What?"

"She was staying at her uncle's, not exactly a safe place."

"Did he hurt her?"

Eyes red, Hale shook his head. "No, nothing like that. She was a free spirit, a bird of a girl, flitting here and there. And she loved me." Hale seemed to examine the fireplace, looking beyond Willa toward something yet to be seen.

"I can't imagine anyone not loving you." Willa rested her hand on his, but he didn't upturn his palm to hold it back.

"On the day she died, I told her the hard news. That I couldn't pursue adoption. I'd come to see that her uncle truly loved her, that she belonged with him, and my interfering caused heartache for him — and for her, though she didn't know it. She hollered at me. Put her hands on her hips. Said blood didn't make a family, friendship did."

"I'm sorry," Willa said.

"So she ran out the front door. Said she was going to Margie's to play." He said these things as if Willa had been entangled with his life, as if she'd know exactly who Margie was. "And she ran into the road as a truck loaded with building supplies motored past."

"Oh no."

"She just ran, Willa. Trucks like that have become background noise in the rebuilding of New Orleans. And she hadn't bothered to look both ways, so she ran. Killed instantly." Hale removed his right hand from under hers and rubbed his face with both hands. When he pulled them away, his hands shook. He tried to steady them on his jeans, but they tremored anyway.

"When?"

"The same day your mother passed."

She slipped her arm around Hale, his strength for once. She said nothing, just let the tears come again, surprised she had more to cry.

sixty

The address, written by Genie, graced the lined piece of notebook paper on the kitchen counter. *SPECK TAYLOR*, it said, followed by numbers and a street name in Dallas. Genie had kept to herself in the carriage house since Mother's death, often performing her duties from afar, haunting the kitchen only when necessary. So when Willa saw the address, she knew. This was Genie's goodbye, and her final gift.

To have three unresolved issues swirling around Willa's mind gave her a headache.

Hale slept now in the embalming room as if he hadn't had a good night's sleep in years. She could hear his snoring clear to her room, and when she did, she prayed, asking God to please make things clear. Hale gave no indication of intentions either way, as if he were her long-lost brother come back to visit.

Speck Taylor took up residence somewhere in Dallas, still alive, still her biological father. With trembling hands, she picked up the paper, wondering if she had the strength to visit him, to say what needed to be said. To make more peace.

And what if she made that peace? This remodeled house with a bed and breakfast sign out front was fully hers now. Even the carriage house would be emptied of Genie in a week, leaving her the sole caretaker. Genie had decided to move on. The thought of it all crushed Willa. Her life in Seattle beckoned, enticing her with salmon, granola, mountains, and sea. How could she abandon it all to live in the town of her undoing? But the thought of selling the place undid her even more.

She poured filtered water into a mug, microwaved it until it steamed, and plunged a tea bag into its heat. Dunking it, she watched the birds flitter and soar outside, singing songs to no one in particular, or perhaps to God who made their song. She thought of Reality, a girl she only knew in one dimension, and how her voice had been silenced forever, killing a part of the Hale she adored.

The central stairs creaked. She turned to see Hale clad in pajama bottoms and a white t-shirt, his hair askew, his blue eyes tired.

"Hey," she said.

"Hey yourself."

"Want some tea?" She extended her cup, still virgin, to him. He took it.

He drank slowly, his left hand holding the mug, his right leaning onto the counter. Steam swirled between them, the birdsongs the only words between.

"I got this," she said. She lifted the paper so Hale could read it. She'd already spilled her entire story to Hale last night as they rocked on the porch under a starlit sky. Though sympathetic and encouraging, he held himself distant then. Didn't even reach her way when she cried yet again.

"Are you going?" Hale took another drink.

"I was hoping you could come with me." Her voice sounded smaller than a chirp. She was a baby bird, waiting for Hale to bring her a worm. Her soul remained opened and anticipatory, but nothing dropped in.

"I'll have to think about it," Hale said.

"I understand."

"Really? Because I'm not sure you do."

Willa walked past him, pointed to two large chairs in the parlor, and sat down.

For a long time Hale didn't sit. Finally he shrugged his shoulders then slumped into the chair facing hers.

302 / MARY DeMUTH

"What don't I understand? You tell me." She felt the edge
slicing through her voice, but didn't temper it. With everything
spilling out of her, with all the mysteries solved and her heart
raw from death, she had no more energy to be polite.

He shook his head. No tears came, but they looked as if
they threatened. "I didn't tell you the real reason I said no to
Reality."

"Which was—"

"You."

"What? What did I have to do with that? You've been
incommunicado, Hale. No words. No texts. No letters, even.
I'm as much a part of your life as your dentist."

"I saw one last week." Hale smiled a bit when he said it,
crazifying her even more. How dare he look enticing at a time
like this?

"Great. Well, then, I'm less than your dentist, apparently.
Tell him I said hi."

"He's a she, Willa."

"Wonderful."

"Listen, will you?"

Willa tapped her left foot on the wood floor, waiting.

"You may think this is terribly unromantic, but God told
me to pursue you. Even from Louisiana."

"How did you do that, exactly?"

Hale put a hand up, as if to stop her snarkiness. "I didn't do
a good job. Didn't obey."

"Great," she heard hysteria in her voice. "So now you're all
about loving me against your will? I'm a God project for you?
Something you have to obey?"

"No."

"What is it then?"

"Have you ever been rejected?"

Willa rolled her eyes, letting go of any propriety. "Um, yes.

By my mother. By my real father. By Daddy in a roundabout way. By you."

"That's true. But have you asked someone to marry you, someone you cherished like your own flesh, only to have her turn heel and run away from you like you were some sort of freaky specter?"

Willa sighed. "You're not a freaky specter. More like a mummy." She hoped the insertion of Egypt would unravel the tension.

"It's not fair to pull the Egypt card."

"Sorry."

"But from my research, Egyptians tended to marry for love and stay happy. There's some good precedent there. But I've allowed you to distract me down a rabbit trail. I need to tell you what went on in Louisiana."

Willa felt his words in her stomach. It soured in response. Couldn't what he did in Louisiana stay there? "Do I really need to know this?"

"Yes. You do. Because you were there."

"I was?"

"You were the specter haunting me."

"I'm sorry."

"You should be."

"What's that supposed to mean?"

"Only that you've bewitched me, Willa. Captured me."

She thrilled at his words, but kept her heart walled. She said nothing. Waited.

"God told me, very specifically, that I was to spend my time in New Orleans praying for you, pursuing your heart that way."

"Thanks," she said.

"Only I didn't pray. I didn't have the soul for it. I poured my life into homes and needs and Reality. I spent most of myself there, trying to numb your rejection. And little by little, I lost you. After our last visit, I convinced myself that I didn't need you and you didn't need me."

She nearly said, "I need you," but kept those words inside. Instead she said, "So you let go. Like you wrote."

"Yes and no."

"You're a conundrum, Hale."

Hale stood. Paced the room in bare feet, his tea long since finished. "I know. That's me. Mr. Conundrum."

"Kind of rolls off the tongue," she said.

Hale stopped pacing enough to stand in front of her, pull her to her feet, and stare directly into her eyes. "You're not easy to push out. Not easy to forget." He placed warm hands on her shoulders.

She closed her eyes, anticipating his kiss, but she felt his hands leave, heard his footsteps walk away. She turned to see him mount the stairs, leaving her alone in the parlor with one hundred thoughts, one thousand questions, and one million regrets.

The birds chattered outside, as if they spat commentary on the whole sorry affair while Willa sat back in the chair and hugged her heart to herself, telling it to risk, to initiate a run up the stairs into Hale's arms again. But her heart said no, and her feet wouldn't obey without its mandate.

sixty-one

"He's asked me to marry him."

Willa stared at Genie, engulfed in her fluffy chair in the carriage house. "Rheus?"

"Well, who else but Rheus? You see a line of suitors lining up recently?"

"I'm excited for you," Willa said.

Genie showed her the ring, a simple gold band, no diamonds.

It made Willa's naked finger seem out of place. She folded her hands on her lap, covering her ring finger. "When will you leave?" Willa asked.

"That depends on you and what you want to do with the place."

Willa looked out the bank of windows toward the pecan tree, the house, the road beyond. "I don't know."

"Well, you'll need to hire another caretaker. I happen to think Rebbie would do a fine job. She could use the kitchen for catering and free you up to go back to your life in Seattle. Start things new."

Willa remembered Rebbie's invitation to live with her, then thought of her vacant life in Seattle. With Hale probably leaving soon for Louisiana, and having left her interior design clients back in Seattle, did she have a life in the Evergreen State? "I know she'd do a great job," Willa said.

"I can approach her if you'd rather me handle it," Genie said.

"That would be great."

"You're not going to sell the place, are you?"

"Not just now. I really can't say about the future, though. I never fancied myself an innkeeper."

"It's been in the Muir family—"

"I know. Oh, how I know." Willa stood. "I need some time to sort this all out, to sort out my life."

"When does Hale leave?" Genie stood, paced toward the door, and opened it.

"He hasn't said. But I sense it'll be soon. I'll be visiting your brother today."

Genie pulled Willa into an awkward hug, then released it. "He doesn't look like his picture," she said. "Be prepared. But I've told him you're coming. He wants to see you, if that's any consolation."

"It is. Thanks."

Willa descended the stairs. She expected the door to shut behind her, but it didn't. So she turned and looked up. Genie stood in the threshold, tears running down her softened face. "This has been like a home to me these many years. Please take care of it."

Willa nodded, then left the carriage house.

Under the pecan tree, she stood in the place Speck Taylor, her father, petted her head so many years ago. A lifetime ago. She wanted to be brave, wanted to meet him without tears, matter of fact, but pinned to the earth right now, her bravery drained through her feet, watering the pecan's roots. She had to see him, had to face whatever her heart endured. Rooted to the ground, she felt entirely alive—aching, longing, hoping, searching. Was that grief's goal? To anchor you to yourself, to pull you into the messiness of life? To make you pay attention?

She watched her windows from under the tree's branches, wondering how long she'd live in that room, and who she'd be when she finally decided to leave everything behind.

sixty-two

Hale insisted on driving to the AIDS hospice house, something Willa didn't protest. But since his silence had screamed all through the day, she didn't know what kind of company he'd be. Still, a quiet Hale next to her was better than facing her father alone. Hale played the latest Aaron Spiro release on his iPod, filling the rental car with terrific voicings, rocking guitar, and steady drums.

The volume didn't permit conversation, and for that, Willa celebrated. So much tinkered in her head that she'd rather not let it out into the air between them. Thoughts of what she'd say, what her father would say, whether it would devastate or hearten her, all mixed with wildly swaying emotions about Hale, his nearness, his distance. Plus grief over losing Mother, deciding on the house, and adjusting to Genie's moving plans. All these worries fought for supremacy while Hale motored down Interstate 30, seemingly oblivious. He tapped his fingers on the steering wheel, occasionally singing a line along with Aaron.

Turning south on Interstate 35, Hale exited shortly after. They drove down a main road, a sketchy area of south Dallas, where crumbling brick apartment buildings, tired-looking minimarts, and strolling pedestrians made for a hodgepodge of humanity. To her right, a car idled next to a man standing on the corner. His hand plunged into the passenger side of the car, and the occupant thrust something his way. Quick as a wink, the drug transaction was a distant memory, the man walking away as if nothing happened, the car speeding ahead.

Hale turned down the music. "Did you see that?"

"Yes," Willa said.

"You nervous?"

"About the drug deal?"

"No, about seeing your father."

"Yes."

Hale turned left, then parked in a small fenced lot in front of a converted hotel—the AIDS house. "We're here," he said.

He reached over, touched her hand, then let go. "I'm praying," he said.

"Aren't you coming with me?"

"Yes, but I don't need to go in the room with you. That's private, don't you think?"

Willa nearly cried. "I need you there. Please come with me."

Hale nodded, but he didn't say anything.

They checked in at the long-countered main desk flanking the right-hand side of the entrance. "He's in room 251," the lady said. "Mr. Taylor knows you're coming."

"He does?"

The lady leaned forward, her hands in front of her on the countertop. Willa took note of impeccably groomed hands and beautiful red fingernails. "His sister Genie let him know."

"That's good," Willa said.

"We love Mr. Taylor here, ma'am." Her words sounded like a half-warning, half-invitation.

Willa nodded and headed toward the staircase in the back. Hale followed alongside her.

She paused at room 251. Felt her heartbeat in her neck, throbbing. She leaned against the wall outside, her vision blurring. She closed her eyes.

"You can do this." Hale's voice sounded blessedly normal,

connected, as if he divorced himself from his distance for this one occasion.

She opened her eyes, found his. His blue irises matched Daddy's. She wanted to stay there, wrapped in comforting blue, but Hale averted his eyes to the open door, as if to say, "It's time."

So she told herself to walk. One foot, then the next. She commanded her blurred vision to calm down, her heart to stop pattering. She felt Hale's presence behind her, so she willed him to follow after. He did.

Seven steps in, she saw him. Speck Taylor. Her father. Wasting away on a twin bed, his face turned toward the downing sun.

"Mr. Taylor?"

He turned, agony on his face, pockmarks on his arms. "Is that you?"

How she stood by him so quickly she couldn't figure out—like love had transported her there. "Yes," she choked.

"My beautiful girl."

Willa found the chair next to his bed, wondering at the irony. Her third time to sit in this place, to hold a dying parent's hand, to feel her heart burst with grief. His gray-green eyes took her in. His hair, silvered, wisped around his ears. His complexion, scarred, hinted at a shade of gray-yellow. "Mr. Taylor?"

He nodded. He seemed to know. To understand she couldn't call him Daddy or Father or Dad.

Willa looked over at Hale then, seated next to the wall. His eyes captured hers; something like love passed between them. Not the tickle-your-toes kind of love, but a deep, abiding, friendship love—the kind of love you experience when friends share grief. She turned her attention back to Speck. Her father.

"I'm sorry," she said.

"For what?" He tried to pull himself up, but Willa could see his weakness. She tried to prop him with a pillow.

"I don't know. I'm just sorry is all." Tears wept down her cheeks.

Speck cleared his throat. Coughed. "I don't deserve your visit."

"What do any of us deserve?"

"I wasn't the daddy you needed. I left you."

"You couldn't help it," she said.

"If I were a stronger man, I would've fought for you. But I gave up on you. And your mother."

"It's done now. We can't repaint the past."

"No, I don't suppose we can. But please don't say you're sorry. It's me who's sorry. I've got a lifetime of sorries to atone for."

She held his hand now, marveling at how frail, how human it was. His long slender fingers mirrored hers, except with age spots and papery skin. His lips, thin like hers. His frame, similar. In some ways it was like looking into an age-transformation mirror, seeing what you'd look like in thirty years or so. Only she hoped she wouldn't die of AIDS, wouldn't have to live with the same regrets that Speck wore tonight.

"I loved her," he said.

"I know."

"And I loved you."

She didn't respond to that, because how could she? She couldn't say, "I know." Not with authenticity. As silence filtered between them, she remembered what must've been his words. *You'll find home one day.* She drank in his eyes then, understood their green, and wondered where the ring was he once looked through. She squeezed his hand.

He licked dry lips. "I suppose love is a word you think I

throw around. And you'd be right, I suppose. Because I wanted freedom, and I worshiped recklessness and laziness. Little girls should be worshiped, but I ran away."

"Yes, you did," she said. Willa thought of her life, wondered if her running away from Hale was recklessness. If her not wanting to make a decision about the house equaled laziness. Had she become Speck Taylor? But as she looked at him, she didn't feel angry. Instead, she felt strangely proud that he had the guts to come clean. To say the truth undecorated. "Thanks for being honest."

Tears streaked down Speck's pocked face. He turned toward Hale. "Who is this?"

Hale stood. "I'm Hale," he said. "A friend of Willa's."

Speck let go of Willa's hand and took Hale's. "Nice to meet you," he said.

Hale returned to his seat.

The word *friend* pestered Willa, but she told herself to lock that away to think about another time. Right now was Speck's time. Her time. Their time.

Speck's eyes fluttered shut, then opened. "I'm sorry," he said. "They say I'll just keep getting sleepy until it's time to go."

"To the hospital?"

"To heaven."

Heaven took her breath. Winded her. Willa swallowed.

"Don't worry about me. I've made my peace, finally. Seems God had to strike me with AIDS to get my attention. And boy, howdy, does he have it now. It brought my life into perspective. Showed me my ways. Made me sad for all my wanderings. But happy too. Because now the wanderings mean something. Every straying is a lesson I hold closer to me, learn from. I only wish I could live and breathe without so much regret weighing me down."

Hale left after he said those words. Willa watched him leave, but then returned her eyes to Speck. "All of us live with regrets," she said.

Speck rolled more toward her, took both of her hands in his. Held them tight between his. "I'm dying with mine."

Willa said nothing, but she held his alligator-green gaze, while tears trickled down her face. She didn't wipe them away.

She pulled out her picture. "This is us," she said. "Right?"

He held it close, blinked a few times. "Yes. Genie let me visit a few times, when your parents weren't at home. We played a few times. Colored. I pushed you on the swing."

"I think I remember," Willa said. "But there was another time. You saw me later, when I hid in the utility shed next to the house. You had a flashlight. Said something about my eyes." Willa tried to keep steady, but now that the picture of that memory lived between them, she felt the rejection as if it happened right now.

"I vaguely remember," he said, his voice distant. He closed his eyes, opened them. "Whatever I did that night was a mistake. Most likely I was high. I'm so sorry." Speck Taylor pulled in a breath, tears wetting his face. "Folks say things to others on a whim that they really mean for themselves."

Willa wrapped arms around herself as Genie did on the porch. Protecting her heart, most likely. "Once you told me I'd find home."

Speck nodded. "And have you?"

"I really don't know. With Daddy and Mother gone and you … here—it's hard to say. Home seems farther away than ever."

Speck cleared his throat. "I'm not a smart man," he said. "Not a good one either by most standards. But I have one thing going for me: I can warn."

Willa wondered what he'd say. Would he ridicule her?

Whenever Mother had that tone it meant only one thing: verbal thrashing. And what did that have to do with home?

Speck's eyes emanated peace. He said, "You live your life, you hear me? Live it well. Follow after the ones you love, no matter how long the road is or how tired you get. I lived in my own hell because I didn't chase. I don't want that for you, you hear me?"

Willa nodded.

"Now I don't have much time. Dinner's coming. But I want you to know this. I love you. Today. Right now."

Willa withdrew her hands, covered her face. She wept there, shoulders moving, sobs crushing, the world of her past colliding with today with such force she felt the quaking inside. Speck had inaugurated her fault line with those words. Buried her pain with his words. When she resurrected to the room, removing her hands, the sun's angle warmed Speck's face. He smiled. His eyes smiled.

She smiled back, touched his shoulder, then stood. "I love you too," she said.

"It's how it should be," he said before his eyes fluttered closed.

sixty-three

Willa couldn't locate Hale, so she haunted the front desk waiting for him to show up. A group of people came through the doors carrying trays of food and smiles. "Who are they?" she asked the girl with the beautiful nails.

"They come from Rockwall once a month."

"That's where I live!" She wondered at the sudden feeling, that Rockwall was where she *lived*, the place she once called home. Could it be home again?

"Well, you should meet them. They call themselves the Supper Club. They bring bags of toiletries to the residents every month and make a homemade dinner. With that trailer out there, it looks to be barbecue tonight."

She turned to see a trailer pulling an enormous grill in the parking lot with a group of men fussing around it.

More folks brought in gift bags, food, and smiles. Older couples. Kids. Teenagers. All converging here. From Rockwall, of all places.

"The residents love this group," the counter girl said. "They don't just feed them. They spend time. Ask after their stories. Play games. Dance."

"Sounds like a great group of folks."

"They are."

Hale appeared now, placed his hand on her shoulder.

"Where were you?" she asked.

"Around," was all he said.

She didn't press him, as she knew enough about Hale that

he'd probably gone visiting. His heart never seemed complete unless he hung with what he called "his people." The broken. The downtrodden. The needy. She wondered if maybe that was why he remained her friend when the romance left him. Maybe he still felt the need to rescue her.

After saying goodbye to the front desk girl, they passed by the behemoth grill. Hale, of course, introduced himself to the lead barbecue man. They spoke a hidden man language, the language of wood fire and smoke and meat, while Willa waited. Back in the car, Hale kept his silence while Willa cherished the visit in her heart. A peace settled into her, as if everything in her life started to make sense. Even without Hale's affection, she knew, somehow, that she would be okay. And that maybe Thomas Wolfe was wrong. Maybe you could go home again. As they sped east down Interstate 30, the sun at their backs, she felt the irresistible pull.

sixty-four

With much effort and the aid of a walker, Speck Taylor walked her down the aisle.

Genie beamed beside him, but not as much as a scrubbed clean Rheus Aldus who stood beneath the pecan tree that May afternoon. They publicly spoke words to honor and cherish, in sickness and in health. Hale, in for a quick visit before flying back to work, performed a song with a loaned guitar, his voice lifting the pecan's leaves and giving the birds a run for their money. Willa never would've imagined that only a few months after encountering a scowling Genie on the wide front porch of the Muir House, that she'd be her only attendant—and a niece at that. In a strange cycle of events, and a memory-filled hole, Willa smiled when Rheus and Genie kissed with sweet passion under the peek-a-boo sun.

The small congregation clapped. Folks set up tables where the wedding had been, throwing on a wild variety of table-cloths and mismatched dishes. Rebbie hurried through the kitchen, in and out of the back door, hauling salads, crudités, little quiches, vegetables.

The sunshined afternoon proved Rockwall's worth. Late spring in full force now, a gentle breeze wafted honeysuckle while a passel of interesting guests mingled with terrific food for what Hale would crown the quintessential community. He walked beside Willa as she filled her plate again.

"Hungry?"

Willa laughed. "Hiring Rebbie was the best thing I ever did."

"It appears so."

Hale loaded his plate too. They dined under the pecan tree, chatting with Speck who looked a little less yellow-gray, though his condition continued to be grave, according to Genie. When they finished, Hale gave Rheus a hug, shook Genie's hand, and congratulated them.

"The song was perfect," Genie said. "I don't know how to thank you."

"Just live happily ever after," Hale said.

Rheus put his arm around Genie's shoulder. "I intend to see that happen," he said.

As they cleaned up and retired the tables and linens, Hale leaned into Willa, a whisper of a breath. "Can you get away?"

"Yeah," she said.

He touched the small of her back, maneuvering her through the yard to his car.

"Where are we going?"

"You'll see."

She opened the window, letting in hot humidity. Near-summer wafted in while Hale skirted downtown. He turned left toward the courthouse, then passed the old Methodist church, Rebbie's dream. "I love that building," he said.

"Me too. That's the place Rebbie wants to buy and establish an artsy bakery. A hangout place for Rockwall. I hope she does."

Hale tapped his fingers on the steering wheel to the beat of a song she didn't know. Ethereal and Irish it sounded. They stopped at Harry Myers Park. "Don't get out," he said.

He ran around the car, opened her door with a flourish. "Welcome to the park," he said.

She smiled. "Um, thanks?"

He led her toward the woods. She remembered her time with Blake, how terribly it ended, how quirked her stomach became in the aftermath of his words, his actions. That same flutter existed now, but she wasn't sure why.

They walked serpentine-like through meandering trails. A long corridor of trees flanking either side cathedraled them. Willa felt the holiness. Hale took her hand. It felt natural there.

He pulled her down a steep ravine to a rough-hewn out-cropping of rock, a perfect place for two people to sit. The sun couldn't find them here, which felt refreshing. Hale turned to her. "How are you?" he asked.

"Shaken and tired."

"How so?" Hale pulled his knees to his chest, wrapping his arms around them.

"I have no roots, no stability."

"You do, Wills."

"I'm unwanted." The rejection from years of living life in her childhood home collapsed on her. Truly a home for the dead, a place where memories died, then resurrected with a vengeance.

"Even if everyone on the face of this earth turned away from you, you'd still be wanted."

"You've been fickle, Hale. You haven't exactly been there for me."

"I'm not talking about me. I'm talking about Jesus. He's been there. In every memory, every mystery, every shame, every disappointment."

"If he was there, then why didn't he step in and make the adults in my life act right?"

"Hard question. I don't know. Wish I did. But I do know that he made you. And he loves you. And even if everyone left, he'd still be there."

"I feel like a mistake." Silence followed, stillness pregnant with grief.

Hale leaned against the earth behind him. "Don't say that, Wills. No one's a mistake. Particularly not you. You're here, aren't you? Alive. Beautifying the world one house at a time."

"Maybe that's why I decorate. Why I'm obsessed with homes."

He brushed away a strand of hair from her face, tucked it behind her ear. "I consider it a selfless act — you who can't seem to find home, wishing it for others, giving it to them."

"I'm tired, Hale. Weary of looking for home."

"I know." He pulled something from his pocket. "Maybe this will help."

He pushed a folded inside-out envelope her way.

Her heart shuddered.

She opened it.

Inside, a heart locket.

"What is this?" Not a ring. She told herself not to cry. Not to be disappointed.

Hale smiled. "Look inside."

She did. A picture of him. A picture of her. Both smiling. "Thanks," she whispered.

"There's a story behind it."

"I know. You're making up for the one I broke."

"Yes and no." He took the locket from her and fastened it around her neck.

"What do you mean?" She told herself to breathe. To wait. To listen.

"The ring I gave you? The portal? I had it melted down to make this."

So it was friendship after all. He'd melted his intentions — a nice gesture. "Thank you," she finally said.

"I want you to always remember me, to remember there

was a time when a man wanted to marry you, that he saw such beauty and potential there."

"Saw," she said.

"See," he countered. He lifted her to her feet. He scrambled up the embankment, then stooped to help her up.

She pretended not to see his hand, preferring to claw at the dirt and dust her knees than to take his hand. This was Hale's The End to their story, she knew. His clever way of letting her down easy. A melted ring. Her melted heart. As they walked in silence to the car, she knew she deserved it. She'd run away. Played fickle with his generosity. What did she expect? Hadn't he said that even if everyone left, Jesus would be there? She sent a silent prayer Jesus' way, begging for the wherewithal to withstand another goodbye. How many farewells would she say in her life?

They drove toward town, the Irish music still lilting through the car. Hale stopped in front of the abandoned church.

"Why did you stop here?"

"I like the stained glass. Don't you? I wanted to take a few photos."

"I'll wait here."

"No, please come. I want to take one of you too."

To remember her by, she thought.

They stood in front of the stone steps looking up at the blue sky. "Let's see if it's open."

"It's not," Willa said. "Rebbie and I have tried. She's called a real estate agent, but we haven't been able to get an appointment to get in."

"Sometimes it's worth the risk to try," he said. Hale walked up the stairs and opened the door. "See?"

Willa looked around. Would they be trespassing? Was this legal? Now that she'd decided to reframe her life in Rockwall, make it her home, she had to think of the implications. The Rockwall police were happy to issue all sorts of tickets and citations, she knew. That's how the streets got maintained around here.

But Hale disappeared inside. She sighed and followed him into the darkened church.

He stood at the altar, arms wide. "Look at this, will you?" Stained glass preened from the sun's advances, scattering prism light everywhere.

"It's beautiful."

Hale sat on a dusty front pew, then patted the seat next to him.

She sat. "We shouldn't be here, Hale."

"The Egyptians –"

"No more about the Egyptians. You can't convince me they had stained glass and pews."

"No, but they did have marriages."

"And your point is?"

"Well, this is a place for marriages, wouldn't you say?"

Willa fingered her necklace. No marriages in sight for her. Hale had made that clear.

Hale dropped to one knee.

Willa gasped. "But the necklace."

"A ruse. To elongate the proposal.

Willa's tears came as natural as a spring rainstorm then.

"Don't cry."

"I can't help it."

"You know I love you, right?"

"You do?" Willa's heart catapulted inside.

"I've always loved you. That's why I have this."

He pulled a velvet box from under the pew, opened it. A simple gold band.

"Where did you—"

"I asked your father's—Speck's—permission that first day you saw him. And he gave me this ring. The ring he would've given your mother. Told me to take care of you."

"But—"

"No buts, Willa. Will you marry me?"

She threw her arms around him, nearly toppling him to the musty floor. "Yes," she said.

He slipped the ring around her finger, lifted her up, and smiled. "I told you I was your home, Willa. It just took a long journey to get you there."

As they drove toward the Muir House, Willa marveled at the circle of completion. The ring started this whole awful, beautiful adventure. It dangled in altered form around her neck, covering her heart, while a piece of her past, painful but redeemed, held her finger.

The house no longer loomed, no longer felt disconnected from her, no longer kept its mysteries. It lived and breathed before her, a place she could start over, create family, welcome community, and cherish life alongside her best friend. When Hale pulled in and cut the engine, she sat for a minute, taking the house in, noticing its peeling paint, the crooked stairs. So much like her soul.

And yet, still standing.

discussion questions for book clubs:
the muir house

1. Willa believes she'll be okay once she knows the truth about her past. In retrospect, do you believe she is right? Why or why not?
2. In what ways does The Muir House reflect Willa's heart? In what ways is it different?
3. How did your opinion of Genie change throughout the book? Did she become a sympathetic character? Why or why not?
4. What qualities did you like in Blake? What did you dislike?
5. In what ways does Hale show his weaknesses?
6. How does your impression of Willa change by the end of the book? Has she changed? What steps has she taken that show growth? What indicates that she still has some growing up to do?
7. How does Willa's trust in God evolve throughout the book?
8. What role does Rheus play in the unfolding of the book's events? If you could flesh out his backstory, what would it be?
9. Willa's father seems to be supportive and amazing, but his image tarnishes toward the end. Why? What happens? What clues in the text alerted you to the change?

10. Which characters embody evil? Or can any of them be characterized that way?

11. Rheus helps restore physical memories to folks. In what ways is Willa's memory restored?

12. How was the dinner outside behind the house a picture of positive community? What was awkward about the dinner?

13. What makes you trust or distrust Blake?

14. How does Willa justify not visiting her mother? Or does she?

15. What is Willa's biggest fear? Hale's? Genie's?

16. What role does written communication play in this book? In the age of texting and electronic communication, how did this device enhance the book?

17. Recount all the rings in the book. What does each one mean? What happens to each one?

18. What did you enjoy about Rebbie's view of life? What puzzled you about her?

19. How did your beliefs about Willa's mom change? Why?

20. The central theme of the book deals with truth setting folks free. In what ways did the truth set Willa free? In what ways did it not?

21. Pretend Willa never found out about her empty memory. Would she still have been able to move on with her life? Why?

22. Hale's patience seems heroic. What five qualities do you appreciate about him? What makes you want to shake him?

23. What is redemptive about Willa's journey?

24. Is it possible for a broken person to find love? If so, how can one move beyond the past?

25. What twist in the plot surprised you?

26. When Willa meets her biological father, do you believe her daddy-hole is filled then? Why or why not?

27. How would your feelings have changed about the ending had Willa ended up with Blake?

28. What do you think will be the next thing that happens in the book? Will Hale and Willa marry soon? Where will they live?

Publish your thoughts!

The Muir House ends in an open-ended way, leaving a spot for you to fill in what happens next. If you'd like to connect with other readers and devise alternate endings, click over to *The Muir House*'s Facebook page:

http://www.facebook.com/TheMuirHouse

There we'll have giveaways, contests, and lots of author-reader interaction.

acknowledgments

Patrick, I appreciate your steady hand, your sacrifice for our family, and the stability you bring to my life. You've been the best parts of Hale. Sophie, I wish you weren't going away to college, but I know God has huge plans for you away from Rockwall. I get excited just thinking about the adventures he has planned for you. Aidan, my steady son, you teach me so much about dedication to craft as you excel in music. Thank you. Julia, someday you'll pen stories; I can see it. Your creative, empathetic heart will exceed my storytelling ability. You're a genius.

Leslie Wilson and D'Ann Mateer, you both found things I missed in this manuscript. Leslie, thanks for being the queen of Rockwall. D'Ann, I know that soon I'll be holding your novel in my hands. I can't wait.

Sue Brower, thanks for loving the idea of this story from the beginning, for coaxing it from me.

Esther Fedorkevich, you've been a tireless worker on my behalf. Thanks for your coaching, kindness, empathy, smarts, and cheerleading.

Thank you, prayer team, who prayed me through: Ashley and George, Kevin and Renee, Carla, Caroline, Cheramy, Colleen, Jeanne, D'Ann, Darren and Holly, Dena, Dorian, Elaine, Erin, Ginger and JR, Helen, Katy, Denise, Anita, Diane, Cyndi, Lesley, Leslie, Lilli, Liz, Marcia, Marcus, Marilyn, Marion, Mary, MaryBeth, Michael and Renee, Pam, Don, Paula, Rae, Rebekah, Becky, Sandi, Sarah, Shawna, Sue, Susan, Tiffany,

Tim, Tina, TJ, Tracy, Twilla, and Heidi. You have blessed me beyond what I could write on the page.

Jesus, thanks for remodeling me.

Daisy Chain
A Novel

Mary E. DeMuth

The abrupt disappearance of young Daisy Chance from a small Texas town in 1973 spins three lives out of control — Jed, whose guilt over not protecting his friend Daisy strangles him; Emory Chance, who blames her own choices for her daughter's demise; and Ouisie Pepper, who is plagued by headaches while pierced by the shattered pieces of a family in crisis.

In this first book in the Defiance, Texas Trilogy, fourteen-year-old Jed Pepper has a sickening secret: He's convinced it's his fault his best friend Daisy went missing. Jed's pain sends him on a quest for answers to mysteries woven through the fabric of his own life and the lives of the families of Defiance, Texas. When he finally confronts the terrible truths he's been denying all his life, Jed must choose between rebellion and love, anger and freedom.

Daisy Chain is an achingly beautiful southern coming-of-age story crafted by a bright new literary talent. It offers a haunting yet hopeful backdrop for human depravity and beauty, for terrible secrets and God's surprising redemption.

Available in stores and online!

A Slow Burn
A Novel

Mary E. DeMuth

"*Beautifully and sensitively written, her characters realistic and well-developed. Mary DeMuth has a true gift for showing how God's light can penetrate even the darkest of situations.*"

– Chuck Colson

She touched Daisy's shoulder. So cold. So hard. So unlike Daisy.

Yet so much like herself it made Emory shudder.

Burying her grief, Emory Chance is determined to find her daughter Daisy's murderer—a man she saw in a flicker of a vision. But when the investigation hits every dead end, her despair escalates. As questions surrounding Daisy's death continue to mount, Emory's safety is shattered by the pursuit of a stranger, and she can't shake the sickening fear that her own choices contributed to Daisy's disappearance. Will she ever experience the peace her heart longs for?

The second book in the Defiance, Texas Trilogy, this suspenseful novel is about courageous love, the burden of regret, and bonds that never break. It is about the beauty and the pain of telling the truth. Most of all, it is about the power of forgiveness and what remains when shame no longer holds us captive.

Available in stores and online!

Life in Defiance
A Novel

Mary E. DeMuth

In a town she personifies, Ouisie Pepper wrestles with her own defiance. Desperate to become the wife and mother her husband Hap demands, Ouisie pours over a simple book about womanhood, constantly falling short, but determined to improve.

Through all that self-improvement, Ouisie carries a terrible secret: she knows who killed Daisy Chance. As her children inch closer to uncovering the killer's identity and Hap's rages roar louder and become increasingly violent, Ouisie has to make a decision. Will she protect her children by telling her secret? Or will Hap's violence silence them all?

Set on the backdrop of Defiance, Texas, Ouisie's journey typifies the choices we all face—whether to tell the truth about secrets and fight for the truth or bury them forever and live with the violent consequences.

Available in stores and online!

ZONDERVAN®
.com

Thin Places
A Memoir

Mary E. DeMuth

In this moving spiritual memoir—*Thin Places*—Mary DeMuth traces the winding path of thin places in her life, places where she experienced longing and healing more intensely than before. From surviving abuse as a latchkey kid to discovering a heavenly Father who never leaves, Mary's story invites you to a deeper understanding of your own story. She calls you to discover new ways to look for God in the past so that you might experience him more profoundly in the present.

What if you could retrace your life and discover its thin places—places where the division between this world and the eternal fades?

"Thin places are snatches of holy ground, tucked into the corners of our world, where we might just catch a glimpse of eternity. They are aha moments, beautiful realizations, when the Son of God bursts through the hazy fog of our monotony and shines on us afresh. He has come near to my life. I will tell you how."

Available in stores and online!

Share Your Thoughts

With the Author: Your comments will be forwarded to the author when you send them to *zauthor@zondervan.com*.

With Zondervan: Submit your review of this book by writing to *zreview@zondervan.com*.

Free Online Resources at
www.zondervan.com

Zondervan AuthorTracker: Be notified whenever your favorite authors publish new books, go on tour, or post an update about what's happening in their lives at www.zondervan.com/authortracker.

Daily Bible Verses and Devotions: Enrich your life with daily Bible verses or devotions that help you start every morning focused on God. Visit www.zondervan.com/newsletters.

Free Email Publications: Sign up for newsletters on Christian living, academic resources, church ministry, fiction, children's resources, and more. Visit www.zondervan.com/newsletters.

Zondervan Bible Search: Find and compare Bible passages in a variety of translations at www.zondervanbiblesearch.com.

Other Benefits: Register yourself to receive online benefits like coupons and special offers, or to participate in research.

ZONDERVAN®

ZONDERVAN.com/
AUTHORTRACKER
follow your favorite authors